RAGGEDY ANN HEART

HEATHER McPHAUL

ISBN: 1-4196-8627-5
ISBN-13: 9781419686276

Library of Congress Control Number: 2007910188
Visit www.booksurge.com to order additional copies.

To those colorful folks in West Texas
without whom I would have no desire
to tell a story, much less a story to tell.

PROLOGUE

Three-year-old Lindy was playing with her favorite doll, Soft Baby, when, after grave contemplation, Momma decided to seize the moment.

"There's the girl I love more than anything in the whole world," said Momma.

"I love you this much," Lindy said, spreading her wings as far as they would go.

"And you love Soft Baby too, don't you?"

"Yes," answered her only child, nodding.

"She's so sweet and soft and lovable."

"Yes." Lindy nodded again.

"Would you like to have a real life soft baby?"

"Nope," she shook her head, emphatically.

"I mean like the McNamaras' new baby. You know, Shelly's little brother?"

Lindy's face contorted the way it did when threatened with a spoonful of Pepto-Bismol. "Yucky."

"What's yucky?"

"Babies are yucky."

"Babies aren't yucky. They just need a lot of attention and love."

"I only want Soft Baby." Lindy clutched Soft Baby to her torso.

"Just because we get another baby doesn't mean you can't keep Soft Baby. She could never be replaced. No one in our family could ever be replaced." It was time to get to the point. Momma injected excitement into her voice: "In a few months, you're going to have a baby brother or sister."

Lindy looked blankly at her mother. "No," she said matter-of-factly.

"It can be fun to have a little brother or sister."

"No."

"Lindy..."

"No, thank you."

"You'll like having a little brother or sister."

"No, Mommy, I won't!" Lindy screeched.

"Don't be a brat. I refuse to love a brat," Momma said tersely.

Lindy quickly switched to another softer, more momma-friendly tack complete with quivering lip. "Why do I have to have a brother or sister? I like it the way it is now. Me, you, Daddy, and Soft Baby."

"Well," Momma started, "your father and I wanted to grow our family so we decided to have another child."

"Couldn't we get a dog instead?" Lindy proposed.

"It's not the same thing," Momma admonished.

"I know. It's better." Lindy flashed a toothy smile, trying to sell it.

"A brother or sister is someone you'll have with you your whole life," Momma replied.

"No, Mommy, not a good idea," Lindy stated simply.

Momma took a deep breath, summoning her patience. "Look, sweetheart. We're going to have a baby and that's just the way it is. I expect you to be a good big sister."

"This stinks," Lindy said.

"Fine," Momma said. "Then we'll keep the new baby and find an orphanage for you."

"No, Mommy, no!" Lindy screeched. "I'll be a good big sister, I promise I will. I promise!"

"That's my big girl," Momma said.

"I love you, Mommy, I love you!" Lindy threw her little limbs around Momma's neck for a big bear hug.

"I love you too, sweetheart," Momma said. "And your new little brother or sister is going to love you as well."

Lindy released her grip on Momma and stared her in the face. "Will you love the new baby more than me?"

"Of course not. No one will ever love you like I do. I love you this much." Momma reached her arms out wide and hugged her little jewel.

"I love you too, Mommy." Lindy giggled into Momma's bosom.

"Just like nobody will ever replace your Soft Baby, nobody will ever replace my Lindy."

Momma held her Lindy. Lindy held her Soft Baby.

~

Four months later, Soft Baby was left in a Dallas hotel room after a visit to Momma's sister and never seen again. Lindy was beside herself. But mostly she was beside Momma, crying, wailing, mourning. A funeral was held for Soft Baby, sans body, after which Momma bought a Simplicity pattern for a rag doll from the local nickel-and-dime-store. As quickly as she could, she stitched together a homemade Raggedy Ann complete with a red-stitched heart that read, "I love you." It took a long while—three whole days—but Lindy finally warmed to the doll. Soon, she was loving the stuffing out of her new baby, and before she knew it the irreplaceable Soft Baby had been replaced.

Momma's baby was due next month.

~

Lindy stared at the TV in the hospital waiting room while Dad stood outside smoking a fine cigar from south of the border—Juarez. Jo Francine Logan was an hour old, and Lindy and Dad were waiting to catch their first glimpse of the new addition. *I Love Lucy* played on TV, the episode where Lucy gives birth to little Ricky. Lindy was glued to the tube like a fly to a cow patty. The most terrifying thing was the way Lucy looked at her newborn baby. With such love. That's when Lindy decided she hated this show.

∾

A crowd had gathered outside the picture window where rows of newborns nestled in their hospital cribs. Lindy heard "oohs" and "aahs" coming from the crowd, but didn't understand what all the fuss was about until Father held her up so she could see through the glass. Jo Francine Logan slept front row, center.

"Isn't she beautiful," one of the women said.

"A little angel," said another.

"Aren't you Joe Logan?" the first woman asked Father. And before he had nodded, she added, "Your baby is simply precious."

It was then that Lindy realized they were talking about Jo. The thing was, they were right. Your eye couldn't help but go to her. She *was* beautiful. Unlike the rest of the infants her skin wasn't splotchy red, but smooth and cream colored. Her head was perfectly round and crowned by delicate wisps of brown hair. She even smiled in her sleep.

Lindy stared at her baby sister and felt a swelling of pride. "She's my baby sister," she said, and the women began cooing and fawning over *her*.

"You love your new baby sister, don't you?" said woman number two.

"Who couldn't love such a widdle, biddy bundle of joy?" the first woman said in a baby voice.

"She'll be such fun to play with," said yet another woman.

"A little doll baby."

"I'm her big sister," Lindy said proudly.

A nurse scooped Jo up out of her bassinet and carried her out of the nursery, and Lindy felt the spotlight dim as the women turned their bodies in the direction of the baby and away from her. "I'm her big sister," she said again. But no one cooed this time.

"There she is. The girl I love more than anything in the whole world."

That's what Momma always said to Lindy. Lindy whipped around to see Momma roll up in a nurse-propelled wheelchair. But Momma wasn't talking to Lindy at all. She was talking to the baby who had just been placed in her arms. "Hello, Jo Bean."

"Maggie, we were just admiring your beautiful baby," the annoying leader of the pack said to Momma.

"This is Jo Bean," Momma said. "I nicknamed her that 'cause she's thin as a string bean."

Lindy tried to wave to Momma, but ended up bonking Father in the nose.

"Dammit, Lindy. Knock my glasses off, why don't ya?" He set Lindy down on the floor while he straightened his frames.

The commotion caused Momma to look up. "Lindy. Come look at your beautiful baby sister."

"Well, Maggie," said the woman who would not clam up, "we have to go. Take care of this little one."

"Oh, I will," Momma assured Mrs. Busybody. "I love her more than anything in the whole world."

Momma gently cupped the baby's face and that's when Lindy knew. She was only three and a half and couldn't articulate it, but she knew. That foot-long imp was no angel. It was a family-wrecking ball. It had stolen all of Momma's love and left squat for Lindy. Lindy had known her little sister, "Jo Bean," for all of five minutes, but she could already tell this was one bean that needed to end up the way all beans do: being picked, shucked, and boiled.

In fact, Jo's name was fertile soil for Lindy's budding hatred of her sister. Lindy knew her own name was weird. Nobody could ever get it right. Kids would call her "Wendy" or "Cindy" and old folks would just say, "Huh?"

But "Jo"—Jo was a cool name. A short, to-the-point name. A tomboy name.

Jo Francine was supposed to be named Joseph Franklin Logan, Jr., because Father was willing to bet the house that his second child was going to be a boy.

Father had never been very lucky.

By the time the doctor announced that they were having a girl, all the Logans' friends and family—not to mention the soon-to-be-parents themselves—had gotten used to the name. So Momma and Father just dropped the "e" off of "Joe" and settled for "Jo." Not short for Josephine, just Jo. Easy to pronounce "Jo." Jo Bean, Momma's lean little love machine.

~

The baby had been home for months and Momma could sense that Lindy was still not comfortable with her younger sibling. Call it Momma's intuition. Call it Lindy's repeatedly asking "Is it time for Jo to go live in the hospital again?"

Momma had been waiting for Lindy to outgrow this phase. Now she was determined to help it along. She asked if Lindy wanted to hold the baby. Lindy did not. She asked if Lindy wanted to feed the baby. Lindy did not. She asked if Lindy wanted to change the baby. Lindy definitely did not.

Momma thought the golden icebreaker might be upon them when she saw Lindy playing with her Raggedy Ann. "Why don't you show Jo Bean your Raggedy Ann heart?"

"She can't have my Raggedy Ann," Lindy replied, clutching the doll to her chest.

"No. *Your* Raggedy Ann heart." Momma pointed just below Lindy's left clavicle. "The one in here that says 'I love you.' Like on your Raggedy Ann."

Lindy had no such heart. Not when it came to Jo.

"Do I have to?" Lindy asked.

Momma nodded. "Try for a little bit."

Momma perched Lindy on the couch then sat down beside her with the baby.

"The nurses at the hospital could take care of her forever and ever," Lindy said.

Momma sighed, her patience waning. "Lindy, stop it. This is Jo's home. I want you to start loving your sister like I love you. Before I take a hairbrush to your backside."

Lindy clammed up. She hated Momma's blue hairbrush more than she hated Jo.

"I want you to try holding her." Momma carefully placed Jo in Lindy's lap while still supporting the baby's head. "You don't need to be so stiff, honey. She won't break." Momma reached for Raggedy Ann and laid the doll in Jo's arms. The doll was almost as big as tiny Jo. The baby latched onto the rag doll's yarn hair and started to chew its red strands. "Oh, look. She loves your Raggedy Ann."

"Not my Raggedy Ann," Lindy whined.

"She won't hurt it." Momma beamed. "Isn't this precious?" This was a Kodak moment. "Are you OK with her?"

Lindy nodded rigidly, afraid the baby might break if she moved at all. Not that she cared; she just didn't want to be yelled at for being the one to break her.

"Are you secure enough to hold her by yourself while I run get the camera?"

Another rigid nod.

"Be right back.

Lindy sat stiff as a board, unable to prevent this rodent from gnawing on her doll's head. This was her train of thought as the baby begin to cough, then gag, then vomit. The whole ugly incident was over in a matter of seconds.

"Momma!" Lindy screamed bloody murder. "Momma!" Jo joined her sister by screaming baby bloody murder.

Momma ran in, frantic. "Is the baby OK?"

"She threw up and it stinks," Lindy cried.

"Is that all? Lindy, you scared the hell out of me. Babies throw up all the time. Here, I'll take her. Watch the baby's head." Momma scooped Jo up and the vomit-covered Raggedy Ann landed in Lindy's lap. "I'm so sorry, sweetheart."

Lindy shrugged that's OK, but there was no need because Momma was talking to...

"Jo Bean. I should've burped you better after your bottle." Momma headed for her bedroom with the baby.

"Momma?!" Lindy hollered, incredulous.

"Oh, Lindy. Go to the bathroom and take your clothes off. I'll be there in a minute to run your bath."

"But Raggedy Ann!"

"Rinse her off in the sink then throw her in the washing machine. She'll be fine. She's a rag doll."

Lindy could hear the sounds of cooing and fawning floating from Momma's bedroom as the stench of baby puke wafted into her nostrils. It made her want to throw up herself. Why *couldn't* stupid Jo Bean grow up in the hospital with the nurses as mothers?

As she listened to Momma making a big to-do over her stinking little sister, Lindy grew certain. She was not quite four and couldn't yet articulate it, but she knew. Momma loved the baby more. Or, worse, the baby was loved and she wasn't. Well, Lindy wouldn't have it that way. Lindy wouldn't let the baby get all the love and attention. No matter what—no matter what—Lindy would make Momma love her again. Even if it took the rest of her life.

CHAPTER ONE

Twelve-year-old Lindy arose on the morning of July 3, 1976 overwhelmed by a solitary feeling: doom. She had teased herself with optimism ever since Father had broken news of THE MOVE. But, alas, Lindy's optimism never took hold—false optimism never does—and this morning a black cloud of pessimism set in...landed...no, crashed down upon her.

Perhaps it was because she had spent the night on the floor in her sleeping bag, her bed having been moved to the new house the day before. Or perhaps it was because Father had thrown open her bedroom door at 6:00 a.m., letting the brutal light from the hallway pierce her dreaming eyelids. Then again, maybe it was the dream itself, in which Momma expressed her desire to not move at all by nailing Father to the living room wall with a shish kebab skewer.

Whatever the culprit, now that she was awake, her negativity only increased. Momma loudly clanged an impromptu dinner bell as she exclaimed that it was time for breakfast—their last meal before moving "out of civilization." It was clear from the sound of Momma's voice that, instead of banging on her pot, what Momma really wanted to ring was Father's bell.

Lindy put on her glasses. She had gotten Father's vision genes, which meant she was as blind as an underground mole, so putting on her glasses was her first act every morning. She had also gotten Father's teeth, just crooked enough to warrant a mouthful of metal braces. Lucky her, Little Miss Four-Eyes-Metal-Mouth. Jo, of course, had gotten Momma's twenty-twenty eyesight and piano keys-straight teeth. Jo was so hateable.

Lindy pushed herself up from the floor and went into the bathroom, only to find Jo washing her face. Jo turned off the water and cheerily looked up to see Lindy in the mirror.

"Good morning, sleepyhead," Jo said, her cheeks dimpled with an ear-to-ear grin, reminiscent of Liz Taylor in *National Velvet.*

Lindy ignored her sister. There was something wrong with people being that chipper at six in the morning. Or maybe there was just something wrong with Jo.

Lindy used the bathroom, then hurried out. That was one of Momma's many insisted-upon phrases—"use the bathroom." The idea that certain words used to describe body parts or bodily functions were vulgar—like "pee" and "tinkle"—had been passed down among the women in her family for generations. Likewise, "poop," "number two," and "BM" were never used (although Lindy's paternal grandmother did use the clinical "BM"). Momma's family's word was "stinky." It needn't make sense to the rest of the world; "stinky" was deemed least offensive to the delicate sensibilities of Momma and her ancestors.

Lindy flushed the commode, washed her hands and then skedaddled. As she left, she wondered: did her hatred apply to eight-year-olds in general or just to Jo? But, Jeez Louise, who wouldn't sicken of a life-sized China doll with blue eyes as big as Frisbees, who prissed around all day in lace and heels, wore her silky brunette hair in a *That Girl* flip, and wanted to grow up to be a model like Cheryl Tiegs?

Lindy had her share of TV idols, but they did more than flit their way down a runway. If Lindy could wish herself into a celebrity, she would be someone inspirational—like David Cassidy. The way he strutted his stuff on *The Partridge Family,* the meld of his husky voice with those moving lyrics, the bell-bottoms on that maroon velvet costume, the puka shells. Now *that* was cool. Lindy parted her dishwater-colored hair down the middle, but could never get it to feather quite like his. Unlike Jo's bouncy curls, her hair had less body than dental floss. Had it not been for the Coke-bottle lenses that magnified her mousy brown eyes, her looks would have no distinction at all.

~

Lindy searched her closet for the perfect moving attire and settled on a T-shirt and jeans. Or shorts? Maybe she should wear shorts. She looked out her window to confirm her wardrobe change. Not a cloud in sight and already the sun pounded the parched tan grass. Before noon the temperature would top the hundred-degree mark. That is unless the thirteen-month drought broke and sewed up the cracks in the ground.

Welcome to West Texas.

Lindy wasn't sure if she liked West Texas or if she was just used to it. Familiarity is often confused with affinity. Lindy did know she wasn't too crazy about the flat, dry landscape. It produced no greenery at all and no trees except for the mesquite which were shriveled and sunburned and only good for flavoring a barbecue. But on days when the spring winds picked up the loose dirt from the cotton fields and blew sandstorms so thick you couldn't see in front of your face, Lindy despised the place. The flying granules stung as they pelted your skin and it was impossible to close your mouth tight enough to keep the grit from getting in between your teeth. On these days she cursed this western quadrant of the Lone Star State and didn't care who heard. Yet if Lindy had caught anyone outside the area—north of Amarillo or south of Midland/Odessa—putting down even these worst aspects of her homeland, she would have fought a verbal war defending the place. Two rules—strangers do not bad-mouth your home and they do not insult your family. Only a member of your family could insult a member of your family. Lindy wasn't sure if she liked where she lived, but dad gum if she wasn't loyal to it.

With the exception of occasional visits to Lubbock, the hub of West Texas, Lindy had lived every day of her twelve years in the small town of Jessip. That was now only hours away from being past tense. Lindy and her family were moving thirty miles north to a farm in Boudine, Texas. Actually they were moving to Grady County—Boudine was the one and only town in the county, a fact that secured its placement in the *Guinness Book of World Records.*

The majority of Grady County's few hundred residents did not live in the town of Boudine, so the school was called Grady, not Boudine. And because the Logans would not live in Boudine, their address would be Route 1, Treat, Texas because, well, because their edge of the county was close to Treat and that's how the post office could locate them. So Lindy was moving from the only home she'd ever known to a route in a town that wasn't even in the county, to a county that didn't even have but one town, to a town with a school that was named after the county—it would take years for Lindy to get this all straight. By then, she was certain to have lost all contact with civilization and it with her—how could civilization find her? She was moving beyond hell; this was what was called hell and gone. Jessip would no longer be referred to as home. It would be called either by name or by the generic "town." The farm—Grady, Boudine, Treat, Timbuktu—was going to be home.

Lindy could sense Momma's mood the moment she walked into the kitchen and she knew what to do. Shut up. Even Jo was perceptive when it came to Momma. Both girls quietly concentrated on breakfast. Momma's dinner bell was purely a statement of her burden; the girls made their own breakfasts, which consisted of pouring milk on their Fruit Loops. Since the breakfast table had been moved out the day before, they ate standing up at the kitchen counter. Most people would move all their furniture and belongings on the same day, but then again most people could afford to hire movers. Father could afford to borrow his friend Smiley's cattle trailer for free and pay a couple of farmhands migrant wages to help him move the big furniture.

Father stood beside the girls at the counter, finishing his cereal, but he only added to the silence. It was what he added best. The three looked as if they were lined up to face a firing squad. For their dining entertainment, Momma banged around the house, packing (or repacking) boxes containing items with the most potential for making noise: brass knickknacks, trivets, Father's collection of classical music albums. Granted, Momma's shuffling of the albums wasn't so much for noise as for her own vindication; she hated this uptight music as much as she hated this move. Father didn't stop Momma from manhandling his prized collection. Odd, since such an action would usually cause retribution equal to someone harming his own blood kin—even if the manhandler was his own kin. But he stayed put, methodically ingesting spoonful after spoonful of cereal.

Momma finally tired of repacking and retreated to her bedroom to make up her face. Father drank the remnants of his cereal milk and strode over to the box of albums. He casually picked up the box and carried it out to the cattle trailer. Free from scrutiny, he surveyed the contents for damage. He expected the worst—cracks, chips, dents. He found only a bent corner of an album jacket. He breathed a sigh of relief and cursed himself for not taking this box with the load of big furniture he moved yesterday. He placed the box deep inside the truck bed, pulled the pen out of his shirt pocket and wrote "fragile." It probably wouldn't help, but it made him feel better. He went back into the house on automatic pilot ready to continue carrying out boxes.

The girls were finishing their breakfast. At least Lindy was. Jo hadn't touched her cereal. In fact, she was talking to it. Not out loud, but silently, mouthing the words. Lindy stared. This was a new one.

Jo finally looked up. "Fruit Loop people," she said. As if that explained it.

"What are you talking about?" *Nutcase,* Lindy wanted to add, but didn't.

"You know the dust at the bottom of the cereal box that gets into your cereal? They're the Fruit Loop people."

"You're the only Fruit Loop I know."

Jo ignored her. "And when you add milk they come alive and use the loops as life preservers. I like to give them plenty of time to float to safety."

Then she paused. A moment of silence perhaps for all the Fruit Loop folks fighting for their lives in the tidal waves of milk.

"This bowl had an especially large amount of people because it was the bottom of the box."

Lindy sat there, judging her sister and empathizing at the same time. Truth was, Lindy had her own set of quirks. The difference between her and Jo was that she had the good sense to hide her freakiness. Lindy had felt a weirdness welling up in her for some time, but she had managed to quash it until recently. On a trip to the new mall in Lubbock, Momma had let Lindy buy a new shirt. But it wasn't until she had brought it home, cut off the tags and hung it in her closet that she realized the shirt had some flaw she couldn't see or place. Yet that unseen flaw gnawed on her. It cried out to be returned to the store and replaced with a "perfect" model. So the next time Momma went into that store, Lindy tagged along, hiding the imperfect shirt under her own. Without telling a soul, she made the switch while pretending to try on clothes in the dressing room. She left the store shaking with adrenelaine, yet also at peace. The new shirt was no different than the first—neither had been worn—except that the new shirt didn't reek of an undefinable (and invisible) imperfection.

~

"What are you girls doing sitting on your bowhunkuses?" Bowhunkus was less vulgar than ass, butt, or hiney.

Momma stood there, face made up, dressed casually fashionable, her hair swept up like Grace Kelly's in *High Society.* At least Momma claimed that as the inspiration for this do. Nothing inspired Momma like movie stars. "Wash your cereal bowls and we'll pack them in the kitchen boxes."

Momma proceeded to whip everyone into a moving frenzy. When she set her mind to it, Momma could move mountains. Today, she was just gonna move a house. She bribed the girls with homemade brownies if they worked together. They did. She bribed Father—who didn't eat sweets but also didn't need bribing—with his favorite meal of chicken-fried steak and mashed potatoes. Like most women in the South, Momma used food as motivator, comforter, and cure-all. Within the hour, the rest of the house was loaded into the vehicles and ready to roll.

"Which one of my best friends is gonna ride with me?" Momma hollered to both Lindy and Jo.

"Me! Me! Me!" yelled Jo, always quicker on the draw.

"Jo spent all yesterday with you," said Lindy, referring to the haircut that Momma gave Jo that turned into an "afternoon of beauty."

"Nuh-uh, liar," Jo whined.

"Girls. Why don't you draw straws?" Momma dug a toothpick out of her purse, pulled a lint ball from one of the points, broke it in half and hid both ends behind her fingers. "Lindy, you pick first."

Lindy drew the short one.

"I win! I win! I win!" Jo yelled, too enthusiastically.

"We'll do some unpacking together tonight," Momma said to Lindy, as if that could compare to a day of beauty.

So Jo accompanied Momma in her old yellow 1958 Ford Fairlane, a cool car twenty years ago with its aerodynamic fins and bad attitude that was now just an old clunker with cracked vinyl seats and rusted metal dents. Father pulled the cattle trailer behind his pickup truck. Lindy rode with him in the cab, along with her basset hound, Lulu. Lulu, five years and fifty pounds of lethargy, sat on Lindy's lap putting out just enough energy to breathe. Not that Lulu wasn't healthy, she was just a basset hound. And a surprisingly agile one when she wanted to be. Her short little legs could carry her tri-colored body at a much faster clip than could Lindy's long two. But this was one of those times she preferred to act like dead weight.

Lindy kept her attention on the lump of flesh that was her pet basset in order to distract from the awkwardness she felt around her father. Lindy always called her dad "Father" just as she always called her mom "Momma." These monikers summed up Lindy's relationships with her parents. "Father" felt as stiff and formal as "Momma" felt warm and loving.

In the cab of the pickup, as was status quo, Father and Lindy didn't talk easily, not by a long shot. Lindy couldn't imagine Father talking freely with anyone, but she had seen him with his friends at the John Deere store and he seemed to chat quite nicely. Maybe it was her. She admitted to being a little afraid of him. His temper could flare to life with the intensity of a firecracker, and Lindy didn't want to push it. Not that he would hurt her. Not physically. But he might hurt her verbally. He might admit what she already knew but could ignore as long as it went unspoken: he didn't love her.

Father's attempts to make conversation with his daughter were as erratic as his temper and more excruciating. Watching her father's fidgety discomfort as he grasped to make small talk shredded Lindy's nervous system. She would answer with short responses because she didn't think he was interested in long ones and because her fear of rejection always lingered. Ironically, this had the exact effect Lindy did not want—she came off as disinterested herself. When Lindy initiated the discussion, she would try to engage her father in topics a twelve-year-old girl finds mind-boggling but a thirty-seven-year-old father finds stultifying. Father would clam up and his lack of participation quickly turned Lindy's attempt at dialogue into an uneasy monologue. He couldn't understand why his daughter always wanted to talk about *things*, disconcerting things like Vietnam, religion, *The Brady Bunch.* His idea of an enjoyable conversation was to talk about *nothing.* In short, their time together was spent distancing the other. Lindy disguised her anxiety with short, disinterested answers and Father hid by withdrawing inside himself. And both wondered why the other was always so defensive.

"Land sure is dry," Father said.

Let the games begin.

"Uh-huh."

"Sure could use some rain."

"Yep."

Pause. Silence. Deadly, unbearable silence. Lindy could tolerate only a few seconds. It was her turn to try. "Father?"

"Yes, Daughter?"

"You ever think about dying?"

Father stared straight ahead. "No."

"I do. What if the world ends soon?" That was his cue. He didn't pick up on it. "Or what if we get into another war and it's a nuclear war and it's all over and we're all burnt to a crisp in a matter of seconds?" Nothing. "Or if Armageddon comes like in Revelations and I'm not prepared or forgiven or... thirteen?" Lindy glanced over at her father for a response. She decided to give it one last try: "You know, I can really relate to Jan on *The Brady Bunch,* fed up with hearing 'Marcia, Marcia, Marcia.' Just like all I hear from Momma is 'Jo, Jo, Jo.' I mean, give me a break." She smiled, proud of her analogy.

Father looked over at his daughter, his brow furrowed as if viewing an enigma. Then he turned back to the road and caught a glimpse of something. "Maybe that there's a rain cloud."

~

Joe Logan looked uncannily like the Scarecrow in the movie *The Wizard of Oz*. He was thin and brittle and sported the classic farmer's tan—sun-browned from the shirt sleeves down and the neck up with a torso so white you had to wear shades. He was not a man of many words, but he was a man of many emotions. He just didn't know how to express them. He worked long, lonely hours in the company of only his tractor. As a farmer, he had relatively little cause for human contact. This was generally OK, but when he had a hankering for such interaction there was usually an equipment part he could do to replace and would travel to the John Deere store in Jessip for a bit of socializing.

Joe didn't own any land and that called for him to make his living as a farmer the hard way: leasing land from owners. He paid to farm the land and got seventy-five percent of the profits. But given the sad state of cotton prices, a lessee needed more than one piece of land to make a living. Most men could barely muster the time to farm two leases. Joe farmed three.

That is until last year when two of the owners decided to sell their land. The first sold his outright and informed Joe after the fact that his lease would not be renewed. The other told Joe of his plans and asked if he had an interest in buying the land. Interest, yes. Money, no. Money was a constant source of marital conflict with the Logans. Maggie, his wife, found solace in shopping sprees, even if only to K-Mart. Joe found solace in saving money, which was hard enough to do with two kids. Kids cost a lot of money. And Maggie got all their affection anyway. What did they need him for?

Joe's last lease was with his friend, Smiley McCorkle. Smiley and his wife Vernice had been friends with Joe ever since he first got into farming. Smiley was a jovial sort, always smiling (hence, his nickname). He was also a mentor to Joe early on, advising him in the ways of the land and the men who work it. Smiley warned that farming was full of ups and downs, usually correlating with the ups and downs of cotton prices. Joe heeded the warnings, and his experience indeed confirmed that, in farming, when it rains it pours. Unfortunately, that applied mostly to problems and only occasionally to actual rainfall.

Since Joe couldn't pay the mortgage on his house from the money he made on only one lease, Smiley offered to let the Logans live in his parents' old house. His mother passed away years ago, and his dad had lived there until his death a few months ago. The house was on the same property that Joe farmed, only a few hundred yards away from Smiley and Vernice's house. Smiley and Vernice never had any children of their own, and Smiley was an only child, so there was no one else to live in the house.

Smiley's mother had grown up dirt-poor in the Depression and believed in full-out ownership and not owing a cent to the bank. So she had insisted they pay off the mortgage and not borrow against it for any reason. His dad paid off the deed early and gave the paper to his wife as a surprise fifty-sixth birthday present. She died two weeks later. But she died happily owning the house.

After his dad's death, Smiley had inherited the house and he didn't feel right about charging his friend rent. But Joe didn't feel right about not paying rent. So they settled on a nominal amount of money to be paid monthly in the name of rent.

Blaaammm! It sounded like a gunshot. Father steered the pickup to the side of the road and surveyed the damage. Blowout. Momma pulled up behind and stopped. Father hunkered down to check under the trunk and confirmed his fear, a fear worse than just having a blowout. He hadn't replaced the spare tire in his pickup truck. What was his rule? As soon as you use something, you should replace it. He scolded the girls numerous times for breaking that rule and now he cursed himself breaking it too. He took Momma's place in the driver's seat of her car and promised to be back with a new tire as soon as possible. The female contingent stayed behind in the pickup, guarding the open-topped cattle trailer that held all of their earthly possessions. Even with the windows rolled down, the pickup truck was two degrees warmer than hell so they sat drinking from the sixteen-ounce Thermos of ice water that Father religiously carried with him. Jo drank so much, she eventually had to use the bathroom in the bar ditch beside the road. Momma and Lindy stood between Jo and the pavement, sort of a human outhouse. An hour and a half later Father came back from town with a tire. In another half an hour, that tire was on the truck and the vehicles were once again moving. Momma had not spoken to Father since leaving the house.

That pretty much summed up the morning.

The afternoon was worse.

Momma started speaking to Father.

The Logans arrived at their new home while the sun was still brightly shining. A mile away, the house looked hopeful. Or perhaps they looked upon it hopefully. By the time they pulled into the gravel driveway, their hope was gone.

"What a dump." Momma's words were appropriately to the point; Bette Davis couldn't have said it better.

The house was a shock. That is to everybody but Father, who already knew the house. Maybe he was shocked at one point; now the man was numb. He didn't seem to absorb any of Momma's verbal zingers. But she kept slinging them anyway. About the lovely carpet, which was glitter gold shag where their furniture had been, but was brown matted-down clumps everywhere else. About the modern kitchen appliances that were at least three decades old. About the wall-to-wall aroma of old people and cigarettes. About the roominess of the tiny two-bedroom, one bathroom house. Her sarcasm dripped bitter bile. You could've seen its residue on the floor if there hadn't been so many stains on the carpet already.

Lindy felt her usual discomfort at this latest of Momma's tirades. Par for the course, Father said nothing and the girls tried not to make the situation worse so they too zipped their lips. But at her core Lindy was tired and wished Momma would lay off Father.

Jo tugged on Lindy's sleeve. She was excited. Lindy groaned. This could only be bad news. "What?"

"We get to share a room," beamed Jo.

Great. Lindy hadn't shared a bedroom with Jo since they were little kids living in that house on South 13th. Well, at least with the twin beds from Jo's old room, Lindy wouldn't have to sleep with her.

"The room's too small for my twin beds so Father moved your full size in there." Lindy rushed to the smaller of the two tiny bedrooms. Jo was right. The room barely fit Lindy's full-size bed. She peered into the master bedroom across the hall. Momma and Father's queen size fit with just enough room to walk around the bed. The bathroom, the one they all had to share, contained the basic necessities—sink, commode, shower/bathtub combo—and more: cracked linoleum curling up in the corners, permanent mildew stains on the ceiling, rusty faucets, peeling paint, and not enough privacy for a near-to-be-teenage girl.

Lindy wandered back into the living room and listened to Momma's outburst with renewed vigor. The woman was right, gosh darn it. This place was a teensy-weensy hell hole and they were all gonna kill each other before it was over with, or even before it began.

With her new point of view, Lindy saw her mother as a Holy Roller evangelist laying down the truth and the way for the people, hard as it may be to hear. Lindy practically started swaying to the message. Tell it like it is, Mommasita—my master, my leader, my lord of all. *Hallelujah and amen!*

CHAPTER TWO

A couple of hours later, about suppertime, the doorbell rang. Momma was in the middle of a rant about what a sloppy housekeeper the last tenant had been—the last tenant, of course, being Smiley's elderly father. Momma stopped cold when she heard the arrival of company. Father answered the door. Smiley and Vernice stood on the stoop. Vernice held a Pyrex casserole dish covered in foil.

"Welcome." Smiley extended his hand.

Father returned the shake. "It's good to be here."

Momma whisked over to the doorway. "Please come in. Joe'd have you standing there all night."

"We don't want to stay long," Vernice said, entering. She spoke in a soft voice that intoned sincerity. "We know you're tired. Just wanted to bring you something to eat so you didn't have to cook." She indicated the casserole dish.

"You didn't have to do that, Vernice. But since you did, let's heat it up. Can y'all stay for dinner?"

Vernice shook her head. "We're gonna skedaddle and let you start unpacking."

"Well, we have to stop unpacking long enough to eat. You might as well eat with us." Momma's logic made sense and the McCorkles agreed to stay.

"As long as you'll give us orders and let us help with whatever," Vernice added.

"It's a deal. Let's go heat this up."

The women headed into the kitchen. The men settled in on the couch, clearly ordering themselves to relax. Momma turned the oven on and its rusty door squeaked when she opened it.

Vernice couldn't ignore the hinges' shrill screech. "I want to apologize for the state of the house. Smiley's father didn't much care for visitors and made it easy to oblige. I didn't realize it was so...*worn* 'til I came in to clean up the other day." She smiled at the look of surprise in Momma's eyes. "Believe it or not this is cleaned up."

Momma instantly felt guilty about her bitter tirade of before. "I appreciate your help."

"I can come back tomorrow and help blast through the second layer of crud. This place needs a woman's touch at the very least and a bulldozer at best." Vernice sighed. "Smiley's mother would roll over in her grave if she knew how her husband let this place go to hell in a handbasket. Heck, she's probably giving him hell right now." And on that, Momma joined in with a smile of her own.

∾

Lindy liked Smiley. He treated her like a person, not like a kid. She had met Smiley on her trips to the farm with Father. A short, tiny man with a basketball belly, he had a merry, round Santa Claus face. He was always jovial, but never picked on or teased her with stupid jokes like most adults did. But perhaps what Lindy found most fascinating about Smiley was his weird lower lip that bulged in that soft spot above his chin. For years, she just thought he was born with a deformed, protruding lip. When she mentioned that to Father he laughed so hard the beer he was drinking nearly bubbled out his nose. Smiley's lip wasn't deformed, he said; it housed a permanent pinch of Red Man chewing tobacco.

Now that Lindy had met Vernice, she was even more intrigued. If Smiley was a miniature Santa, then Vernice was his little Mrs. Claus doll. But that wasn't her most captivating feature. Vernice's pinkie and the finger next to it on both hands were wrapped together in skin like one big crooked finger. The joints underneath the flesh were clearly for two fingers. It looked as if a doctor were to cut the webbed skin down the middle she'd have two fingers like everybody else. Unless this deformity also had something to do with chewing tobacco.

As curious as she was though, Lindy tried not to look. She didn't want to be rude. Still, during dinner, her eyes would lock on Vernice's hands. Now as she was drying dishes, her eyes kept doing the same thing.

"Would you like to touch them?" Vernice asked Lindy, kindly.

Lindy was horrified. She had been found out. "I'm sorry. I didn't mean to stare." Her heart was pounding a mile a minute and it reflected in her shaking voice. The only saving grace was that Momma couldn't reprimand her because she had left the room to put Jo to bed.

Vernice leaned in to tell a secret. "My two little toes are the same way."

"Could a doctor fix 'em?"

"My parents couldn't afford 'acts of vanity' as they called it. I eventually accepted my digits by deciding I didn't want to be like everybody else."

Lindy thought about this. She wanted to be special too, but as a singer or movie star. Not because she had webbed feet.

"And, no, I don't swim faster because of them." Vernice smiled.

Lindy smiled too. Something about this soft-spoken woman just made her want to.

"I thought I was never gonna get her to lie still." Momma breezed in. "She's so anxious about being in a new house. So where were we? Oh, Vernice, I was gonna ask you—who are the people to know out here?"

~

Margaret—Maggie—Franklin Logan knew she couldn't do anything about having to move to this godforsaken place, but that didn't mean she had to like it. She was, however, going to make the best of it. Even in the boonies there were bound to be people who cared about the same things she did—culture, art, society. To Maggie, culture, art, society meant one thing—Hollywood. She could quote lines from old films and describe down to the accessories what her favorite screen heroines were wearing when they said those lines. She knew every bit of gossip printed about Tinsel Town—affairs, illegitimate children, sexual preferences. She was an avid reader of fan magazines, though she hid this "common" vice and would never admit to it. She empathized with the older stars she had grown up worshiping, but the new stars she chastised for being radical, liberal idiots. She cried when the newly widowed Doris Day realized her husband of seventeen years had embezzled her fortune, and she berated the anti-war efforts of Jane Fonda. Poor Henry was such a good father and what did it get him? Hanoi Jane and easy ridin' Peter. It just wasn't right.

When Maggie was a little girl, the whole family loved going to the picture show after church on Sundays. Each week the picture changed at the Rose Theater in Turnip, Texas, and each week for only a quarter per kid and two for adults, the Franklins sat tenth row from the front on the left center aisle.

From western shoot-'em-ups to grand musicals to tragic love stories, they went to be not only entertained, but uplifted. Maggie would never have told her mother, but she was far more inspired by the beauty and athleticism of Esther Williams than by the preacher's sermon that morning.

When teenaged Maggie became obsessed with Hollywood beyond the screen, her parents began to worry. They forbade her the purchase of movie magazines and chided her fascination with Sodom and Gomorra. If they had known of her secret desire to actually go to Hollywood, and live amongst those Communists, they would have shipped her off to the convent—or the Methodist equivalent.

Maggie truly loved her parents and had always been a good girl; she would never do a thing to hurt them—including running off to Hollywood against their wishes. Still, her dream nagged at her. Dreams were meant to be lived. If Maggie could go to Dallas or Houston and get a few local commercials, then her parents would see how well she handled fame. They would see she was mature. They would let her go to Hollywood. And Maggie saw no reason this couldn't happen. At eighteen, she was beautiful and had the proof with not one but two "Most Beautiful of Turnip High School" titles (after winning her sophomore and junior years, she understood the judges felt obligated to give the title to someone else her senior year; nevertheless, the memory conjured up emotions akin to her own personal holocaust). Maggie knew she needed exposure. Which is why long before graduation from high school, she had applied to enter the Miss Texas pageant.

The state prequel to the Miss America pageant rolled around in the summer of 1959, and Maggie Franklin as Miss West Texas was named second runner-up. One of the judges, a talent scout out of Dallas, asked if Miss Texas and her four runners-up would be interested in coming to Big D for screen tests that would be sent to several big-time Hollywood agents. The queen and her court were all interested except for runner-up number three who was engaged to be married and couldn't bear the thought of leaving her fiancé. Maggie couldn't imagine giving up her dream for a man; of course, it was just as well for this girl—her talent had been organizing a closet in five easy steps. Clearly housewife material.

Maggie was anything but. She knew she had acting talent, and she knew it came across on her screen test. She had been the star of all four of Turnip High's annual plays, and had even been named "Most Talented Turnip" her senior year. Yet the more time that passed without word from the talent scout, the more she began to question her talent. She found herself anxiously chanting a mantra under her breath—you are talented, you are talented, you are talented—like a cheerleader rooting for a team on an unexpected losing streak. So why hadn't she heard from the talent scout? He said the agency representatives would call if they were interested. Why wouldn't they be interested? Hollywood should be calling. Hollywood was her calling.

Maggie's mother, Lurleen, was getting caught up on her mending the day of the fateful phone call. She was alone in the house and that's the only reason she picked up the phone. A woman asked her to hold on for a Mr. So and So, and not being familiar with this business cordiality, Lurleen almost hung up. But before she did, Mr. So and So got on the line and identified himself as being an agent from William Morris in Hollywood. He was glad to reach someone at home; his secretary called twice yesterday and nobody answered. That's because nobody was home yesterday, Lurleen said flatly. Lurleen had driven Maggie around town trying to find her a nice dress for job interviews. Job interviews in West Texas. Lurleen wanted her daughter to be a secretary, preferably at a church; Maggie had been the most accurate typist in her class. And why in the Sam Hill was Hollywood calling anyway?

That's when Mr. William Morris stated his purpose—he wanted to sign Mrs. Franklin's daughter to an acting contract and since she was under the age of twenty-one, he needed parental approval. He said he wanted Maggie to meet with several film directors and start working in bit parts to build her resume and get her ready for starring roles. But what Lurleen heard was that he wanted her daughter to whore around with a whole town of Red perverts before being thrown out onto the cold, hard streets of Hollyweird and left for dead. Lurleen gained her composure enough to thank Mr. Morris for his diligence in reaching them, but was sorry to have to decline his offer. The fact was her daughter was no longer interested in being in pictures; she had decided to work in the church. Lurleen hung up the phone, grateful that God had chosen her to answer the phone and not Maggie. It would be over her dead body that Maggie would ever go to Hollywood, but it was best that her daughter never know the heathens had called for her anyway. The way Lurleen saw it, she had just saved her baby from a life of sin and regret. Lurleen had never been more proud of herself as a mother.

At the time of the call, Maggie was not scouring the churches for secretarial jobs as she was supposed to be, but sitting in her row at the Rose absorbing Marilyn Monroe's performance in *Some Like It Hot.* Her laughter during that movie healed her soul (more than the preacher's negative hellfire and damnation ever did), and purged all the insecurities that had crept in the last few weeks. She had Marilyn Monroe's beauty *and* her timing. Maggie simply needed to keep the faith.

But, as the months went by and time distanced itself from Maggie's shot at stardom, her faith faded. Self-doubt moved in and set up house. She stopped going to the movies so often, until she finally stopped going altogether. If she couldn't be a part of the movies, she wanted no part of the movies.

She became a secretary at the Church of Christ despite the fact that Lurleen thought they were a little radical—they dunked instead of sprinkled.

Two years later, while secretly moonlighting in Lubbock department stores as a demonstrator of household products that ranged from pots and pans to toilet bowl cleaners, Maggie had still not found more than the most fleeting of local fame. But she had found Joe Logan, who upon meeting this graceful clerk with the movie star looks, decided to ditch his unhappy stint as a car salesman in Jessip and try his hand at farming in Turnip. After all, his beloved was a farmer's daughter and would surely be happy as a farmer's wife. They married that year and in 1964 had a daughter named Lindy.

As far as Maggie knew, Hollywood never called.

~

Lindy lay in bed that night staring at the ceiling. It was the combination of the day's events and Jo's atrocious snoring. This eight-year-old cherub made noises in her sleep that would scare the most macho of men. Lindy would not sleep as long as she shared a bed with this freak of nature. How could Jo sleep anyway? Wasn't she upset about this move? This turmoil that was now their lives? Stop being so overly dramatic, Momma had said to Lindy a gazillion times. Well, this crisis warranted the drama. Her sister was snoring like a lumberjack.

Lindy sat up in bed, clutching her pillow and rocking back and forth. Her eyes glanced from her pillow to Jo's vibrating lips. What if she snubbed out her sister's snores forever? Would the court consider it premediated murder and ship her off to live in a cell with Charles Manson? Or would they understand the anguish she'd suffered and praise her for performing a public service?

As Lindy toyed with the idea of homicide, Jo's enlarged adnoids got their second wind. In lieu of braving the storm, Lindy took her pillow and walked into the closet. She closed the door behind her and lay on the floor beneath their newly hung clothes. This slightly muted Jo's hacksaw impersonation. Lindy buried her head under the foam pillow and willed herself to fall asleep. Instead, she fell into nightmare after nightmare, the worst of which had her showing up at her new school naked as a jaybird.

Lindy fought through the deep waters of the horror and forced herself awake, still bubbling on its surface, unsure of where she was. *The closet floor... the new house...yes, that was it.* She felt the relief of remembering, and just as quickly she didn't want to remember anymore.

She walked into the kitchen and was surprised to see how organized it was. Momma must have stayed up into the wee hours of the morning. Their kitchen clock was even hanging above the sink. Six-thirty. Lindy hadn't known her father to sleep past six o'clock in years. Was it from exhaustion or did Momma finally skewer him like a shish kebab?

"Mornin'." Father's voice. *Guess that answered that.*

Lindy turned to see her father standing in his boxers and T-shirt, hair disheveled and in desperate need of coffee. "Mornin'."

"Do you know where your mother put the coffee?" The poor man was completely disoriented in a domestic situation. His culinary skills consisted of boiling water for coffee and pouring milk on his dry cereal.

"Um, well..." Lindy tried to think like her mother. She opened two cabinet doors below the countertop and realized her mistake; Momma would never put the coffee canister below—pots and pans go down, cans and spices go up. Lindy found the coffee on the middle shelf to the left of the sink.

Father had started the water heating, stopping to note where Lindy found the coffee. Forgetting would cut his kitchen know-how in half.

"Thought we'd have a cookout tonight. Since it's the Fourth and all," Father said.

Lindy nodded. It was indeed the Fourth—the bicentennial, no less.

"Celebrate our move," Father continued. "I've got a special spot picked out. The bar ditch at the end of the section."

Lindy mustered a fake smile. The bar ditch? The dirt ditch alongside the road? What were they gonna cook, earthworms and asphalt? Maybe the man needed his coffee before he could think clearly.

Father didn't tell Momma or Jo about his special celebratory spot. He just told Momma to get together the fixin's for hot dogs and s'mores. She was certain the family had been invited to a bicentennial barbecue.

So when Father pulled the pickup off the road only a mile and a half from the house and announced this as his special spot, Momma's balloon burst.

While he readied the campfire with sticks and old newspapers, he prattled on about when the girls were little and the whole family would travel out to the farm to roast weenies. The dirt bar ditches just to the sides of the country roads were ideal for such cookouts, the fires being easily contained. Father glanced at his wife, hoping to share the memory, "We've always known how to have fun without much money."

Momma looked at him, blankly. "When are we gonna learn how to have fun with it?"

This abruptly ended Father's chatty streak.

In silence, he set everyone up with their own weenie to roast. Father roasted two at a time and ate them both. Momma couldn't finish hers, so Lindy did it for her. Everyone but Jo wanted to skip the s'mores. She set three marshmallows ablaze before consenting to Father's help.

No more fireworks went off that night. Not Momma, not Father, not even the bottle rockets

Father had purchased. The family returned home to watch the bicentennial festivities on TV. The rest of the country looked vibrant, colorful, happy. Every American burst with the exuberance of fireworks and celebration. And life. In fact, it appeared that life sizzled everywhere that night but in Grady County. In Grady County, in the house of the Logans, life fizzled.

~

Lindy awoke in the middle of the night with a severe case of hot dog poisoning. The rest of the family quickly followed suit. Their one toilet was standing room only. In her wildest dreams, Lindy could never have imagined that much pain and suffering coming from a package of weenies. She swore not to eat hot dogs ever, ever, *ever* again. Hot dogs had been her favorite thing in the whole world.

Life continued to fizzle.

CHAPTER THREE

Except for a couple of days here and there, living in town had allowed Lindy to escape hoeing the vast rows of cotton in the summer and tromping the newly stripped cotton in the fall. But now they were moving out to the farm. She would be expected to work all summer hoeing cotton and after school in the fall tromping it.

Of the two, hoeing was the worst. The Public Land Survey System had determined the farm to be one square mile or a section of land, which is equivalent to 640-acres. One acre contains 43,560 square feet, and, of that, weeds seemed to cover 43,559 square feet. They grew everywhere the cotton did, only with deeper, tougher roots. And the weeds towered over the newly budding cotton plants. To kill the weed, the entire stubborn root had to be pulled out of the ground. That meant chopping at a weed until the hoe stuck in it like a hatchet, then pulling with all your might and praying the entire root retreated from the earth. The weeds deserved their names of devil's claws and iron weeds. Iron weeds were akin to cutting a one-hundred-pound barbell with a nail file. Devil's claws literally sprouted an evil two-clawed hook that would latch onto your boot and not let go. Many a time, Lindy would come home from the fields with so many devil's claws clinging to her boots it looked like she was dragging Rosemary's baby.

These wicked weeds were one reason to wear boots in the fields. Another was rattlesnakes. Rattlers looked for refuge from the West Texas heat anywhere they could, including under the leaves of an overgrown weed. If a rattler struck, its fangs couldn't pierce the leather of a boot. Lindy had never run upon a rattler herself, but Father had hacked several to pieces with a hoe or just plain shot 'em in half with his rifle. The mere thought of the repulsive reptile from the story of Adam and Eve made Lindy want to retch. Why on God's green earth, Lindy wondered, would anyone choose to spend a summer battling devils and dirt when one could be dipping Dilly Bars at an air-conditioned Dairy Queen? But no matter what the city girl in her wanted, Lindy was stuck in the country now. Her summers would never be a series of ice cream breaks at a local fast-food restaurant, but a string of red necks and farmer's tans.

~

Whereas Lindy focused on lemons, Jo made lemonade. Her method of hoeing cotton made the whole rotten chore bearable, enjoyable even: take lots of breaks. Unlike her sister, Jo had up to this point been completely able to avoid Father's sporadic efforts to recruit his daughters as hoe hands. She chalked it up to her status as the baby of the family. And her ability to use that status to the *n*th degree. Jo figured there were equal advantages to being the oldest and the youngest. You just needed to know how to take advantage of those advantages. But when it came to chopping cotton, the baby defense would no longer fly. Jo was almost nine and old enough to help with the chores. This would put a big dent in Jo's summer plans. She was in training to be a model.

Jo prepared for her career hands on. She looked in the mirror constantly. She posed. She puckered. She strutted. And all with an eye toward being a future runway queen and cover girl. She dressed up in glamorous hand-me-downs—beauty is in the eye of the beholder—and would try on Momma's makeup when Momma was in the mood to give permission. All of this pampering and primping drove Lindy crazy. All the more reason for Jo to love it.

Jo had pampering on her mind when she reached the end of the cotton row. It was time for one of her breaks. She plopped gingerly onto the ground to keep the loose dirt from flying up into her face. Dirt would clog her pores. Jo lifted the Thermos of ice water and drank 'til her stomach was full. She had read that top models always drink plenty of water to flush out the impurities in their systems.

Then she turned the Thermos upside down and let the water flow onto the ground, mixing with the dirt until she had a nice muddy pool. It was time for a mud facial. Jo had read that models believed in daily facials, and she saw this as a perfect time to incorporate the ritual into her own daily routine.

She applied the mud to her face, perched her bottom (Momma said to never use the tacky *butt, buttocks,* or *rear*) atop the Thermos to avoid snakes and turned her face toward the sun.

Nice day, Jo seemed to think. *Yes, it is, the voice in her head said. See, we can make anything fun, the thought bubble responded. Life's not worth living if it's not fun, agreed the voice.*

"What in the heck are you doing?" Lindy demanded, and Jo almost jumped out of her skin. It was jarring to have your internal dialogue so rudely interrupted.

"I'm cleansing my pores," Jo said, irritated at being sneaked up on. She had forgotten about Lindy being all the way back in the field. It took so long to get down the row when you actually did the work of hoeing. "You could use it to get rid of those blackheads in your T-zone."

Lindy felt her nose. Her blackheads weren't that bad. "What I could use is some water if you'd move your bottom."

Jo did move her bottom and handed the near-empty Thermos to Lindy. "What did you do, pour all the water on the ground?"

"No. I drank some too."

Lindy swallowed the last drops in the Thermos. "That's all the water. We just got started. Father won't be back to pick us up 'til lunch time."

"That's only a couple of hours. We can make it."

"I'm not just gonna let you sit there. You're gonna help me hoe this field."

"I'm just taking a break. You're not my boss."

"Father's our boss and he's gonna kill us if..."

"I have a theory...why do they call it chopping cotton when you're chopping weeds?"

"You are such an ignoramus."

"I know you are, but what am I?"

"Shut up."

"No, you shut up. Killing the roots is dumb. No matter what you do there'll still be new weeds next year."

"Why don't you tell Father this?"

"I don't think he'd understand."

"Gee, I guess that's 'cause it's stupid. If we don't kill the roots of these weeds now they'll grow back even before next year. Like in a couple of months."

"In a couple of months, we'll be in school. Father won't make us hoe cotton while we're in school."

Lindy was shocked. As much as it hurt to admit it, there was a certain logic to that.

Jo continued: "It's much faster to chop the weeds off at the ground. That way it looks like I'm following Father's instructions and if he finds out I'm not, well, then, I guess I just misunderstood. After all, I am just a little kid."

Incredible, Lindy thought. *She has all the bases covered.*

"I'm telling you it makes hoeing a lot more fun," Jo said in summation. "You have time for facials."

Lindy had always known Jo was devious beyond her years—after all, most of the time Jo's deviousness was used to get Lindy into trouble. But Lindy only saw how she could benefit from this scheme.

"You know, maybe I should take a break for the rest of the morning. I mean we are out of water and all. I wouldn't wanna parch." Lindy raised the corners of her mouth into a wicked grin. Jo returned the favor.

The rest of the morning Jo spent cooling her eyes with the chilled cucumber slices she had brought from the kitchen and shucking her face free of the crusted mud pack. Lindy sang show tunes, largely from *The Sound of Music,* her favorite since she had first seen the film as a toddler. Lindy had never been to New York, but she dreamed of the Broadway stage. It sounded like the most magical place in the world and her greatest passion was to be a singer in Broadway musicals. But in her heart of hearts, she knew Broadway was too lofty a goal. She would have to settle for being a world-renowned pop star.

Lindy was writing songs in her head constantly. A lot of the time anyway. At least the few minutes a week she felt the rush to be a star. Of one thing she was sure, any hit song had to have the word baby in the chorus—the more times the better. Lindy would get the chorus in her head and keep repeating it over and over until she could run home and pick out the tune on the piano. As for her voice, she exercised her naturally gifted instrument by singing along with her eight-track tapes, but that was when she had had the privacy of her own room. Now she didn't know where to perform her vocal stylings of the latest Linda Ronstadt, Olivia Newton-John, and Carpenters' hits. Perhaps every morning in the cotton fields.

So it came to pass that in the hot July sun in the fields of West Texas, Jo became Twiggy working the Paris runways and Lindy became Julie Andrews running through the Austrian Alps. Lindy decided Jo was right, this made hoeing a lot more fun.

~

Father picked up Lindy and Jo from the field each day at noon. Each girl made sure she was hoeing furiously when he drove up. Noon was lunchtime for them all and the end of the workday for the girls. Since the summer sun was a scorcher in the afternoons, Momma had talked Father into requiring their daughters to work only the first half of the day. The summer afternoons were the girls' to enjoy however they chose. They usually chose to enjoy them in front of the television set.

Lindy loved television. She memorized every facet of each week's *TV Guide*—from the articles to the program listings. She knew the schedule of each network seven nights a week plus the selection of syndicated shows during the days. Most of the time, Father didn't bother to look up TV listings, he just asked his daughter. She was a walking *TV Guide.* She knew which shows got cancelled, which got renewed and which got changed to a different time slot or night. She knew when regular programs gave way to specials, and this information came in especially handy during the holiday season. She even knew how to tell time by when specific programs broke for commercials.

Television offered a more fascinating world than Lindy had ever seen. Momma and Father were always telling Lindy to stop watching so much TV, to go play outside, to go do this or that, to live life. But the life she lived through television was more exciting than anything she could live in the desolation of West Texas.

The year 1976 was an especially good one for TV. The Winter Olympics had aired in February, and after watching them Lindy wanted to be Dorothy Hamill. Or at least be her best friend. Or at least have her haircut. Momma wanted Lindy to keep her hair long. Lindy begged. And begged. And begged. Lindy kept her hair long.

Lindy fell into a depression after the Winter Olympics ended. The only way she pulled herself up by the bootstraps was the realization that the Summer Olympics were coming up toward the end of

July, which was now only a few days away. It was good to have something to live for.

Olympics or not, there were always sitcoms. First run, rerun, and syndicated. Every hour of every day. Lindy's lifeblood. These people were more than funny. They were friendly. They were loving. They were family. What they experienced, Lindy experienced. Where they lived, Lindy lived. Where they went, Lindy went. When the Bradys vacationed in Hawaii, she was there. When Laurie Partridge got her braces, she was there. When Endora turned Darrin #1 into an animal, she was there. Ditto, when Endora did the same to Darrin #2.

Lindy even thrilled to the theme songs of her favorite shows. Who couldn't love the catchy little ditties that introduced *The Brady Bunch, The Partridge Family, The Monkees,* and, especially, *The Mary Tyler Moore Show?* That 20-inch tube definitely turned Lindy's world on with a smile.

The only time TV let her down was just after the closing credits of a favorite show. Her friends disappeared and the consolation that they would air again next week was no consolation at all. What Lindy had looked forward to all week long was over in a few short minutes, dumping her back into reality and leaving her to fend for herself. It was like being in class with the most popular girl in school. Her personality draws you in, you feel better about yourself just being in her presence, but when class is over, that's it. She leaves, you go your separate ways. No good-bye, no nothing. She doesn't even know who you are.

Despite the occasional separation anxiety regarding certain programs, TV was the one constant in Lindy's life. It talked to her when she was lonely, it cheered her up when she was down, it took her mind off herself. She didn't have to be perfect when she watched the tube, it accepted her as she was. It gave everything and took nothing. It was the best friend in the world.

Jo watched television simply because it was always on. The only program she begged to watch was the annual Miss America pageant.

Par for the course, the girls sat in front of the TV this summer afternoon as well. Jo sported attire appropriate for watching reruns of *I Dream of Jeannie*—Momma's petite chiffon formal from her coronation as Turnip High's Most Beautiful 1957. The dress was not that much bigger than Jo. It was hard to imagine it had ever fit Momma. Lindy lounged in her version of TV watching apparel—a frayed T-shirt and denim cutoffs.

"This isn't so bad, is it?" Momma whirled in like a dirt devil, dusting the TV. "Oh, I'm sorry, I didn't mean to interrupt your program. I'll wait 'til the commercial."

"It's OK," Lindy said, trying to steer her eyes around Momma.

"Y'all watch too much TV anyway." Momma resumed her dusting. "Living out here isn't so bad, is it? Y'all get to work outside. I'm gonna start a garden. Grow our own fruits and vegetables. We'll can 'em, preserve 'em, make whatchamacallit...jam...jellies...jam... Vernice'll show me how, I'm sure. It'll be fun." Momma's voice cracked on "fun."

"Do you need us to help, Momma?" With the cleaning, Lindy meant.

"No. Y'all worked in the field all morning. You deserve to sit and relax. It is your summer vacation after all."

Momma moved just past the TV to the knickknacks decorating the shelves of the entertainment center. "Just think, when school starts, this community will probably liven right up. With football games and social events of some kind, surely. There'll be lots of new people to meet. I mean, what are there? A couple hundred people that live in the county, at least?"

Momma suddenly got quiet, gazing off into some internal netherland. Too late, Lindy realized this was the calm before the storm.

Momma's voice was even, yet cutting: "Why can't you girls be like those nice kids on TV? *The Brady Bunch* girls would feel guilty sitting around watching their mother clean the house all by herself."

"They have Alice," Jo said.

What a moron, Lindy thought. *Just throw kerosene on the flames, why don't ya.*

Momma was incensed. "I wanted to help my mother with the cleaning. And I always did, without being asked."

Lindy picked up the cue. "We'll start with the bathroom." She turned to Jo. "Come on."

Jo followed, chiffon dragging the floor. "I have to change."

"Yeah, do something about your clothes too," Lindy shot back. She led Jo into their room, then turned on her. "'Alice'? You are really stupid."

"I know you are, but what am I?" Jo stuck out her tongue in quick snake-like darts. "This is your fault. You're the one who asked if she wanted help."

"You're the one who brought up being a housekeeper."

"I did not. I brought up Alice."

"She's a housekeeper on TV, you dummy!"

~

Maggie worked as a housekeeper for some of the wealthy families in town—one of the bank presidents, the owner of the Piggly-Wiggly, and the only Jew in town who was also the only lawyer in town. She cleaned the kind of houses she had always dreamed of living in, houses that were large but not too ostentatious. Houses in which every bedroom had its own bath, and rooms were so plentiful that the extras had been turned into offices and game rooms. Sometimes

Maggie pretended it was her own house she was cleaning—cleaning herself just for the fun of it, because she never had to do it, because the help had the day off.

Maggie didn't mind the work of cleaning houses. She minded the class to which it relegated her. And this she minded to her core. The one upside of moving to the farm was that it presented a new community that would not view her as a cleaning lady, a servant, *the help.* She intended for these new neighbors to see her as another housewife who took care of her house only. She would not advertise her skills or take on new houses outside of town. And she did not want the well-to-do ranch wives who lived in the county to know of her status—or lack of it—in town. She only wanted one thing—to feel equal.

~

The bathtub passed the test. Lindy ran her finger along the porcelain. Except for the crack under the faucet it was smooth as a baby's butt. Amazing what Comet and backbreaking scrubbing could do. The toilet had been soaking in the cleanser and was ready for its turn. Where was Jo? Lindy was not getting stuck cleaning the whole bathroom by herself. Jo had probably gotten sidetracked deciding upon the proper wardrobe for bathroom cleaning. Lindy grabbed the toilet brush and headed for their bedroom.

But the giggling she heard came from Momma's room. Momma and Jo sat on the bed picking through a mound of clothes.

"Come in." Momma motioned to Lindy. Lindy did, leaving the brush in the hallway.

Jo's face dropped when she saw Lindy. "Momma wanted me to help sort through her clothes."

"Some of these things are just atrocious. I've got to give them away." To prove her point, Momma held up a sixties' pantsuit so loud it screamed. She tossed it in the "out" pile where it landed with several other outfits that hadn't been worn in years. She claimed each piece to be out-of-date or god-awful—which they were—but there was another reason she was forced to do away with such antiques. She had gotten too damn fat. She would never admit it; she couldn't even acknowledge it to herself. Her identity was wrapped up in being Miss West Texas 1959.

"I'm helping her," Jo reiterated.

"I heard." Lindy forced a smile.

"I was ready to burn the whole lot, but Jo Bean saw the potential in several outfits."

"I have an eye for these things." Jo was humble about her enormous gift.

In lieu of gagging on Jo's humble pie, Lindy thought of the rhyme she and their cousins used to tease Jo because of the nickname Momma had given her: "Beanie, Weanie, the Fartin' Meanie." *Ah, the good old days.*

"She does," Momma confirmed. "Jo Bean really does have an eye for these things." She pulled up another item. "What do you think about this?"

Jo turned serious, examining the possibilities. "I think it needs just a little splash of color. How 'bout that scarf?"

"This one?" As Momma reached for it, Lindy took this opportunity to back away. Fashion was not her forte, and she couldn't stand this best friend act between Momma and Jo.

"Where are you going?" Momma had caught her.

"I haven't finished cleaning." Lindy stared at her sister, "And neither has Jo."

"It doesn't matter," Momma waved it away, now as awash in calm as she had earlier been in rage. "Take a load off. You girls've been working hard this morning. Why don't we have a tea party and do our hair the rest of the afternoon?"

Jo looked to Lindy, who muttered a hesitant "O-kay." A tea party was good. Doing hair could be very, very bad.

But to Momma it was the remedy. "I don't need new clothes, but a new hairdo...I found a picture of a do...it would look so cute on me...where is it..." Suddenly, she was deep in a sea of torn-out magazine pages.

Lindy looked at Jo and mouthed "No." Jo shrugged and said, "Maybe just a tea party, Momma?"

"Oh, no," Momma said. "Hair's the fun part. Now, where're my scissors?"

She went in search of her shears as her daughters shook their heads almost imperceptively.

~

Jo and Lindy had purposely glued themselves to the television and that's where Father found them when he came home for supper. There was no other activity in the house, far as he could see. Certainly no activity in the kitchen. He stepped in front of the TV and changed the channel to the news. The girls let out a groan to signal their discontent, but didn't push it. You never wanted to set off Father's temper.

"Where's your mother?"

"We're on our own for supper tonight." Jo was being helpful.

"Is she here?"

"Uh-huh." Lindy pointed to the bathroom.

Father narrowed his eyes, confused for only a second. Then he knew.

Momma stepped out of the bathroom and into the living room. It wasn't far to step. "Hi, hon."

There was a brief pause that matched Father's slight intake of breath. "Hi," he said genially. But it was too late. He knew it, the girls knew it, and, most importantly, Momma knew it.

"You hate it." Momma nailed him.

"No, no. It's just..."

"It's Dr. Seuss hair," Jo chimed in. She was being helpful.

"I knew it. It's awful. It's not even close to blonde. I must've been crazy to think I could get beauty shop hair color out of a do-it-yourself rinse." Momma toweled off a drip of solution from her forehead.

"It's nice," Father said.

"It's green," Momma replied.

"Like *Green Eggs and Ham*," Jo said. Lindy shot her a look.

"It is a little green," Father agreed. "But the cut is..." He paused, searching for words.

"Too short." Momma began to wail in a fashion similar to Lucy Ricardo. "I look like an artichoke!"

"No you don't...much." This was Father, trying to help.

Mother wailed louder.

"Look, go to the beauty shop if that'll make you happy. I want you to be happy." Father was trying, bless his heart.

"Oh, no," Momma countered. "I don't want to hear you complaining about how poor we are."

"One visit to the beauty shop won't break us."

Lindy wanted to encourage her mother in this direction. "The beauty shop can save it. It's not so bad." *Yet.* Lindy knew that if her mother tried to repair it, it would only get worse.

"No," Momma said. "I can do this. I'm going to do this. Come hell or high water." *Or burnt to-the-root hair*, Lindy thought. That's what happened the last time. All Momma's hair broke off and for months she wore scarves on her head like some sheik. Nothing like having a bald-headed mom for kids to make fun of. Lindy's new classmates would have a field day with that.

Momma threw TV dinners in the oven for everyone but herself, then was off to the bathroom. One more rinse of color would remove her hair's lime green tinge and another would bring her to the intended blonde. Momma was certain of it. Her family wasn't.

Lindy had almost finished her aluminum-enclosed square of apple cobbler when the scream came from the bathroom. It was expected, but jarring nonetheless. Father, Lindy, and Jo never knew what to do during these crises and this time was no exception.

Suddenly, Lindy surged with bravery. "I'm going in." She looked to Father. He didn't budge. Lindy made her move. Jo followed. Their adrenaline pumped as they closed in on the disaster, driven by that twisted human quality that forces us to gawk at the wreckage of other people's accidents.

Momma stepped into the hallway ahead of Lindy and Jo and made an announcement. "It's orange. Your mother has orange hair. Or according to Jo's Crayola 64-pack, burnt sienna. Welcome to the farm." She returned to the bathroom and slammed the door.

Momma didn't open the door until later when Jo threatened to pee in her pants. "Don't say that," Momma said as she let her youngest in. "Say 'it's an emergency.'" Jo came out and reported that Momma was trimming her hair more. Father said nothing, but decided to go to bed early. The girls were determined to stay up. It was Friday night and they didn't have to get up early to hoe the next morning. They got weekends off.

Momma emerged before Johnny Carson had signed off on *The Tonight Show.* She sported an orange-hued crewcut. Momma supposed she had too many chemicals on her hair already, what with her perm and three previous tints. This last color not only turned her hair a color that would make Sunkist proud, but made the strands heat sensitive. The blow-dryer sent the abused hair flying like fluffy seeds blown from a dandelion. Momma had no choice but to cut it and start from scratch. Momma showed her daughters the welts on her head from the chemical burns and downed four extra-strength aspirin within the hour. She took the bottle of painkillers and went to bed. She didn't get up until Saturday afternoon.

Momma staying in bed for days at a time was also a pattern familiar to the girls. They knew it was in their best interest to tiptoe around the house and let Momma remain buried under the covers. She wasn't going to get out of bed until she was good and ready to get out of bed, and it behooved everyone to accept that. Momma's hibernation was less about sleeping and more about escaping. But when she took herself out of commission, a funk fell over the house. Lindy couldn't shake her sick feeling of guilt and wondered if she had in any way caused her mom's depression. In her gut, Lindy knew that's what it was—depression—but she called it "Momma's mood."

When Momma arose from her mood in time to make Saturday night supper, Lindy held her breath. Would this Momma be Dr. Jekyll or Mr. Hyde? Momma's respites didn't necessarily put her in a better state of mind. In fact, they oftentimes had the opposite effect.

"Didn't you girls make dinner?" Momma said with more than a hint of sarcasm. The girls didn't answer. There was no right answer.

"Well how 'bout if I make a peach cobbler for dessert? It'll match my hair color."

Three cheers for Mr. Momma Hyde.

Momma's mood lightened further as she made supper. She was serving her family to purge her guilt after almost twenty-four hours of neglecting them. The girls chatted with Momma in the kitchen, alternating one at a time so that they each got Momma's undivided attention. The one not being doted upon would go into the living room and watch television. The funk lifted from the house. It was a wonderful evening.

CHAPTER FOUR

Sunday morning held a distinct ritual in the Logan household. Certain Logans were not as fond of the ritual as others. Momma hated it. Father loved it. Of course, it was his ritual.

On the Sabbath, Father would rise before anyone else in the house. He also rose before anyone every other day of the week. What made this morning unique was the ritual. This was the morning that God hath made. This was also the morning that Father playeth his records. He started by dusting the jackets of his alphabetically arranged classical albums. Then he placed the morning's first selection on the turntable. With the volume low, he sat in his La-Z-Boy and conducted the orchestra. At that moment, he had it all. His body commanded the authority of a maestro, and his face revealed the smile of a little boy. Nothing made a man swell inside like Ferrante & Teicher. That was classical music.

When it was time for the rest of the house to get up, Father abandoned his weekday habit of rousing the females out of bed by knocking on bedroom doors, announcing times and, inevitably, turning on overhead lights. Classical Sunday was special and, as such, it required a dramatic, fiery awakening. So as the music crescendoed, Father cranked up the volume. The boisterous strains filled the house. He would be conducting full-out by this point, one arm leading the musicians as the other made morning coffee. As the orchestral bass vibrated the knickknacks that lay on the stereo speakers, Father thought how much he would appreciate being woken up this way.

Momma always refused to make breakfast until Father turned the volume down; she had long ago given up trying to make him turn it off. He would turn it off when he was ready to turn it off and not a moment before. It was the one time Father exercised his stubborn control, and the one time Momma let him. If he didn't stop her from staying in bed during her moods, she wouldn't stop him from raising the dead with his damn—darn—classical music.

Father did turn the volume down a notch so Momma could hear herself think enough to make breakfast. She continued to bitch about the music—she allowed him to play it, but she couldn't stop nagging him about it—and she continued to scream over "that noise." Lindy didn't think the music was as noisy as Momma's yelling above it, but she would never say that. She didn't want her mother's anger to shift away from the music and onto her. And Lindy would never, ever admit to her mom that she liked the music. At first, Lindy had sided with her mom, as usual. The bold music jarred her bones. Then when it stopped scaring the heck out of her, it began to grow on her. Not because of the music itself, but because of the tradition. She found comfort in the stability, in the expected behavior. Every Sunday morning Lindy expected Momma to complain about the classical music, and she expected Father to play it anyhow. And every Sunday morning they never let her down.

~

Jo had still not finished her breakfast cereal when it was time to head into town for church. Numerous Fruit Loop people floated in the milk, battling for their lives as Father lifted Jo out of her chair and carried her to the car. Jo's blatant abandonment of the Fruit Loop people upset her greatly. The whole ride in, she could concentrate only on what was to be her newfound reputation as the savior who couldn't deliver. What if Jesus had let his people down like this? Let them drown in a giant bowl of rainbow-colored milk and fruit holes? He wouldn't be the Jesus she was going to church to worship today, that's for sure. She felt herself spiraling downward, drowning in her own giant bowl of guilt and sorrow. Nothing could make her feel better, not even Momma's offering to let Jo read her copy of *Good Housekeeping* with Christy Brinkley on the cover.

Jo was a Fruit Loop people murderer.

~

Momma had managed to cover her carrot top surprisingly stylishly with one of her famous scarves. She looked like a trendsetter, instead of someone who had tried too stubbornly to follow the trend. Some of the women in church even complimented her new style; others said nothing, obviously threatened by trendsetters.

The Logans had been attending the First United Methodist church in Jessip since before the girls were born. Father always sat at the end of the pew with Lindy next to him, then Jo, then Momma. The girls had each learned at an early age to sit still in church, and given the dull-as-dishwater sermons, that was no easy task—even for adults. But Momma's stern looks quieted a fidgeting girl real fast, and her pinches downright paralyzed one. In their younger days, the girls were allowed to occupy themselves by drawing pictures on back of the blank checks that the banks provided in the pews. With the pencil stubs also found in the pews, the girls sketched numerous portraits of stick-figure Logans. Stick-figure Jo and stick-figure Lindy were barely indecipherable, stick-figure Father was distinguished by his glasses, but drawing stick-figure Momma was the most fun. In those days, Momma sported the requisite beehive. But even then she couldn't help occasionally butchering her hair, so it was never able to grow long enough for a natural beehive. She wore a hairpiece, long strands of hair that matched her color. And if her color changed, she would buy a hairpiece to match that color too. She had accumulated several of the fake hair accessories. To achieve a beehive, she braided the piece, twisted it up into a hive and pinned the whole thing on top of her head. It became known as Momma's topknot. The height of the topknot was always exaggerated in the girls' drawings, often running off one check and continuing onto another.

Capturing the artistry of Momma's topknot helped the girls to survive many a sermon.

As Lindy grew older she sincerely tried to listen to the sermons. She was too old to draw in church—that was for babies. But the pastor didn't make it easy to pay attention. He alternated his speech between monotony and melodrama. Just when his monotonous tone lulled you to sleep, his voice suddenly crescendoed to a melodramatic intensity acceptable only in the pulpit. These moments frightened Lindy, partly because they jarred her awake, and partly because they were all hellfire and damnation. Yet it never once dawned on her that the preacher's routine was a lot like an actor's performance on a daytime soap opera. The only difference was that one made her roll with laughter and the other scared her to death. After all, this wasn't just a bad actor in the pulpit; this was a man of God.

Lindy didn't know what to think about God and would never tell anyone she wondered if He even existed. But she was afraid of death—that she knew—and if there was life after death and if God was the way there then she was gonna believe in Him. It only made sense, therefore, that she had to believe in the men God had chosen to spread His word. She had to revere and respect them. She at least had to fear them. That's what they preached from the pulpit every week.

"God is love," a typical sermon would begin. Birds chirped in the background, sun glistened through stained-glass windows; then, in the blink of an eye, black clouds descended and the Garden of Eden morphed into the bowels of hell. "Fear God, fear His wrath, fear His plagues, fear His famines, fear His fires, fear His destruction...did I mention plagues? Oh, well, as long as you *fear Him.*" The preacher would pause, then regain his composure. "Now go with God. Remember God is love."

Messages of fear and sorrow pervaded the church—the stained-glass window of God violently casting out the angel who became Satan, the dirges that reverberated like death escaping from the organ pipes, the stringent stoicism of the entire ritual. The implication Lindy took from all of this was that God loved the perfect. Fear of God kept you in line, kept you on the road to perfection. If you attained perfection, you had less to fear because God loved you, unless of course you stepped out of line and became imperfect, then God stopped loving you and you must fear Him all over again. It was a vicious cycle. Lindy was striving to be perfect. She wanted God to love her. She wanted to live on in heaven. But she was exhausted by the constant threat of losing God's love and inevitably slipped off her tightrope of perfection. She feared the God of fear. It was harder to love the God of love.

The one good thing about church service was that Lindy sat by Father every week. All her life she wanted to be Daddy's girl and this was as close as she got. Church didn't allow for alienating conversations. As they sat in silence every Sunday, Lindy managed to convince herself that her father loved her. She waited for a confirmation, like him putting his arm around her. When he finally did, usually as an excuse to ward off sleep by stretching during the sermon, Lindy froze, becoming a statue, barely breathing, repressing sneezes, willing away itches. She knew Father would take any movement on her part as a sign that she was uncomfortable and remove his arm. And she wanted her daddy's arm around his girl. Not that Lindy was wholly comfortable—suppressed movement and inhibited breathing is no picnic—but she was comforted, which was much more important. So if Lindy didn't move and didn't breathe, then Father's arm would stay over her shoulders until they stood up to sing a hymn. And for those few moments she would be Daddy's girl.

~

"Sing out. You have beautiful voices." Momma leaned over to her daughters as the congregation rose for a hymn. "Page 301, 'Holy, Holy, Holy.'" It was Lindy's favorite. It was the catchiest hymn she knew.

Jo refused to really sing. She mouthed the words but the sound that emerged was barely a whisper. Jo equated her voice with a frog's. No, a frog's was better.

Lindy knew she sang like an angel. It was the only quality of hers she had any confidence in at all. So while Jo let her song be drowned out in the sea of voices, Lindy let her voice sail. She belted the words—"Holy, Holy, Holy, Lord God almighty"—and the melody of Lindy rose above the din like an angel.

Lindy looked up from her hymnal. A little girl stood on the bench before her, smiling up at Lindy. She couldn't have been older than two or three; as soon as her mother saw her errant daughter, she spun the child around to face front. Momma chuckled.

Church service let out at exactly twelve noon. One minute past and the parishioners got restless. The pastor didn't dare destroy his illusion that his congregation was glued to his every word so he never held them late. He had learned the hard way. As a young minister just out of seminary, he liked the sound of his own voice a great deal and expected his followers to feel the same. When one Sunday, he went not five, not ten, but fifteen minutes after twelve and even the most devoted parishioners began to leave—in droves, it seemed to him—well, he never kept them past the hour mark again. Nothing destroyed a shepherd's ego as much the sight of his sheep wandering out to pasture while he was still speaking.

The reason for such promptness was simple. The Methodists had to—*had to*—arrive at K-Bob's before the Baptists. K-Bob's was Jessip's steak house, not the only one, but the only one that was fancy. It was part of a chain. No greasy spoon after Sunday church. K-Bob's sported three dining rooms (each large enough to accommodate a rural school's Future Farmers and Future Homemakers of America banquet), a huge salad bar housed in a covered wagon that boasted everything from bread and butter pickles to banana pudding, and a diverse menu that offered meat in every form imaginable—fried, filleted, and fingered.

Now, it wasn't that the Methodists minded the Baptists dining at K-Bob's. They just minded the Baptists dining there before them. Truth be told, the Church of Christ always let out their service the earliest and got to K-Bob's first. They mined over the salad bar, but nothing like the Baptists. The Baptists were, well, they were pigs. They were massive in number. They far outnumbered the Church of Christ. Heck, the Baptists outnumbered everybody, although the Methodists liked to think themselves a closer second than they were. The other of the Big Four, the Presbyterians, also headed for K-Bob's post-church, but there were hardly enough of them to amount to a spit in the bucket. The only ones who made a big dent in the food stock were the Baptists. And whoever came to eat after them had slim pickings. The Methodists did not want to be eating hamburgers because the Baptists had ordered all the ribeye.

~

Four minutes after twelve and Father was still visiting with the men outside the church. Momma stood with the girls.

"Go tell your father to hurry up. The Baptists are gonna let out any minute." Jo ran for her father as instructed. Momma waved good-bye to several departing congregation members, ad-libbing "How are you," "Good to see you," and "See you next week."

Lindy felt a tug at her hem. It was the toddler who had been so fascinated by her singing, and her cheeks still dimpled with the same giddy smile. "You sing loud."

"She means you have a beautiful voice," the little girl's mother tried to clarify in an apologetic tone. She held onto her daughter's hand.

Momma turned her effervescence toward these strangers. "No need to apologize. It's hard to rein her in. She thinks she's a singer." Momma rolled her eyes and extended her hand. "I'm Maggie Logan. I sing the solos on special occasions—Christmas, Easter. Hope you'll keep attending."

The young mother reeled back ever so slightly. "I'm Kristina Coughlin. We just moved here from Tulsa. I don't know which church we're gonna join," she said quietly. "We're shopping around."

"Tulsa, huh? Oral Roberts country. He's Methodist, isn't he? Well, regardless, this is the biggest church in town, outside the Baptists. But you don't wanna get lost in that crowd. If you don't watch it, they'll turn you into a lay-lay before you can say 'Praise the Lord.'"

"'Lay-lay'?"

"Lay witness. Baptists are big into that. 'Spread the word, spread the word.' Won't go to heaven unless you're sprinkled with Baptist holy water, as if their tap's better than anybody else's. I say give it a rest. It does make me wonder what else they're into—speaking in tongues or that charismatic crap. They come off pretty cult-like."

Kristina's brow furrowed. "Uh, well. I don't know if this is a permanent move. I really miss Oklahoma."

"Well, who doesn't love the musical? But, really, is that reason to stay there?" Momma chuckled at her joke.

Kristina didn't seem to hear, as she was frantically eyeing the crowd. "Um, excuse us. My husband is waiting." She pointed in his supposed direction and scooped up her little girl like it was a matter of life and death.

Momma scrutinized their backs and called out, "Be sure to come and hear me sing." She turned to Lindy. "Okies. They can be so rude."

Ten after twelve and the doors to the Baptist church across the street opened. The congregation poured out like bees to honey.

"Good Lord," Momma grabbed Lindy's wrist and pulled her toward Father. "If we don't get to K-Bob's right now, there won't be a spoonful of fruit cocktail left at the covered wagon."

But Lindy didn't hear a word she said. She was thinking about her singing. She wondered why she no longer felt as confident. It was nothing she could put her finger on.

~

Momma encouraged Father to drive through two rather pinkish traffic lights—pink being the transition from yellow to red—and, as a result, the Logans arrived at K-Bob's in record time. They waited in line for only a few minutes before being seated and were thrilled to see they had beaten the bulk of the Baptists who now stood in a line that ran out the door. Momma had the feeling of leading a charmed life. She ordered the all-you-can-eat salad bar and, while standing in line for the covered wagon, spotted the McNamaras sitting in dining room number one finishing their meal. The McNamaras always arrived early. They were Church of Christ. Momma did not want to give up her place in line to the impending masses so she waved until she got Lindy's attention.

"Shelly," Momma mouthed loudly, pointing to the other dining room. "The McNamaras. Get up. Go say hi."

A hot rush of panic shot through Lindy's veins. Shelly McNamara was her best friend since kindergarten. They knew everything about each other, sharing sleepovers, secrets, sorrows. But right now, there was only one thing Lindy knew—there was no way she could talk to Shelly.

That's because Shelly *had* been Lindy's best friend. Past tense. The cold, hard truth was: Shelly lived in town. Lindy now lived in the boondocks. They could no longer be best friends. With the move came Lindy's new unbreakable rule—no friends from town. She couldn't bear to be reminded of her old life when she was so ashamed of her new one. Not that she was as embarrassed of living in the boondocks as she was of being so poor that she had to live in the boondocks. She was certain Shelly wouldn't want her as a friend, not now; and with that, Momma agreed.

Yet, Shelly had already written Lindy once in the week since the move, and Lindy was surprised to get the letter. Momma didn't think she would ever hear from Shelly. Lindy shrugged and said Shelly's mother probably made her write it. And with that, Momma agreed.

Shelly's family was fairly well-to-do, at least in Jessip's terms. The McNamaras loved Lindy, but weren't so fond of Maggie, at least Shelly's mother wasn't. So with the move, Momma suggested Lindy dump Shelly as a friend, start anew in Grady. Lindy mulled it over and decided that, yes, she was unable to fit together the oil of her old life with the vinegar of her new. She had moved only days ago, yet it seemed like an eternity. The farm was a mere thirty miles from town, but it might as well have been on another continent. Lindy didn't want to forget the time she and Shelly caught the huge goldfish in the stream by the YMCA. She didn't want to forget yakking at slumber parties or trying to levitate each other or gorging themselves on Morton's frozen honey buns. She didn't want to ache for her best friend until she was all ached out. And because she didn't want to do it, she knew there was only one solution: cut all ties with her old life. She would force Shelly McNamara out of her blood. With that, Momma agreed.

Now, sweat broke out around Lindy's hairline, leaving the stringy mess clinging to her forehead like a flat octopus. Judging from the clamminess of her palms, she suspected her temperature would blow the mercury out of the thermometer, and she wished she could blame her symptoms of the flu. Ah, to have the flu. It sounded like the best diagnosis in the world.

But she didn't have the flu. She had come down with a case of homesickness. This crippling geyser of emotions usually burst forth every time Lindy was forced to spend the night away from Momma. Lindy was afraid Momma would die when they were separated and she would never see her mother again. She could not survive that. When Momma died, Lindy wanted to die too.

She thought she had gotten a hand up on her homesickness. It had been years since the forced sleepovers at her grandparents' house during which Lindy cried herself to sleep. Her wails always cut a planned weeklong visit down to one night, and her grandmother would drive her home the next day. On one visit her grandfather drove her the two-hour round-trip home at three o'clock in the morning. By the time she was six, her grandparents stopped inviting Lindy to spend the night.

Shelly's was the only place Lindy had ever been able to spend a homesick-free night. Lindy was thinking about this as she meandered up to Shelly's table.

"Hi, Shelly. Hi, everybody," Lindy managed, nodding nervously. "My mom saw you over here."

"Hi, Lindy," said Mrs. McNamara. "How are you doing?"

"Good." Lindy nodded while looking at her shoes. Her shoes bounced up and down in her frame of vision.

Shelly smiled. "How's the farm?"

"Fine," Lindy said, still nodding. She couldn't stop nodding. She was nodding like one of those stupid bobbing-head dolls.

"Are you OK?" Shelly asked.

"Yeah," Lindy said. Nod, bob, nod. "Are you?"

"Uh, yeah. I meant is your head OK?"

"A little case of whiplash. During the move. No big deal."

Shelly's mother spoke up. "You should have your momma take you to the doctor, sweetie. Your head shouldn't keep doing that."

"How are y'all doing?" Momma stood there smiling, her all-you-can-eat plate full of salads from potato to Jell-O. For the first time since her head had started its Katherine Hepburn impersonation, Lindy breathed. She was saved. Momma had stepped in.

"Hello, Maggie," said Mrs. McNamara. "We were just telling Lindy to have you take her to a doctor for that head bobbing."

"It's not doing it anymore," Lindy said quickly.

"No, it's not doing it anymore," Mrs. McNamara noted. "Well, maybe as a precautionary measure."

"I'll consider myself advised," Maggie said. She turned to Shelly. "You two will have to keep in touch. We're still close enough for you both to get together."

Lindy smiled at Shelly, focusing not on her eyes, but outside her ear. She wondered where she had gotten the idea to dump Shelly as a best friend.

Lindy ate less than half her chicken fried steak, and Momma took the rest home for supper. It was one of the rare times Lindy actually adhered to her self-imposed diet plan.

Momma eventually stopped harping on the McNamaras and six months after moving to the farm Lindy got around to writing Shelly. She never heard back. At that point, Lindy considered the friendship over, but felt more like the dumpee than the dumper. And with that, Momma agreed.

CHAPTER FIVE

The Saturday afternoon movie matinee was *Bathing Beauty* starring Esther Williams. Personally, Lindy preferred the thrills of competitive swimming in the Summer Olympics or, better yet, of watching Bruce Jenner win the decathlon. That he was a hunk didn't hurt either. Lindy had even replaced her poster of David Cassidy with one of the decathlete, as a sign of maturity. After all, she was on the brink of adulthood; her room decor needed to reflect that. But the Olympics had ended a week ago, and the only choice for weekend afternoon viewing today was old movies.

Momma, on the other hand, was in heaven. Yes, her animosity against Hollywood had lasted several years. But eventually her love affair with the movies picked up where it had left off. She concluded it was petty to reject Hollywood because it had rejected her; that was forgetting the golden rule. The truth was she couldn't survive without Hollywood; it was the only thing in life that invigorated her.

"Now that's a movie star," Momma said of Esther Williams at the commercial break. Watching old movies, Momma was born again. As much as anything, old celluloid was her religion. They washed away her sins. They made the impossible seem possible. They connected her to a world she desperately wanted to believe existed. They gave her hope to go on in the world that really did.

"I used to think Lolly looked just like Esther Williams," Momma continued as she lounged in Father's La-Z-Boy. "And Birdy like Loretta Young." Lolly and Birdy were Momma's older sisters. Lolly was thirteen years older than Maggie, Birdy eleven.

Lolly's name was a hybrid of Laurie Lee. As a teenager, Laurie Lee decided she wanted to change her name. Laurie was too common and Lee too masculine so she came up with LaLe which she pronounced with a French accent. Everyone refused to call her that until one day when her toddler sister Maggie called her "Lolly." This was easier than the mouthful "Laurie Lee" and close to the name LaLe had given herself, so the parties compromised and the name stuck. As an adult, Maggie often wished she'd dubbed her eldest sister Lala, which she felt was appropriate since Lolly was always off in Lala land. Anyone who considered white patent leather go-go boots suitable footwear for their father's funeral was off in Lala land.

If Lolly was as colorful as a parrot, Birdy was dull as a sparrow. Birdy's God-given name was Bertha. But Bertha never really fit her; the name was much too big. Instead of being a Big Bertha, this Bertha was quite the opposite. She looked like a twig and was the pickiest eater ever born. This earned her the nickname Birdy as a child. The name still fit her as an adult—she never ate more than a few bites in a meal and remained thin as a rail, and if it weren't for the fact that she hen-pecked everyone to death, not a soul would notice she was present.

The girls had heard Momma's Lolly-to-Esther Williams and Birdy-to-Loretta Young comparisons a hundred times. "My sisters were so beautiful. I thought they were as gorgeous as movie stars."

"You were the most gorgeous," said Jo.

"Not nearly...," Momma said, smiling.

"You're the one who won all those beauty contests," Lindy said. "You were almost Miss Texas."

"I was Turnip High's Most Beautiful. Twice."

"You coulda been a movie star," Jo insisted.

"I coulda been."

"You only had to say yes when Hollywood called."

Momma couldn't help telling her daughters the story of her brush with fame, and she couldn't help lying about it. In her version, Hollywood did call. She turned them down, opting for a family instead of movie stardom. Momma told this story so many times, she almost believed it herself. Momma was still a good actress.

She was also chock-full of what-ifs. What if she hadn't waited around for the call that never came? What if she had just gone on to Hollywood? What if she had believed in herself, truly believed? These what-ifs filled her memories until she had no choice but to shut the memories off. Regardless of any what-ifs, that was a long time ago and there was nothing she could do about it now. She tried to stuff these feelings back in their box. Once freed, they were so unruly. Uncontrollable. Messy. But they weren't cooperating today. Damn hormones. They must have something to do with this. They always added fuel to the fire.

The movie came back from commercial seconds before Momma's eyes welled up with tears. She lowered her head, hoping to dry up before the girls saw. But they sensed something was wrong. The girls glanced at Momma, then turned to the TV screen for an explanation. There was no sign of movie death or tragedy or even romance, just Esther's big Technicolor water finale. The girls peeked back at Momma, now blowing her nose. This was not her standard modus operandi. Hiding all day under the bedsheets, yes. Breaking down, no. They didn't know what to do. They froze like two deer in the headlights.

Jo asked aloud what both girls were wondering. "What did we do?"

"Nothing. Just hormones," Momma managed with a teary-eyed smile. "And Esther Williams. Lolly looked so much like her."

~

Esther was emerging from the synchronized circle of bathing beauties for the last time when Father walked in with the mail. He knew not to speak until "The End" appeared on the screen, so he waited until then to hand Lindy the envelope that was addressed to her. She opened it and silently read:

⁂

> You and your family are invited to a swim party for the Grady County seventh-grade class at Amber Donovan's house. Date: August 15. Place: See directions. Please RSVP.

⁂

A phone number and map accompanied the invitation. Amber's house was marked with a red dot. Like Lindy, Amber lived in Grady County, but her address was someplace else. Route 2, Box 80, Stickley, to be specific. *Compared to Treat,* Lindy thought, *Stickley must be a metropolis. It had two routes and a box number.*

The thought of meeting her new classmates scared Lindy to death. So she decided not to think about it. She would not give it the time of day. *Would not, would not, would not.*

Yet, she couldn't not think about it. Only seconds after receiving the invitation, her brain was stuck in this sick and twisted cycle. *Scared to death, don't think about it, must think about it.* Just imagine the mush her brain would be by tomorrow. Lindy suddenly noticed a pen-point-sized stain on her white T-shirt. It might as well be the size of an extra large pizza. With stinky anchovies. She must erase her blemish with Clorox.

"That's not a letter from Shelly McNamara, is it?" Momma's question stopped Lindy in her tracks.

"It's an invitation for a swim party." This delay only made Lindy jones for the bleach more.

"A swim party! How exciting! Stop tugging at your shirt. Anybody I know?"

"One of the girls in my new class." *Clorox...Clorox...Clorox...*

"Who?"

"I don't know. Amber somebody."

"Let me see," Momma said, snatching the invitation.

"I don't even have a bathing suit!" Lord, how she needed her bleach fix!

Momma's face lit up like a light bulb. "Hold your horses, I'll make you one. I have lots of material I bought on sale at the dime store in Jessip."

Lindy stopped clutching her shirt. "Can you have it ready in two weeks?"

"Of course. We'll pick out the material tonight." Momma loved coming to the rescue. She loved focusing on a project. She loved having a distraction from all those what-ifs.

Lindy calmed down, her need for bleach washing away like one of those grimy stains in a detergent commercial. *Why did she make such mountains out of molehills?* Now thinking rationally, she saw that a squirt of Spray 'N Wash probably would be enough to do the trick on her stain. It was, after all, only a pen mark.

~

After dinner, Momma and Lindy looked through the fabric and agreed that the lime green-and-white-checked terry cloth was perfect for Lindy's first bikini. There was even enough cloth for a cover-up to go over the suit. Momma went into town the next day and bought a Simplicity pattern for a bikini and hoodie cover-up. She took her time sewing the suit, and when she finished, the craftsmanship outshone anything store-bought. Not a stitch was out of place, even the material's green and white checks matched perfectly at each seam line. Momma was so proud she glowed.

Lindy, however, was not at peace with the suit. Something about all the time Momma put into it made her feel guilty. Shoddy craftsmanship would have been hunky-dory with her. She didn't care about the checks matching at the seams. She didn't care about every stitch being in place. She did care about her suit passing as store-bought.

Lindy stressed so much that she began hemorrhaging internally. After an afternoon episode of *Bewitched*, she went to use the little girl's room and pulled down her new white summer shorts to find her panties covered in sticky red blood. "Momma! Help! I'm dying!"

Momma cracked open the bathroom door. "Goodness gracious, sakes alive. What are you screaming for?"

Lindy looked down. "Take me to the hospital. I'm bleeding."

Momma followed Lindy's eyes. "You're not dying," she said, with a small chuckle. "It's that time of the month."

"What?" Lindy wondered.

"You know," Momma whispered, "menstruation."

Lindy looked up. "You mean, the curse?"

"Don't say 'curse.' That's a dirty word."

Lindy later learned that "period" was also unacceptable in the house unless referring to punctuation. So the monthly cycle was referred to as "that time of the month." Certainly Esther Williams would evoke such a euphemism.

"Here," Momma said. "I'll help you put this on." She handed Lindy an inch-thick pad and an elastic belt with small hooks.

Momma slid the cotton on either side of the pad into the hooks, harnessing them firmly into place, making what resembled a skeletal pair of panties. "Now step into this."

Lindy did as she was told. "You'll wear this under your panties," Momma instructed.

Lindy looked at herself in the mirror. She thought of a National Geographic show she had seen about instruments of torture for women in third-world countries and wondered if this contraption had been one of them.

"Do I wear this under my bathing suit too?" Lindy asked.

"Oh, no, sweetheart. You can't wear this in a pool."

"But Amber's pool party is next week!"

"Don't worry, you'll have stopped by then."

"How long do I have to wear this?"

"Four, five days tops."

"And then that's it?"

Momma nodded. "Um-hum."

Lindy signed in relief.

"Until next month," Momma added.

"I'm going to have to wear this every month?!"

"That's why it's called 'your time of the month.'"

"Will it ever stop?"

"When you're having a baby." Momma smiled. "Didn't you read that book I gave you?"

"Not yet."

"Well, maybe you should. Now you get dressed and come on back to the TV. There's a Loretta Young movie about to start."

Lindy slumped onto the commode. News that the mattress hammocked between her legs would not be necessary come pool party time left her tepid at best. This curse—that's what it really was—sounded like a raw deal all the way around. Lindy didn't want to bleed into this antiquated apparatus every month.

And she certainly didn't want a baby. What other good news was in store for her?

Lindy cleaned herself up, then dug out a book from under her bed—*Welcome to Puberty.*

The more Lindy read, the more horrified she grew.

What was in store for her? Turns out, puberty held quite a few pitfalls: Hips that widen into child-birthing conduits. Hair that grows in places only Europeans want to show off. Breasts that balloon into Wonder Woman-type missiles. Lindy realized this hell was already beginning. Store clerks were guiding her out of the boys' clothing section and into the "young miss" aisle. The other day, Momma tearily presented her with her first razor for girls, a pink plastic circle molded to look like a flower with, surprise, a blade in each petal.

And, despite twenty-four-hour vigils begging God to reverse the trend, Lindy's breasts continued to grow. This was the most upsetting. She tried hiding her ever-expanding bust by hunching her shoulders, but she still sensed boys gawking and girls snickering. What horrible sin had she committed to deserve to be the only twelve-year-old on earth with cleavage?

Plus, her shirts betrayed her snowballing secret. Two little nipples, perky as can be, pierced into her one hundred percent cotton T-shirts. She was naked to the world just like in her nightmare where she arrived at school and only then realized she was wearing nothing but her birthday suit. Momma had even mentioned the other day that they needed to go shopping for "lungholders." (Lungholder was Momma's name for the crass sounding "bra.")

Lindy couldn't even escape the effects of her blossoming bosoms after dark. The last time she spent the night with Shelly, Lindy noticed Shelly's dad looking at her breasts through her nightgown. Suddenly, her innocent childhood nightgown with the flowers stitched onto the chest made her feel like Vegas showgirl twirling her tassles. Until she finagled some heavy-duty flannel pajamas, slumber parties were definitely out.

Lindy sighed and shut the covers of *Welcome to Puberty*. This was an awful, disgusting thing that was happening to her. Yet Lindy was too exhausted right now to decide how to combat this blight engulfing her. The only thing she knew was this: as soon as puberty opened its arms and welcomed her, she wanted to spit in its face and run screaming.

CHAPTER SIX

The day of the party dawned to find Lindy blessed. The curse had indeed vanished along with the volcanic pimple on her chin and the fever blister on her lip. Miracles did happen.

She fitted herself into the bikini and looked at her reflection in the mirror, not just being perfunctory, but scrutinizing. Her hips weren't gargantuan, her privates weren't grotesquely hairy, and her breasts weren't yet the size of watermelons. Why was she worried? She didn't have anything to be embarrassed about.

"I'll be in the car," Momma hollered. It was time to leave. *Holy crap,* Lindy really had to go to this thing. Her internal cheerleaders vaporized and took her fleeting confidence with them. Lindy really had to go to this thing.

She heard the ignition roar the car to life, threw on her matching cover-up and hurried to the garage. She opened the door that led to the garage and froze.

Jo sat in the front seat beside Momma.

Lindy wanted to pull Jo out of the car and bounce her on her rear end...er, bottom. Instead, she climbed into the back seat without saying a word.

"Momma said I could come 'cause I never get to go swimming."

Momma had this fantasy that her daughters loved each other, idolized each other like she did Esther Williams and Loretta Young. Instead they were Bette Davis and Joan Crawford.

Momma caught Lindy's eye staring in the rear-view mirror. "I thought I told you. The invitation included families and I RSVPed for three. I didn't even ask your father. I knew he had to work and I thought it'd be fun with just us girls."

And twenty of my future classmates, thought Lindy. Not only did she get to introduce them to her mother's citrus-colored crew cut, but also to the messiah of the Fruit Loop people. With her over-sized mammary glands, Lindy felt like the last circle of a three-ring circus. Her family should be the life of the party.

~

Momma turned off the paved road and onto the long caliche road that led to the Donovans' ranch. From the highway, a huge barn appeared to loom in the distance. But as they neared the sprawling two-story horse hotel, it dawned on Lindy that this building didn't house horses or hay. This was Amber's house. This was Tara. That must make Amber Scarlett O'Hara.

Lindy nervously pulled at a thread on her home-made cover-up and stared at the short strands of orange that escaped the camouflage of her momma's head scarf. Her heart pounded as they neared the mansion. Her organs screamed to stop, turn around, go home. But she couldn't tell her mom that. *Stop, turn around, go home.* What could she say to get out of this? *What? What? What?*

"I think I'm gonna throw up," Lindy spurted.

"Do you have a stomach bug?" Momma glanced over her shoulder.

"Eee-yee-ee-sss," Lindy groaned in her best sick voice.

"Do you need me to stop the car?"

"No," Lindy said quickly, too quickly. "I mean, yes. I need you to stop, turn around, and go home." Lindy instantly regretted saying exactly what she wanted. Deception required a patience that her panic didn't allow.

"Mrs. Donovan is bound to have some Pepto. You can take that and lie down in Amber's room." Lindy panicked. Pepto Bismol always made both her and Jo throw up. Lindy's plan had gone awry. If Momma asked for Pepto, she would be forced to take it, and without a doubt she would throw up. The thought of throwing up in Amber's room made Lindy feel sick for real.

"I don't need any Pepto. I'm feeling better already. It was just gas, I guess." They were less than a hundred feet from the Donovans' palace. Lindy had to think fast. *Plan number two...Plan number two...*

"Oh, Momma. I forgot to tell you about the movie that's on the afternoon matinee today. It's that old movie you always say you can't see enough times."

"What movie is that?"

"You know, the black and white one."

Momma played along. "Of course, the black and white one. I love that one."

"So if you wanna go home and watch it, that's fine with me. Since I'm not feeling too good anyway."

"I thought you were feeling better."

"It comes and goes."

Momma parked the car behind the line of vehicles and killed the ignition. She turned around and faced her eldest daughter. "You're going to go to this swim party. We're here already. If you don't want to swim, you don't have to, but your sister does and we're gonna stay for her. Now do you want me to ask for Pepto or not?"

"No." Lindy didn't need Pepto, the way her stomach was doing somersaults, she was gonna toss her cookies without it.

~

"Hi, I'm Amber. Welcome to my house." The twelve-year-old Judy Garland look-alike answered the door with an authority only wealth could buy. "You must be Lindy Logan."

Lindy managed a speechless nod.

"L squared."

"Excuse me?"

"L.L. Your initials. Two Ls. L squared."

"Oh." *Yes, indeedy.* Lindy did feel square.

"I'm L squared's mother. Maggie. And this is Jo."

"It's nice to meet you," Amber said to Momma, polite as could be. And equally so to Jo—"I've always wanted a little sister. I don't have any sisters or brothers."

Lindy rolled her eyes. *What a kiss-up.*

"Y'all come on in. Amber, give these folks a breather. She'd talk the legs off a chair." The big man with the booming voice gave Amber a tickle. She giggled. "I'm A.J. Donovan. Amber's dad." Mr. Donovan hugged his little girl.

"I'm Maggie Logan," Momma said, offering her hand. "And these are my girls."

Mr. Donovan looked at Momma. "No, ma'am. These girls can't be yours; I thought you were the new seventh-grader in town." Momma giggled and the gentle giant placed her hand on his arm and led her inside in one smooth move. "Here, little darling, let me give you a tour of the old place." Jo grabbed Momma's other hand and followed the magic carpet ride through the house.

So Amber, the only child, was also a daddy's girl. *How fair is that?* Lindy thought. *People with money aren't supposed to have love too; it leaves the rest of us with nothing.*

"Your mom's pretty. Why the orange crew cut though? She joining the army or something?" Amber smiled at Lindy so pleasantly, her sarcasm barely registered.

"It's her Mia Farrow phase," Lindy said protectively.

"Oh," Amber continued. "That must make you Rosemary's baby."

Before Lindy could comment, the hostess quickened her pace. "Let me give you the layout. Food's over there, drinks are next to it, pool's out back. Have fun." Her tone implied she had gone, but she stood appraising Lindy, a stern look on her face. "L squared, you need to stand up straight."

Amber spun Lindy around and gouged her knuckle between Lindy's shoulder blades. Like a shot, her shoulders popped back and her chest thrust forward.

"Much better." Amber smiled proudly, then turned on her heels. She may look like Dorothy, but she was definitely the Wicked Witch of the West.

~

"A.J., you are very modest, but how can you call this house a 'little shack'?" Momma was laughing at every one of Mr. Donovan's jokes.

"You think this is cozy, you should see where my race horses shack up," Mr. Donovan said with a wink.

Truly, the accommodations were breathtaking. The interior was less the palatial southern grandeur of Tara and more the raw Texas rusticity of Reata—Liz Taylor and Rock Hudson's estate in *Giant*—with a touch of Queen Victoria. How appropriate that a little princess should live here.

As they walked through the house, Maggie caught glimpses of a study, a dining room, a game room, a guest bedroom, all done in rich mahogany wood. God only knew what was upstairs. The Donovans were indeed in high cotton. The tour ended up in the den, which led to the pool area.

A.J. opened the sliding glass door and sounds of the party thundered in. Jo made a beeline for the water, but Maggie didn't need H2O. She was soaking in the atmosphere, which included an elaborate buffet, far more ostentatious than warranted by a seventh-grade pool party.

A waitress flowed from the kitchen carrying a tray of bite-sized food. In a thick Texas accent, she asked, "Hors d'oeuvre?"

"Thank you." Maggie took one of the toothpicked thingamabobs, too intimidated to ask what she was about to ingest.

A.J. helped himself and examined the sample as he spun the toothpick. "Horace Derves. That's what I used to call them when I was a kid. Thought they was named after some guy named Horace Derves." A.J. popped it in his mouth and spoke while he chewed. "What are these anyway?"

"Escargot, Mr. Donovan."

"Snails!"

Maggie gulped, but she told herself it was too subtle to be noticed.

"Hmmm," he said as he digested another. "Them little buggers ain't half bad." The waitress smiled—another satisfied customer—and went about her mission of spreading slugs amongst the unsuspecting crowd.

A.J. ushered Maggie outside where several smaller snack tables were arranged around the pool along with coolers of Cokes for the kids and a bar for the adults. A uniformed bartender manned that post.

"My wife selects the Horace Derves for these shindigs," A.J. said. "But we'll be cooking burgers and dogs later on if none of this tickles your fancy."

"Oh, no, A.J. This tickles me plenty."

And it did. For the first time since meeting that talent scout at the Miss Texas pageant, Maggie felt at home. This may not be her house, her pool, her cars, or her family, but this was where she was meant to be. This was the life she was meant to live.

"There you are, A. Your scotch and water's becoming more water than scotch." A woman walked over carrying a highball glass.

"Thank you, Piddle." A.J. took the drink from her and leaned over to kiss this very tiny and dignified woman. "Piddle, this is...oh, hell. Jog my memory?"

"Margaret—Maggie—Logan. I'm L squared, uh, Lindy's mom. Amber's new classmate."

"Oh, yes." Piddle extended her hand. "I'm Amber's mom. Sally."

As Maggie shook Piddle/Sally's hand, her focus narrowed until one question burned in her mind. How in the world did this petite woman and this giant man have sex? Maggie tried to knock the thought out of her head—it was, after all, inappropriate and none of her business—but it kept pushing its way back in. Such positioning—missionary or otherwise—just didn't seem possible. And it sure as hell couldn't be comfortable. Maybe that's why Amber was an only child. A giggle slipped out before Maggie could suppress it.

Mrs. Squished-by-the-Giant glared at her. "Something funny?"

"Nothing. Something caught in my throat." Maggie coughed convincingly.

"I think she's having a reaction to the snails, Ma," A.J. said as he downed his drink.

"They're a delicacy." Sally looked Maggie up and down and then said sweetly, "I guess that's why."

Maggie chose to overlook that comment and barreled on with chitchat. "Your house is divine." That sounded like a word the wealthy would use. She tried to mimic Kate Hepburn's socialite in *Philadelphia Story*. "And your ranch is equally...majestic."

"Guess that means I'm the king of my castle." A.J.'s scotch was taking effect.

"Get another drink, A.J." Sally patted her husband's hand because she couldn't reach much higher.

"Don't mind if I do." A.J. lumbered toward the bar.

Sally turned back to Maggie. There was an awkward silence. Finally, Maggie had to break it. "How long have you lived here?"

"All our lives. My father was one of the original ranchers in the county. A.J.'s family came later, but struck it rich with oil so we let them stay."

Maggie tittered, "That's cute." Sally said nothing, so Maggie continued, "You say you've lived here all your life?"

Sally nodded slowly, as if talking to someone of lesser intelligence. "Yes."

"Well, it is just exquisite."

"What's that?"

"Your home."

"I thought it was divine."

"That too."

"My goodness," Sally said in her best hillbilly-mocking accent. "You have such a highfalutin' vocabulary. We're just simple country folk. Not like you city people."

"I'm not city people. I grew up in Turnip. I'm a country bumpkin too."

"Isn't that divine?" Sally smiled. Her putdowns were getting hard to ignore.

The tension was broken by Jo's screech of "Momma!" as she headed for Maggie.

"Sssshhh!" Lindy whispered after her, trying to avoid a scene. "I told you, you can have it. Stop yelling."

"I snorted water up my nose. Lindy won't let me use her nose plug. She's not even swimming." Maggie shot them the evil eye. Jo shut up instantly.

"Girls, this is Sally Donovan, our hostess. These are my girls, Lindy and Jo."

Sally looked at Lindy. "You're in Amber's class?"

"Yes, ma'am."

"It's the biggest class at Grady. Thirteen boys, four girls. Five counting you. Course the girls run the class," she sniffed, "as it should be."

"Yes, ma'am," Lindy said, plastering a beauty pageant smile on her face like she had seen Momma do so many times. "Just like my momma runs the house."

Lindy knew her joke was brilliant the way Mrs. Donovan cackled. But Momma was not amused. Oh, she beamed her own Miss America smile all right, but she also pinched Lindy's backside, hard. Lindy let out a little yelp.

Sally wiped her eyes with her napkin and glanced at the seventh-graders now cannonballing into her pool. "Grady County has a wonderful school system, but the seventh grade has the best kids. They elected Amber class president. She's also a cheerleader and a starter on the basketball team. Do you play basketball?" she asked Lindy.

"No, ma'am," Lindy said, feeling no longer like a beauty queen but a second-class citizen.

"Oh. Well. You're tall enough. You can learn."

Yeah, Lindy thought, *if I hadn't been absent the day God handed out athletic ability.*

"Why aren't you swimming?" Mrs. Donovan asked Lindy.

"'Cause she has boobies," Jo cracked with the timing of a vaudeville comedian.

"Jo!" Maggie reprimanded her daughter.

Jo deflated. "They laughed when I told them." Jo pointed to a crowd of seventh-grade boys who smiled at Lindy. A couple of them even waved.

"You little creep," Lindy said to Jo. The only thing she had to live for now was mutilating her sister.

It was Mrs. Donovan who saved Jo's life. "Why don't you go take a dive in the pool?" she said to Lindy. "Really give them something to look at. You do know how to swim?"

"Yes," Lindy nodded. She looked at Momma who urged her on. "Here, hold these." She gave her glasses to Momma, then headed reluctantly for the pool. She took off her cover-up, folded it neatly and laid it on a chair.

"Where'd you buy her bathing suit? I thought Amber had tried on every darn one in the state of Texas," Sally said.

Something in Sally's tone made Maggie embarrassed of her once-proud craftsmanship. So she lied. "Lubbock. Hemphill-Wells." It was the fanciest department store Maggie could think of on the spur of the moment.

"Really? I shop there all the time. Course I don't hit their bargain basement."

Lindy stepped onto the diving board. Maggie caught herself praying that for once her daughter would not belly flop. But after several minutes, it appeared Lindy would not jump at all. She stared into the water, wearing not the concentration of an Olympic champion, but the self-consciousness of new kids everywhere.

Gone with the Wind could have been screened in the time Lindy stood on that board. *Gone with the Wind* including the intermission. Perhaps the worst part was that Lindy now had everyone's attention. The kids, the caterers, even the snails were curious. The world had stopped to watch Lindy Logan. Momma knew she was gonna belly flop.

Slowly, Lindy bent at the waist and sprung into the water. Her entrance was effortless. There wasn't the usual drenching deluge that seemed to empty the pool after a belly flop bomb; there was only the delicate spritz of water that followed a dive of Olympic caliber. Maggie gasped. Her daughter had not embarrassed her. Maggie broke into spontaneous applause. Many others in the crowd followed. For all they knew, they had just witnessed greatness.

Lindy surfaced, bobbing up and down like a buoy in the water. It took her a moment to realize the applause was for her. And just as she began to bask in her glory, the applause trickled away. She narrowed her eyes to counteract her nearsightedness and saw the horror in Momma's face.

Lindy followed Momma's eyes back to the pool, squinted harder, and saw, anchored at its bottom, a green and white piece of cloth. Her bikini top. Lindy's budding breasts were floating on the water's surface. Lindy crossed her arms immediately.

Jo yelled out, "She booby flopped!" The crowd erupted in laughter.

Lindy quickly inhaled a gulp of air and dove down as far as she could, determined to drown before ever seeing land again.

It had never dawned on Maggie. Terry-cloth absorbs water, several pounds when submerged. Disaster for a bikini.

Sally turned to Maggie. "I'll get her a towel. Just don't let her dive into the pool with it on." And then Sally walked off, smirking. Hemphill-Wells her ass, she had pegged Maggie's class from the beginning—low.

~

"Stop calling them that. They're not boobies," Momma reprimanded Jo again. It was a hellishly long car ride home.

"Breasts?"

"It's not ladylike to call them anything."

Jo paused. "When can I get a training bra?"

Momma rolled her eyes. "Don't say 'bra.' Say 'lungholder.'"

"When can I get a lungholder?"

"When you get lungs that need holding!" Momma snapped. Finally, Jo got the hint and sat back in her seat.

"She was being snooty to me. I know she was." Momma had thought of nothing but Sally Donovan the entire drive. "She thinks she's better than us and 'the incident' only confirmed her thinking."

Already Lindy's toplessness had become known as "the incident."

"I'm sorry, Momma." It was the first time Lindy had spoken since "the incident."

"It's not your fault. If anything, your beautiful dive just called attention to 'the incident.' But it was not your fault, you hear me?"

"Yes, ma'am."

"Good." Momma took a breath. "If anything, it was your father's fault for forcing me to buy material on sale."

"The material looked cute when it was dry," Lindy said, meekly standing up for her father.

"And if Mrs. Donovan were any kind of hostess, she would have put us at ease after 'the incident.' But then if she were any kind of hostess, she would have had a get-together in the month and a half we've lived here welcoming us to the community. Hell, nobody even brought over so much as a pie."

"Vernice did," Jo piped up.

"Besides Vernice. None of these hoity-toity rancher's wives have shown one bit of hospitality. Well, I'll show them who's the bigger person. If Sally Donovan and her highfalutin friends are too ill-mannered to realize they should have a party for me, I'll have one for them."

In the same breath she added, "Don't tell your father. He doesn't need to know I'm spending money."

CHAPTER SEVEN

That night while Momma secretly planned her party, Lindy executed a plan of her own—Operation Stunt Breast Growth. She confiscated the duct tape from Father's tool box and wrapped it tautly two times around her upper torso, allowing only enough give for breathing room. Except for changing the tape periodically—cleanliness is next to godliness—she vowed to bind her chest with this homemade growth-inhibitor until puberty ended.

The battle ahead of her wouldn't be easy. Her family lineage ensured a bleak future: her mother, her grandmother, and all the women before them had big breasts. She was the recipient of bad genes.

At an early age, Lindy began trying to throttle the big breast gene. She pinched her nipples in hopes that the lack of circulation would cause them to fall off. She beat in her chest with her fists, thinking that would keep them from wanting to pop out. These extemporaneous methods just had to yield results. And they had—bruising.

But despite her hatred of her budding "lungs," it wasn't until that day when the Grady County seventh-grade class glimpsed her bosoms that she fully realized why she hated them. They revealed her secret. She was a slut. Full-figured girls always were.

Look at Jane Russell in those "cross your heart" bras for Playtex. It was Lindy's fault her top came off at the pool party. Not that she yanked it off or tied the knot loosely in hopes of exposing herself. It was her fault *subliminally*. Somehow, someway, she must have wanted it to come off. She must want to be an exhibitionist. A topless-diving, mammary-gland-exposing pervert. The anti-Esther Williams.

She was clearly headed down the path to Hades. Upon reflection, she saw how much of her life had already been spent performing similarly vile and sleazy acts. Because it felt good, she slept with a pillow wedged up high between her legs and sometimes straddled the arm of the couch. Because she was curious, she peeked at the smut articles in Momma's occasionally purchased *Cosmopolitan* magazine. Before puberty, this had all seemed like innocent fun. Now she might as well have neon lights on her forehead, labeling her Deep Throat (which she knew was dirty, but wasn't sure why, since she knew nothing about Watergate).

"You're too big to sit on the couch like that," Momma snapped at Lindy the other day. "You'll break the arm." But Lindy knew it wasn't the sofa arm Momma was concerned about. She could see that Lindy's intentions were no longer pure.

Lindy had always flipped through Momma's *Cosmos*, looking at the pretty pictures. But lately, the moment Lindy picked up a *Cosmo*, Momma circled her near-teenaged daughter like a hawk, wanting to know: "What are you reading?" Inevitably she was reading one of the sexual articles. *Cosmo* only had sexual articles.

"You're too young to be reading that," Momma said as she yanked the magazine from the hands of her firstborn, the deviant. Oh yeah, Momma knew her secret.

So before she became an outright debauchery, Lindy decided to stop reading Momma's magazines altogether, including *Family Circle* (you never knew where one of those cartoons could lead). She gave up the pillow between her legs. And she vowed never to sit on the arm of the sofa again.

She was determined to prove what she knew deep down to be true: she was a good girl. This was Lindy's silent mantra—*I'm a good girl, I'm a good girl*—and she perpetually pleaded her case in her head. But just when her internal judges were about to grant an acquittal, she would incriminate herself in her sleep. Sleep brought dreams, and dreams brought sin.

Like the dream she'd had last night. She was alone with a boy, and she was kissing him. Not two seconds into the dream, Lindy felt a presence. It was the Devil surrounded by his minions of fornication. She was a bad, bad girl. His cloud of depravation penetrated her subconscious, and she fought it as if being suffocated. She forced herself awake, then whispered the name of the Lord Jesus Christ three times to fend off the spirit of evil. But the unclean rarely feel unsoiled again. So she shoveled into her head thoughts of purity like baseball, hotdogs, apple pie, and Chevrolet. Lindy just loved that commercial.

Now as Lindy stared at herself in the mirror, she decided to add another ring of duct tape to her self-made lungholder. *I'm a good girl, I'm a good girl.* But it was becoming harder and harder to convince her own internal judges. She was certain that in Momma's eyes, she was a bad girl.

CHAPTER EIGHT

Lindy studied the school calendar. One hundred and eighty days of school until summer break. An eternity.

Last week, the PTA had sent all parents of school-age children a calendar of the upcoming year's school schedule. It was a courtesy. Only Lindy wasn't feeling so grateful now that she knew what lay ahead. One hundred and eighty school days. And it all started the day after Labor Day. Labor Day was tomorrow.

She imagined reliving the hell that was the pool party. For one hundred and eighty days. "The incident." For one hundred and eighty days. An eternity. There was only one thing to do. Polish her eight-track tapes.

She pulled out Father's cotton handkerchief, the one she used to clean her glasses, and reached for the first tape, The Captain and Tennille's *Love Will Keep Us Together.* Because it was her favorite and she played it the most, she knew there must be fingerprints on the black cardboard cover. She squinted carefully and found one. Its existence proved she was imperfect. She fogged the cardboard with her breath, then polished as if her life depended on it.

Amply distracted, Lindy made a deal with herself. If she promised to go to school for so many days, she could fake being sick and miss so many days. Say a four to one ratio—four days a week at school, one day sick at home. That, plus the weekend, would be three days at home a week on the average. Lindy knew she couldn't fake being sick one day every week—that wouldn't be believable—but she could look forward to one big sick week after the first month of school. It was easy enough to fake a fever for a week of the flu. A sick week here, a day off for the dentist there—for the first time, Lindy was glad she had braces—and she could turn one hundred and eighty school days into one hundred and thirty-five, more or less. One hundred and thirty-five days of school. One hundred and thirty-five days of *perfection.* Was she capable? She rubbed that eight-track with an intensity never before known to plastic.

Lindy knew if she was going to attain any happiness in school, she would have to be perfect. Perfect people were worthy of fame, admiration, and love, and she wanted all three. So since she wasn't lucky enough to be born perfect, she would have to become perfect. This logic had led to her self-penned *Lindy Logan's Bible of Perfect Days.* In the gospel according to Lindy, a perfect day was one in which, among other things, she ironed her clothes, accessorized with the proper belt and small jewelry, spent extra time on her hair to ensure a good hair day, was pleasant and kind and funny and witty to everyone she met, spoke up in class (instead of her usual nervous mumble), looked people in the eye, carried herself well and wasn't klutzy, performed excellent penmanship on all her homework and tests, and stuck to her charted diet plan to lose twenty pounds. *Whew.*

Over the summer, she had gained five pounds, socialized only with the voices in her head, and spent an average of two hours a day alone polishing each of her eight-track tapes. Perfection was still a very distant goal. And Lindy was not one iota closer to fame, admiration, or love.

"There she is," Jo said over her shoulder as she barged into their room.

Lindy looked up. "What do you want?"

"My new classmates wanted to meet you. They heard about your incident at the pool party," Jo said, suppressing a secret giggle.

Lindy glanced into the hallway and saw no one. "Who are your new classmates—the Fruit Loop people?"

"You are so rude. As a matter of fact, you're stepping on Wendy's toe. Would you move?"

"There's nobody here, dingbat."

Jo spoke conspiringly to the air beside her. "I know, Becky, I told you she was a snot." She turned to Lindy, "Just because you can't see them doesn't mean they aren't here. Maybe they don't want to show themselves to a big old weirdo who sits around polishing her stupid eight-track tapes." Jo shared a laugh with her "friends." "They think I'm so funny. Now, we're going to play in the living room so please leave us be."

Jo waited for Becky and Wendy to leave then punctuated her exit with a slam of the door.

Lindy gazed at the indelible fingerprint on the Captain and Tennille tape. They were all out of their ever-loving minds.

~

Labor Day was a double-edged sword. It signified the last day of summer vacation, yet it was also the day to hit the sales. Momma still sewed most of the girls' school clothes herself, but she couldn't resist a really good bargain. Some she stumbled upon, some she stalked like a hunter. Bargains stumbled upon may have been the most thrilling, but those stalked were the most rewarding. Stalking was a matter of patience and will—spotting the prey (the item), charting its course (the markdowns), outlasting the adversary (the store), anticipating the attack (the sale), then beating the other hunters to the kill (the purchase). Patience and will. And the thrill of victory.

Still, some of Momma's best bargains were stumbled upon. That's how it was with plain-pocket jeans. When she discovered that generic jeans on sale cost little more than buying denim material, she vowed never to sew another pair of jeans from scratch. So it came to pass that every Labor Day the girls would buy new jeans—plain-pockets only. Brand names were too expensive, even on sale.

The problem was that nobody wore plain-pocket jeans except for the Logan girls. Or at least that's how it seemed to the Logan girls. Labels on clothes were status symbols, and Lindy and Jo hated the poverty status implied by their label-less jeans. If Momma understood anything it was the desire to upgrade one's station in life, so she made a deal with her daughters. They would buy plain-pockets, and she would doctor them up.

Wrangler jeans were the brand of choice in West Texas, identified by a gold-stitched W on the back pockets. To doctor the generic jeans, Momma removed the plain back pockets with a seam ripper, machine stitched a W with gold thread on each pocket, then machine sewed the pockets onto the jeans again. Every Labor Day night after the Labor Day sale, Momma became a pocket-stitching assembly line readying jeans for the upcoming school days. She was an excellent seamstress—despite her first-time-at-making-a-bathing-suit disaster (but then, she told herself, that was the material's fault, not hers). And with this ingenious pocket doctoring, Momma really worked her magic. She was a one-woman counterfeit jean factory.

As brilliantly as Momma sewed, her true love remained shopping. Her dream of heaven combined a day at Neiman Marcus in Dallas with unlimited credit. Knowing she would never see that heaven in this lifetime, she treated any shopping spree as a big event. Even one to the five and dime in Jessip. As for Lindy and Jo, it made no difference to them whether they hit the biggest department store in Texas or the tiniest thrift shop, shopping with Momma was magical enough to make up for the rottenness of having to go with each other.

Momma had a talent for making small talk to service workers, chatting with complete strangers and putting them at ease. Waiters and waitresses loved her. Grocery cashiers adored her. And store clerks worshipped her.

"Hi, Ida. How you doing?" Momma greeted the clerk at Crawley's, the five and dime at the corner of Jessip's courthouse square.

Ida looked up from her magazine at the counter. Business was slow, especially for a sale, and Ida was delighted to have company. "Maggie. Hi. I'm good. Come for the sales?"

"Is the Pope Catholic?"

Ida smiled at her friend's joke.

The girls were to each find two pairs of plain-pocket jeans to last for the upcoming school year. They began their search as Momma scoured the store for any hidden treasures. Momma was weighing the value versus extravagance of a half-priced coffeemaker when Lindy stepped up beside her.

"Momma?"

"Find something?" Momma was still debating the coffeemaker.

"Can I buy one pair of these real Wranglers instead of two plain-pockets?"

"They're too expensive." Momma put the coffeemaker back. They didn't need it. They had instant.

"One pair won't cost anymore than two pairs of the other. And they're so icky. People can tell they're fake."

"You're imagining things. Nobody can tell the difference after I doctor 'em up."

"I can. They still look dorky."

Momma crossed her arms and sized up her eldest. "Well, then. If you don't like my work, I guess I don't need to stay up half the night sewing W's on your jeans."

"You do a good job, Momma. It's not that. They just don't fit as well. I feel like a dork."

"You look lovely in them and they fit you just fine. I will not waste money just because those others have a label on the butt." Momma only cussed when she got angry. "Butt" was a cuss word. This was not a good sign.

"I'll wear them all the time. It won't be a waste. I promise."

"You need more than one pair of new pants for school."

"I'll be real careful with this one pair."

Momma met her daughter eye-to-eye. "Do not argue with me in public."

"Yes, ma'am." Lindy turned away, head low, mouth moving.

Momma heard the near-inaudible mumble. "What did you say?"

Lindy didn't meet her mom's gaze. "I'm old enough to make my own decisions."

Momma gasped as if to say, Really? "Ida, did you hear what my daughter just said? She's old enough to make her own decisions." She paused for timing. "Isn't that mature for a twelve-year-old?"

Ida laughed. Momma could make the phone book funny.

"Sounds mighty mature to me," Ida teased.

Lindy began to squirm with embarrassment.

"I guess if she's old enough to make her own decisions, she's old enough to pay for them." Momma pointed Lindy toward Ida's cash register. "Go buy your jeans, honey." The "honey" rang with saccharin sarcasm.

"I don't have any money." Lindy could barely hear her own voice.

"Well, I guess you need to work that out with Ida." Momma smiled at her straight man behind the cash register.

Ida picked up her cue. "I can give you a charge account as long as the bank approves your credit history."

"No problem, right, dear? You're twelve. You're old enough to make your own decisions. So since you don't need me, I'll just wait for you in the car."

"Momma." Lindy's voice was barely a whisper. "I'll buy the plain-pockets."

Momma smiled at her daughter. She had won. "I think that's a wise decision. You are maturing."

Lindy headed for the jeans section to exchange the Wranglers for the icky plain-pockets. But as she made the switch, the floodgates opened. "I can't wear these to school," she said to nobody in particular, tears flooding over the dam.

Momma looked at her daughter's heaving body, oozing emotion in public. There was only one thing to do. Save face.

Momma put her arm around Lindy. "Why don't you give me your jeans and I'll check out while you go wait in the car."

Lindy nodded through her tears and handed her momma the two pairs of plain-pockets.

"No one will know the difference. You're gonna have a 'W' on your bottom like everybody else."

She nodded again. "I'm sorry."

"Don't be. It's just me and Ida and Mrs. Kirkpatrick here." Mrs. Kirkpatrick had just walked out of the dressing room and into the emotional distress zone. "Hi, Sharon. How's Bill?"

Mrs. Kirkpatrick nodded. “Fine, thanks.”

“Don’t forget me, Momma. I’m here too,” Jo said.

“I know, honey.” Momma dismissed her youngest and continued her show of comfort. “Us grown-ups understand the emotions that go with becoming a woman...and your first time of the month.” Momma smiled, confident that that would explain everything.

Lindy was mortified. Her momma had just told two strangers about her first period. She might as well have enlarged Lindy’s naked baby pictures and strung them up around the courthouse square.

Lindy headed to the car and waited twenty minutes before Momma and Jo came out of Crawley’s. As Momma started the ignition, she said, “You should have stayed. We found Jo the cutest blouse, seventy-five percent off.”

“That’s practically free, right, Momma?” Jo said.

Lindy said nothing.

They rode in silence to Pete’s drive-through where they each ordered a sweet cherry lime for the trip home.

“Will you perk up?” Momma said to Lindy as they waited for their cherry limes. “You’re depressing me.”

“I’m sorry.”

“Stop saying you’re sorry and try to smile. I mean, really. This is supposed to be our fun day.”

"Yeah," Jo chimed in from the back seat. "Gloomy Gus."

"Now will you cheer up for the drive home or should I have you switch seats with Jo Bean?"

"I wanna sit in front! I wanna sit in front!" Jo whined.

Lindy didn't have the energy to argue. She wordlessly changed seats with her sister, which seemed to make Momma and Jo immensely happy. They chatted the whole way home, like girlfriends at a slumber party. Lindy didn't say a word. Occasionally, Momma glanced at her in the rearview mirror and shook her head. Once, she commented to Jo about the "sulker" in the backseat.

Lindy was a sulker. She was a party pooper. She was the spoiler of their special day with Momma. And she was the seventh-grade dork with the fake W on her butt.

∾

That night, Lindy was in her room polishing the current issue of *Seventeen* magazine when Father knocked on her door.

"Lindy!"

His voice startled her. Except for his morning alarm, he never knocked on her door.

"Come in," she said tentatively.

He cracked open the door. "I want to talk with you and your sister in the living room."

Lindy's heart dropped to her stomach. Her legs turned to Jell-O. This couldn't be good. Anytime Father wanted to talk it wasn't good.

Momma was cooking supper in the kitchen, but when she heard her family congregating without her, she turned down the heat on the burners and joined the assembly.

Father began: "I inspected the fields today where you girls had hoed."

Uh-oh.

He continued: "The weeds are growing back."

Everyone knew what this meant—the girls had not hoed the roots. The girls had disobeyed Father's orders.

Jo pointed at Lindy. "I told her we should do what you said. I told her we should pull out the roots."

"She's lying! This was her idea." Lindy pointed back to her sister.

"That's enough," Father said.

"I'm just a little kid," Jo said, her best Shirley Temple impersonation.

"With the mind of a con artist," Lindy replied.

"Enough!" Father bellowed. The girls snapped to attention. "I had planned to give you both an allowance for your hard work this summer. I can't do that now."

"Oh, Joe, give 'em a little something for when school starts." Momma couldn't hold her tongue any longer.

"They don't deserve it. They'll never learn if they're given something for nothing."

"But they were outdoors in the hot sun all summer long," Momma beseeched.

"Maggie, don't," Father's face was turning red, his fists starting to clinch. Then in one fluid motion, he turned and kicked the side of the television set, leaving the pointy-toed indention of a boot in the wood. Everyone froze. No one wanted to be the thing he kicked next.

"Dammit!!" Father yelled, staring at the evidence of his temper. He stood, breathing heavily, trying to calm down. He felt like Elvis who supposedly made a habit of blowing away hotel room TVs with a pistol when he got angry. Well, Elvis could afford it.

He bent over and pulled on the power button, and the old black and white Magnavox glowed to life. Father released a sigh. Thank God he had only inflicted cosmetic damage. What if he had kicked in the picture tube and irrepairably damaged his only form of entertainment? Under his breath he cursed himself, "Stupid idiot."

"It's fine, honey," Momma said. "I'll go finish dinner. Why don't you go take a nice, hot shower?"

Father shook his head and, without a word, headed into the bathroom. In a second, the shower water was running.

Momma winked at her girls. "Don't worry. I'll get you a little spending money." Then she went back to fixing supper.

Lindy wheeled on Jo. "You liar. No wonder I hate you."

Jo looked up with her big Bambi eyes. "Momma! Lindy said she hates me!"

Lindy clamped her hand on Jo's mouth. "Shut up. Shut up, shut up, shut up."

Momma stepped in. "Jo, why don't you come help me with supper. Lindy, you contemplate your language while you chew on this." She revealed a bar of Lava soap. "Open up." Then she popped the coarse gray block in Lindy's mouth. Lindy's gag reflex made her almost spit out the bitter bar of lye. But she had been here before; if she spit it out, it would only be reinserted after Momma lathered it up on her tongue.

So Lindy contemplated her hatred of Jo. She said what she meant, and meant what she said. She hated Jo, she really did.

But mainly, she hated that her father most likely believed the little snot's lie. She hated that her father probably thought she was the con artist. And she hated that her father had yet another reason not to love her.

By suppertime that night all was forgotten. It was eaten in front of the TV and an episode of *Good Times* let them escape to the Dy-no-mite! world of Jimmie "J.J." Walker. The Logans laughed themselves silly. The only visual reminder of the evening's events was the imprint of Father's boot notched in the side of the television set.

CHAPTER NINE

The next day, Father threw open the door to the girls' bedroom at 6:30 a.m., but it wouldn't have mattered to Lindy if it had been hours earlier. She hadn't slept a wink. Her mind tossed and turned and her body followed suit. Jo slept like a log, lulled into unconsciousness by the rhythm of her own sawing. For once, Lindy was somewhat grateful for Jo's snoring. It gave her mind something to focus on besides the first day of school. Since Lindy was wide awake, she easily beat Jo into the bathroom, although her aching body made her feel like an old woman of twenty. Come to think of it, she wished she were twenty. Then she'd be finished with school.

The school bus driver for their section of the county estimated that he would pick up the Logan girls at a quarter to eight. Their house was the closest on his route to the school, just fifteen country miles away. A country mile, unlike a city mile, meant a wide-open, traffic-free actual mile. No traffic jams to turn a fifteen-mile sprint into an hour-and-a-half drive. At 60 mph, travel time for a country mile was a minute. Just the way God intended.

Lindy and Jo would be the last on the route to be picked up before school and the first to be dropped off after school. It was a small consolation, but, Lindy reminded herself, a consolation nonetheless. The less time spent outside the safety of her own home, the better.

On this first day of school, Momma was up, dressed, and in the kitchen making a big breakfast of waffles and bacon. When Lindy arrived at the table, Father was already halfway through his pecan waffle and Jo was well into her bowl of Fruit Loops, the only breakfast she ate anymore. In fact, she was the only Logan who would even touch the stuff. She had talked Momma into letting her keep the box by her bed at night, and during the day it stayed at Jo's place at the kitchen table. One morning, Father reached for his Shredded Wheat while reading the paper and inadvertently grabbed Jo's Fruit Loops. Jo screamed at such a deafening pitch that even Father was now hesitant to eat cereal in Jo's presence.

Lindy covertly watched Jo meticulously examine each spoonful for cereal dust. As Jo had explained repeatedly, it no longer sufficed to let the Fruit Loop people fend for themselves. There simply weren't enough Fruit Loops to preserve everyone. Now all the dust people had to be spooned to the safety of her juice glass. Still, not all of them could be saved. Some splattered to their death before they reached the juice glass, and those who failed to even reach the spoon drowned in the excess of milk. For these senseless fatalities, Jo would never be able to forgive herself, but she tried to ease her guilt by giving the deceased a noble burial at the end of the meal. All of this—saving the living, burying the dead—considerably lengthened her eating time. Much of Jo's morning prep time went into eating cereal and rescuing its residents. Despite all of this, Jo still convinced Momma to buy another box of Fruit Loops each time the pantry was empty. And it was empty a lot. Jo was up to three boxes a week.

Momma pulled Lindy's waffle from the iron and removed the melted butter and heated syrup from the oven. The heated syrup was something Momma did special for herself and Lindy since Jo only had eyes for Fruit Loops and Father didn't eat sweets. (From what the girls could figure out, Father had overdosed on sugar as a kid. "Too much fruit," Momma said once, as if that explained everything. And since Father explained nothing, Lindy and Jo never quite understood if sugar still made him sick or if it was just a bad memory. Regardless, they grew up with the impression that since their father did not eat sweets, no man did. Dessert was a girly thing.)

"The bus'll be here in fifteen minutes, Jo Bean," Momma said, an urgency in her voice. She knew how long her youngest was taking these days to eat breakfast.

"I only have two more bites," Jo said.

"Oh, that'll only take another hour and a half," Lindy said. Father suppressed a laugh and quickly returned to his waffle. Jo refused to let her focus shift from where it was needed—her cereal bowl.

Lindy was forcing bites of her waffle down her throat, the first time she had been too nervous to eat since she saw Shelly McNamara at K-Bob's, when the squeal of metal against brakes broke her concentration. The school bus had arrived thirteen minutes early. The blood rushed to Lindy's head, and she thought she might faint. Of course, if she did, that'd be grounds for missing school.

"It's here," Lindy said in slow motion, a frightened Fay Wray before King Kong scoops her up into his clutches.

She shot up from the table, almost knocking over her plate, and ran to the bathroom for a breath-freshening gargle of mouthwash. Jo hurried to the kitchen sink and poured out her milk-soaked cereal dust, no time today for a proper burial at sea. Father looked up from his waffle with a giddy the-kids-are-going-back-to-school smile and said, "Have a good day." Momma kissed her youngins good-bye as they walked out the door, and waved a friendly hello to the bus driver which, in her mind, helped ensure her children's safety. The driver now knew her girls had a Momma and that she would be expecting them back in one piece every day for the next six and nine years, respectively.

Before Lindy knew what hit her, she was sitting on a second row bus seat, looking out the window and watching her house get smaller with the increasing distance. Her heart beat to leap out of the confines of her chest. Her temples throbbed to keep pace with the pumping blood. Her attention centered solely on her destination. She was bound for hell.

Lindy's hell was disguised as an innocuous little tan brick building. It wasn't even that little. Yes, it was a small country school that housed kindergartners through seniors, but, thanks to Grady County's oil income, it was no one-room shack. The rooms for kindergarten through eighth-grade were grouped in one wing of the building; the high schoolers owned the other wing. The cafeteria joined the two wings, and an auditorium and gymnasium settled at the far end of the high school wing. A football field and track lay within walking distance. A tennis court rounded out the school grounds. This was not at all like the schoolhouse on *Little House on the Prairie.* This revelation would have made most kids much happier. Not Lindy. At least she could relate to the TV show.

Lindy stepped off the bus and followed the sidewalk up to the school's front entrance.

"Hey, hey. No running," a man said to some kids who Lindy thought seemed far too happy to be here. Then the man turned to her. "You must be the Logan girls."

This was it, the moment of truth. Lindy could run now or fess up. There was no turning back.

"I'm Lindy. This is Jo." *Chicken.*

"I'm Principal Murphy. Nice to meet you both."

Principal Murphy ruled over the elementary and junior high. Because he was largely bald, he looked older than his middle age, but if he had pulled his hair out it wasn't over his own children. He had none. He and his wife, the high school home ec teacher, were alone together amidst 127 surrogate Grady County school children. Perhaps that's why he was bald.

Principal Murphy also had what he considered a dry and witty sense of humor that he often used on unsuspecting and unsophisticated children. This was his favorite perk of the job.

"I need to get your parents' John Hancock on these," the principal said to the Logan girls once in his office. He handed them the paperwork and saw their blank expressions. He loved that. "Didn't know your folks had a pseudonym?" Still, blankness stared back at him. "Just have your Momma and Father sign these." He raised his eyebrows as if to add, *Stupid kids.*

"OK," Lindy said and took the papers from him. She was still wearing her blank look. Not because she didn't know what John Hancock and pseudonym meant, but because she now knew Principal Murphy wasn't the nice man he pretended to be. He was the Grady school's Judas Iscariot. *Once again,* she thought, *welcome to hell.*

Principal Murphy rose from his desk to show Lindy and Jo to their homerooms. Lindy's seventh-grade homeroom was just across the hall from Principal Murphy's office. She hesitated before walking in, so the principal walked in ahead of her.

"Mrs. Westmorland," he said to the woman behind the desk. "I have your new student. Lindy Logan. She's raring to dive in."

This was one time Murphy wasn't trying to be witty or dry, and he didn't know what he had said to make the class burst into almost uniform giggles. Still, he gave himself a mental pat on the back and left with Jo to try and get a chuckle out of the fourth-grade class. Lindy looked at the snickering faces of her classmates. She easily recognized them as the kids from the pool party; they were wearing the same smirks. Lindy inadvertently looked down to make sure her clothes were still on.

"Hello, Lindy," said the woman who was no longer behind the desk, but walking toward her. "I'm Mrs. Westmorland. I'll be your homeroom teacher." She smiled warmly and gently placed her hand on the back of Lindy's upper arm, the fleshy part above the elbow that Momma called "the Merms" because of the hanging flab on that part of Ethel Merman's arm that swung freely during her exuberant rendition of "There's No Business Like Show Business" in the movie of the same name. Mrs. Westmorland led Lindy to an empty desk that sat directly in front of the teacher's desk. From this location Lindy couldn't see her fellow classmates and that was just fine with her.

"Class, I want you to welcome your new classmate, Lindy Logan," Mrs. Westmorland said before Lindy could melt into her seat and become anonymous. Mrs. Westmorland had an affinity for the underdog and decided to take this newcomer under her wing well before the first day of school when she heard about the seventh-grade pool party from her son, Rick, a ninth-grade freshman. He had heard about it at a preseason football practice. For three days in August, "the incident" had been hot high school gossip.

There was a smattering of mandatory hi's and hello's and welcome's, but the loudest greeting came from Trent Smith, a lanky cowboy who was the epitome of gawky teenage cool.

"We already met at Amber's swim party." Trent wiggled his eyebrows and smiled coyly. "Hubba hubba."

This elicited giggles from the girls and snickers from the guys. Trent was quite popular and he knew how to work a crowd, plus he was so cute doing it. Even Lindy had to admit this. She tried to muster a smile to let them know that she was secure enough to laugh at herself, but what appeared on her face more closely resembled the strain of constipation.

"That's enough, Trent," said Mrs. Westmorland, looking directly at him. "Oh, and..." She motioned for him to zip up his fly.

The class giggled and snickered again as Trent checked his fly, but they broke into all out laughter when Lindy wiggled her eyebrows at their leader and whispered, "Hubba hubba."

At that moment of self-gratification, it mattered a little less to Lindy that the 3:30 bell was still seven hours away and there were 179 more school days to go.

~

With 178 days of school to go, it was time for student physicals. No pupil was exempt from the general health examination. Period. Lindy had had such exams in Jessip, of course, but on the second day of school? These people were maniacally efficient. So when Nurse Berkley announced she was taking new kids first, Lindy panicked. She was the only new kid in class, and she had duct tape around her torso. Surely that would be suspect. As the nurse led the new girl down the hallway to her office, Lindy grasped at straws. "I just had a physical. I can get you a doctor's note."

"We have to run a basic exam anyway. Texas law."

"I really have to go to the bathroom."

"Good. I'll need a urine sample," said the woman with the puffy sad-sack face. They reached the nurse's office and Mrs. Berkley handed Lindy a small plastic cup. "You can tinkle in this. The bathroom's in there."

The private bathroom was adjacent to the sick room, a small room with a bed where sick—or faking—students lay down until they felt better or school ended, whichever came first. Lindy planned to spend a lot of time in there.

After locking the door behind her, she placed the plastic cup on the back of the commode and searched frantically for scissors or knives or a sharp object of any kind. Nothing. She would have to rip the tape, like one giant Band-Aid with Super Glue adhesive. This was her original piece of duct tape and she had avoided taking it off for one obvious reason—it was gonna hurt like hell. Why hadn't she thought of that in her haste to come up with a breast reducer? *Damn boobs.*

She pulled her cotton shirt over her head and hung it from the hook behind the door, careful to not let it fall onto the floor, which had seen Lord knows what kind of illness and excrement. Then she reached to her side and fingered the end of the tape. The top layer should be easy, it rested on more tape. It was the bottom two layers that covered skin.

Lindy held her breath and pulled first across her chest, then across her back. NBD. No big deal.

Without allowing herself time to think, she inhaled once again and let the second layer rip.

"Holy Matthew, Mark, Luke, and John!!!!" Like any good little Methodist Lindy had read the Bible, but she never knew much had really stuck until she launched into this pain-filled litany of Holy names. Evidently, she could recite all the books in the New Testament. And at top voice too.

She wasn't even to the Second Thessalonians when the nurse knocked on the door. "Are you

OK, sugar?" The poor child must have one hell of a bladder infection.

"No, I'm dying," Lindy screamed, her statement not at all sarcastic.

Nurse Berkley, sensing this to be the emergency of a lifetime and hero making at that, called upon all of her Florence Nightingale qualities. She found the key in her drawer to open the locked bathroom, plunged it into the knob and threw open the door.

She looked at the sight before her and was fairly certain Florence Nightingale had never seen the likes of this. But then again, she was fairly certain Florence Nightingale had never been a school nurse. There stood a shirtless child, her face beet red, her chest bound in gray duct tape, a long piece of which dangled from underneath her arm.

A classic case of child abuse.

Nurse Berkley immediately sounded the alarm. She alerted Principal Murphy to the *suspected*—a term she used loosely since in her mind she had already tried and convicted the parents—child abuse. He, in turn, called the mother.

Momma was not amused. She happened to be at home—it was her one afternoon off from cleaning houses—and raced to the school. She hadn't abused her child up to this point, but she was going to now.

The principal and nurse had filed a report for the local sheriff, who was called, but hadn't been able to stop by because he was overseeing a cattle roundup and barbecue. Mostly the barbecue.

Momma swore she knew nothing of the duct tape, at which point the authorities at Grady Junior High turned their suspicions on the father. The father, Momma promised, had nothing to do with this either. That's when it was decided to ask the child to name the culprit.

Lindy, as she had when asked three times before, laid the blame on herself. *A pattern of abused children,* said the look on the nurse's face. *Such a brave little soldier.* So it killed Nurse Berkley that, without hard evidence, she had no choice but to release the girl to her mother with a warning, a warning Momma humbly endured, and to suggest rubbing alcohol as an aid in the removal of the remaining duct tape. Nurse Berkley said good-bye to the Logans for now, but promised herself she would get the bastard parents the next time.

Momma said nothing in the car on the way home. The interrogation to which she had been subjected would have made her hate this county more if it had been at all possible. But since she already hated it to her fullest, she only lectured her eldest on having the common sense never to use duct tape—or any construction supplies—on her body again. She promised to take Lindy shopping for training bras that would better hide her impending shape, and Lindy was left feeling, despite the embarrassment, that she had come out of this debacle on top. That is until she spent the evening soaking her upper torso in a bath of rubbing alcohol so Momma could remove the flesh-eating tape quarter inch by pains-taking quarter inch.

Sometime in the middle of the night—the last of the tape was finally removed around 2:35 a.m.—Lindy tried to make light of the situation. The way she figured it, the joke was on Nurse Berkley. She never got her urine sample.

CHAPTER TEN

Soon, Lindy grew accustomed to not fitting in. Her only friend, the only person she liked anyway, was Mrs. Westmorland. The junior high English teacher recognized not only Lindy's awkwardness, but also her intelligence. Lindy had a love for literature and a knack for grammar, and these qualities endeared her to her homeroom teacher. She was quickly becoming a teacher's pet—generally anathema to popularity, but in Lindy's case, her favoritism seemed to actually work out well for everybody. It gave Mrs. Westmorland a student to focus on; it gave Lindy a sense of confidence and comfort; and it got the teacher off the rest of the class's back. For example, when the class read aloud from a book, Mrs. Westmorland asked Lindy to read for a longer time than anyone else. This made Lindy happy; she was a good reader and enjoyed proving it. This made the class happy; they were poor readers and generally didn't give a darn about getting better. This made Mrs. Westmorland happy; she didn't have to spend the entire session correcting the pronunciations of a class that didn't give a darn.

But in the social arena outside homeroom, Lindy couldn't shake her nagging desire to be accepted. Every day at lunch, she followed the four girls in her class through the cafeteria line to their table. She was under no delusions, this was clearly *their* table, and their generosity in allowing her to sit there in no way, shape, or form made any part of it *her* table. She thought about heeding her rebel voice and one day veering from their table to sit alone at her table, dignified and independent. A leader, not a follower. But she ignored her rebel voice and continued following. Her rebel voice was quashed by her voice of insecurity.

So Lindy the follower sat at their table listening to conversations she wasn't really a part of. Every female in the seventh-grade class—Amber, Holly, Kari, and Jenna, or "The Fab Four," as Lindy referred to them because *they* thought they were so fabulous—had lived in Grady all their lives. And with the exception of Jenna, their families had lived in Grady all their lives. Theirs were the preeminent families in the county. No wonder Mrs. Donovan raved about the blue blood of the seventh-grade class.

It's just that all this royalty didn't make it easy for the new girl to acclimate. *But who else was there to turn to?* Lindy wondered. Not the three girls in the eighth-grade class, they were too busy primping in the bathroom and drinking cans of Slimfast to step foot in the cafeteria during lunchtime. And forget about hanging with the high school girls, they wouldn't even talk to the eighth-graders. Her only option was to befriend the sixth-graders, and that was only an option if she wanted to cement her reputation as a geek.

The Fab Four talked about two topics—boys and basketball. Girls' basketball was huge in rural West Texas, and the girls in Lindy's class were particularly gifted athletically, all part of being a blue blood she guessed. That's one reason the Fabs forgave Jenna's lineage for living in Grady only one generation—she was a terrific basketball player. She was the tallest of the seventh-grade girls and, although gangly and awkward off the court, on the playing field she was the star. The Fab Mothers foresaw the future: once their babies reached high school, they were going to win state. As for herself, Lindy had quickly established her ability on the court. She stunk.

The other Fab topic was boys, and this one did interest Lindy more. But it was the bad girl Lindy. The Lindy that slept with pillows between her legs and rode the arm of the couch and read dirty *Cosmo* articles. The Lindy that dreamt of kissing boys and invited the presence of Satan. The Lindy that Momma disapproved of.

All the Fabs had boyfriends, although they often changed from week to week. On Thursdays after the junior high pep rally, they would hide away in the nooks and crannies of the school building and make out with their boyfriends before the start of the football game. And on Fridays after the high school pep rally, they would do the same. They often discussed their make-out sessions at lunch, comparing whose boyfriend was the best kisser. Lindy wondered how they ignored their dirty slut guilt and slept at night. And she was jealous that they could.

"How many boys have you kissed?" It was Amber and she was looking right at Lindy.

"Me?" Lindy looked from side to side, hoping Amber had graced someone else with this question.

"You, L squared. How many boys have you kissed?"

Lindy froze. She didn't want to lie, but then she didn't want to tell the truth because that would make her an outcast. That is, *even more* of an outcast than she already was. She rolled her eyes to the top of their sockets, pretending to mull which kissing partner was better—Harvey the rabbit or Casper the ghost. "Gee, Amber, I can't remember."

Good answer. Neutral, noncommittal, and only a little white lie.

"That many! My goodness, L squared, you're a regular horn dog." Amber smiled at the other three of the Fab Four, and they giggled.

Suddenly, Lindy's answer didn't seem so clever. They thought she was a slut!

"Not that many, really." Lindy tried again to sound nonchalant. It didn't work.

"Then how many, *really*?" Holly was mocking her in the same way Amber usually did. If it weren't for Holly's blonde Crystal Gayle-length hair and shorter stature, she and Amber could be twins. Evil twins.

"I don't know how many," Lindy answered.

"Five? Ten? Fifteen? *Zero?*" Kari said. Lindy had been under the impression that Kari was the best of the bad seeds—she loved to crack a joke and even tried to make Lindy laugh when the other Fabs weren't around—but that impression had come when Kari's jokes weren't at Lindy's expense.

"It doesn't matter. It's nobody we'd know anyway." Amber sounded like she was letting Lindy off the hook.

"Sure it is," said Kari. "He's a movie star. *The Invisible Man.*"

Lindy felt like Kari had read her mind. Or had she confided this information to the one Fab she thought might be a friend? You can bet Lindy wouldn't make that mistake again.

The Invisible Man crack left the Fab Four rolling in the aisles, almost literally. Lindy laughed as well, to prove she was part of the gang. It was a trick she was getting good at.

"What boys would you like to kiss? Here at this school?" Amber had no intention of letting Lindy off the hook.

"I don't know. I haven't really thought about it."

"Come on. There must be somebody you think is cute," Amber said. She was nothing if not persistent.

Lindy studied the peas on her tray as if they could rescue her. "Well, Darius Airhart's kind of cute." And he was. Kind of. His nose was crooked, but his complexion was clear. He had straight blond hair and muscles that stretched the short sleeves of his T-shirt. Plus, Darius was an older man. An eighth-grader.

"He's a calf roper," confided Kari.

"In the junior rodeo," Holly explained impatiently off Lindy's blank look.

"Decent basketball player," said Jenna, meaning he was a so-so person. Talent as a basketball player was her yardstick for measuring a person's character. To her, Wilt Chamberlain was the kind of loyal and moral man that a girl should marry.

"She doesn't need to know everything about him," Amber said. "She's not gonna marry him." Amber smiled pleasantly, and Lindy felt like the girl in the water just before Jaws emerged and gobbled her up. *Da dum. Da dum...*

Lindy's voice quivered ever so slightly. "He's just kind of cute, that's all."

"That's all," Amber reiterated, mocking Lindy's quiver to her henchmen. Then she got up to take her tray to the dishwasher. The other Fab Three followed. Lindy hadn't touched her lunch and was starved, but she got up and followed too. Lindy the follower.

Lindy headed straight for the bus after the 3:25 bell that signaled the end of the school day. Jo was already on the bus, sitting in her second-row seat.

"Hey."

"Hey."

End of sisterly discussion.

Lindy sat two rows behind Jo. It was an unwritten rule that the youngest kids sat in the front of the bus, the oldest kids sat in the back, and in the middle sat all the rest, more or less in graduating order. Any kid could sit in front of his delegated row, but never behind. Unless you were a senior of course. Seniors could sit anywhere. Row four was as far back as Lindy had dared venture, although, as a seventh-grader, she was eligible for row seven.

The high school kids sat in the back four rows, specifically the high school kids that were too cool for the other kids. And there was a Sloan kid on almost every row. That's because there was a Sloan kid in almost every grade. They were obnoxious, unkempt bullies and the nicest thing Lindy could say about them was that they were dumb as fence posts. Occasionally, she could insult them in a way they took as a compliment, but mostly it was best to ignore them if at all possible. Besides, their dad drove the bus so it was best to keep your distance, not for fear of Bus Driver Sloan actually understanding one of these backhanded insults—fence-post stupidity was clearly genetic—but because when he lashed out it was to kill one of his own, which wouldn't have bothered Lindy except for the fact that Bus Driver Sloan couldn't kill and drive at the same time. And she'd be damned if she was gonna die in a fiery crash on this stupid school bus.

Come to think of it, the only time Lindy risked conflict with the Sloans was when they got to teasing Jo. Not that she minded her sister being given a hard time—she enjoyed the game herself—but the Sloans could be vicious. The oldest Sloan boy, almost in high school, would taunt Jo from the back of the bus, calling "Jo Bean the Psycho Machine" over and over again. And on one out-of-the-blue occasion, the youngest Sloan boy reeled back and whacked Jo in the head with a grape Tootsie Pop fresh from his mouth. When he tried to retrieve his sticky confection, it became an intangled mess permanently glued to Jo's hair. He launched into a wall-eyed fit that Lindy heard didn't stop until his daddy took the strap to him at home. Bus Driver Sloan offered Momma the services of his wife in removing the Tootsie Pop from her youngest's lovely head of hair, but Momma declined. She ended up having to cut Jo's pretty *That Girl* do into a Julie Andrews pixie. Despite her tears, Jo still looked like she should grace the cover of a fashion magazine.

What elicited this harassment was that Jo had made no friends in the first weeks of school. To say the pickings were slim was an understatement—there was one other girl in Jo's class of six. Her name was Renee. Jo tried to befriend this lone rangerette, but Renee was jealous of the attention the fourth-grade boys gave to Jo as the new girl in town. Renee had worked this grade for four years (including kindergarten) and didn't care for a new chick coming in and taking over her territory. Renee thought Jo was bossy and prissy and know-it-all. Jo thought Renee was bossy and prissy and know-it-all. They were two peas in a pod. And they hated each other for it. So Jo had no choice but to remain best friends with the imaginary Wendy, now preferred over Betty and Susie.

Complicating matters even further was the fact that Jo was oblivious to the mind-set that labeled chatting with an imaginary person as weird. Maybe because to Jo this person was real. Or maybe because she just didn't give a hoot and holler what everybody else thought. Whatever, she chatted with her friend everywhere. Even on the bus.

"Who ya talking to?" The middle Sloan boy, the fifth-grade Neanderthal, uttered the same words to Jo every day.

"Yeah, who ya talking to?" mimicked his third-grade Neanderthal brother. This was repeated by two more Neanderthal parrots: the second-grade girl and the third-grade girl (the identical twin of the third-grade boy). Only the sixth-grade girl broke the Neanderthal mode. She never said a word, and for this Lindy felt both appreciation and pity. The other Sloans probably gave her a constant tongue-lashing at home for refusing to act like a moron in public.

Then it was time for the eighth-grade Sloan to sing his top-ten hit, "Jo Bean the Psycho Machine," now complete with a deaf-eared tune and daily improvised verses. "Jo Bean the Psycho Machine, you don't know what it means to be clean. 'Cause you don't bathe, in your cave, that is why you stink!"

"Leave her alone," Lindy said. Jo completely ignored the Sloans and would let them nag her all the way home if Lindy didn't interject. Jo's oblivion bugged Lindy almost as much as the Sloans' heckling.

"Who's gonna make us? Your momma?" asked fifth-grade Neanderthal Sloan. His siblings joined in his laughter. This was the funniest joke in the world.

"She's not hurting you. Just leave her alone," Lindy said.

"Goochy, goochy, goo," the third-grade boy tickled the vacant space next to Jo. "She likes to be tickled. Look, she's laughing hysterical."

The eighth-grade Neanderthal got such a kick out of this bit that he left his second-to-the-back-row seat (there were no high schoolers on the bus that day) and walked the length of the bus to tickle the air beside Jo as well. "Tickle, tickle, tickle" he said in a voice that blended the newfound deepness of puberty with the high-pitched giggles of Woody Woodpecker.

"Kyle, sit down, you moron. Leave the little kids alone," bellowed Bus Driver Sloan to his eldest son.

"I'm just making friends," Kyle hissed at the floor. He slapped the back of the seat in frustration and spat into Jo's face, "Ya freak. Ya oughta be in Big Springs." Jo didn't flinch, and Kyle walked back to his row of power.

Big Spring (commonly called "Big Spring*s*" by regional residents unconcerned about oral accuracy) was a nearby West Texas town well known for housing a state mental institution. Everybody knew all the crazies and wackos lived there locked in padded rooms and straight jackets, foaming at the mouth and peeing in their pants. A reference to being placed in Big Spring was the ultimate insult. Any other time Lindy would have defended Jo against Kyle's last statement, but his dad had already shut him up and none of the other Sloans dared pester after that. Still, Lindy daydreamed of killing the brainless lunkhead herself. Nobody needed to hear they should be sent to Big Spring.

CHAPTER ELEVEN

Momma had sent invitations to five of the county's most prestigious ranch wives for what she privately called her "Welcome Me to the Community" luncheon. The time had come for her to obtain acceptance—which to her meant parity—among the county elite.

She had planned her menu for a little over a month and settled upon an English tea theme. Classiness was of the utmost importance and so she opted for appetizers instead of a heavy meal. They were ladies after all. She had gotten up early this morning, rushed Joe out of the house by pretending to be in a ranting and raving mood, and spent the morning preparing the party food. She wanted it all to be as fresh as possible. She cut the crusts off an entire package of white bread for her pimento cheese finger sandwiches, wrapped dill pickles in cream cheese and ham, and broiled cocktail weenies rolled in bacon. After showering and applying her makeup (not too heavy, she didn't want to look cheap), she dressed in her newest casual from K-Mart (a blue light special), then returned to the kitchen to cut the finger sandwiches and slice the dill pickle wraps.

She had brewed several flavors of iced tea and stocked individual bags in case any traditionalists preferred their tea hot. Dessert was a colorful rainbow sherbet with actual Pepperidge Farm Milano cookies. She had splurged. There would be no Piggly Wiggly generic today.

But the topper was the fondue pot. Cheese Whiz melted and kept warm above an eternal flame. Bread squares toasted for dipping. The fondue kit had been expensive—twenty books of Green Stamps—but Momma saw it as an insurance policy. If her luncheon needed a spark, the fun of fondue would break the ice.

The luncheon was scheduled for twelve noon, early enough for her guests to enjoy hours of fun and still get home for their kids' return from school.

~

Lindy and Jo ran off the bus as the brakes were still squealing. They expected Momma to greet them with titillating tales of the day's gathering. So when they entered the house and saw no sign of her, they were a little perplexed. But when they looked at the table and found six empty place settings with six empty plates nestled around a basket of stale finger sandwiches, a broiling pan of congealed weenies and bacon, and a plate of withered pickles and ham, they were downright worried.

Lindy looked into the fondue pot, its everlasting flame extinguished, and with a fondue fork pricked the layer of air-hardened yellow skin that protected the once melted Cheese Whiz.

"Momma?"

The girls found their mother on the commode in the bathroom. She was still dressed in her "Welcome Me to the Community" luncheon attire, but her "Welcome Me to the Community" smile was nowhere to be found. Instead, her serious gaze focused on the heels of her feet. When in a mood, one of Momma's practices was to clip the dead and cracked skin off her heels and then sand the remaining skin with a pumice stone. Judging from the clipped-to-the-quick raw skin, this was some mood.

Momma looked up at her daughters, but continued to sand. "The bastards didn't show up. They didn't even call."

"Bastards"? Was Momma cussing? Lindy had heard that word on TV not long ago and looked it up in the dictionary. *Was Momma talking about illegitimate children?*

"Highfalutin bitches."

Nope, Momma was definitely cussing.

The girls didn't know what to say. They didn't need to. Momma had a lot to say.

She hurled every curse word the girls had ever heard her use—"hoity-toity snotrags"—and some they hadn't like "shit." Both girls let out a gasp when they heard that one. This wasn't any old bad mood, it was a four-letter-word bad mood.

Momma wailed, "You're the only people who love me. The only people who understand me. You're my best friends." She engaged her girls in a group hug and was about to embark on another round of put-downs—"Self-absorbed jackass..."—when the phone rang.

Momma stopped mid-insult.

Maybe it was one of her guests with an apology as to why she didn't show.

She answered the phone. "Hello?" Sweet as pie. "Why, hello, Sally." Sally Donovan, one of the invitees.

"Uh-huh. Uh-huh," Momma could be heard saying on the phone, and as quickly as it had arrived, her joy vanished.

Sally Donovan had heard from one of her friends in town that Margaret cleaned houses for a living. Her Mexican (like most West Texans Sally dropped the "i," changed the "x" to "ss," the "can" to "kin" and pronounced it Mess-kin), her Messkin had moved recently, and she was in desperate need of a replacement. Would Margaret be interested?

Margaret paused. "Yes, Sally," she heard herself say. There was nothing else to say. Her cover had been blown, and the Logans needed the money.

Momma hung up the phone and slowly disappeared inside herself. If Sally knew she was a cleaning lady, the other mothers probably did too. Her secret was no secret at all.

So much for parity.

~

Father came home earlier than expected and walked into Heartbreak Hotel with its six lonely place settings and abandoned fondue. He noticed none of it.

But Momma noticed Father. She had specifically planned her party on a day Father would be away. She hollered from the bathroom, "You were supposed to be helping Smiley with his cattle all day."

"One of the calves was sick. Needs to be hand fed. I brought it home," he hollered back.

Momma suddenly felt enraged. She was mad. At Father. Not just mad. Livid. She'd be damned if he was gonna yell at her for spending money on her party. *Her* party.

She walked into the kitchen where her adversary stood taking a swig from a glass of iced tea—one of the nauseatingly sweet, fruit-flavored luncheon teas. Father's face contorted into that of a man poisoned as he aimed and spit a mouthful of tea into the sink. "What is that?!"

"It's my party tea."

"It's sweet."

"At least something is."

"What party?"

"The party I decided to hold for me. Because I need to meet people in this godforsaken wasteland. Because I need something more than sandstorms and cotton and TV for company."

Momma paused. But she wasn't finished.

"Don't worry. Your precious money didn't go to waste on my frivolous party. Nobody came. Not a damn woman I invited came. So we may be broke, but we get to go down in style. Eating party food and drinking sweet tea. Oh, and I won't let us starve 'cause I'll be making the big bucks as a cleaning lady for Sally Donovan." She smiled to keep from crying, and laughed like she could kill somebody. "Ain't this the life? I tell ya. Welcome to goddamn euphoria. I'm so happy I could choke you." She was looking straight at Father. "I tell you one thing, if this ain't hell, I don't wanna know what is!"

With that, she stormed into the bathroom. Her heels needed sanding.

Father didn't say a word. Not about the expensive new fondue pot or Momma's outburst or anything. Saying a word would only get him into trouble. He walked outside. His sick calf needed him.

~

Momma had fixed way too much food for her gathering. She may have thought she was cooking for five socialites, but she prepared enough for an army. It was an affliction that had been handed down the female lines of her family for generations. Holiday leftovers alone could feed all those starving kids in Africa. So dinner that night was what it would be for the next week: finger sandwiches, fancy pigs in a blanket, dill pickles with poor man's prosciutto, and fondue cheese dip. Father made up a lot of ground since it took four finger sandwiches to equal one normal-sized sandwich and a manly meal required at least eight of the tiny "pains-in-the-butt," as Father mumbled when Momma was out of earshot. Everybody but Lindy ate the weenie rolls. She would touch nothing in the hot dog family after their July 4th contamination. She ate only cheese—pimento, fondue, and cream with the pickles. She would be constipated for the next seven days.

CHAPTER TWELVE

"You wanna play a game? Monopoly maybe?" Jo whispered loudly, a piece of her spittle landing on Lindy's cheek. Momma had retreated to her bedroom and the rest of the house knew not to risk life and limb by bothering her. Of course that didn't stop Jo from having the gall to bother Lindy while she was in the bathroom washing her hands. Hand washing had become a life-and-death pastime.

Lindy let out an exaggerated sigh as she wiped her cheek with the shoulder of her shirt sleeve, her hands still under the running hot water. "Stop spitting on me, you germy geek. And, no, I don't wanna play with you...unless Father's gonna play?"

"He doesn't want to. He's out back taking care of the calf."

"Then I don't want to play either." But Jo did not pick up on her cue to leave. Lindy emphasized the point. "Am-scray."

Jo just smiled. "Will you teach me pig Latin?"

Lindy spoke slowly, to signal that her patience was running out. "Leave. Me. Alone."

"I don't have to leave. This is my bathroom too."

"Oh, for God's sake." Lindy sighed, even more sensationally.

"I'll tell Momma you took God's name in vain."

"And I'll tell Momma you kissed Brian Sloan on the bus." Brian was the fifth-grade Neanderthal Sloan.

"I did not. That's gross. You liar."

"So what? The Sloans'll back me up. They'd love to get you in trouble."

Jo knew her sister had won and there was only one thing left to say. "I hate you."

"I hate you too." Lindy reached for a Kleenex, patted her hands dry, then turned the faucet off with the same tissue, careful not to touch the germ-infected chrome surface.

Jo knew how to get her sister back. She quickly exited the bathroom and firmly shut the door behind her.

"Come back here and open the door!" Lindy shrieked. She couldn't touch the doorknob with clean hands. So she shielded her hand with yet another Kleenex. No poisons could permeate the armor of a Kleenex, and that's why Lindy used them constantly. If she wasn't using them for their mythical antiseptic qualities, she was using them for their intended purpose (she blew her nose and she blew it a lot). Her only fear was that she was using them too much. Momma would kill her if she knew how many of the name brand she went through in a day. Momma always teased behind Father's back that he talked them up as so poor, they couldn't afford the luxury of soft toilet paper. The last thing Lindy wanted to do was give her momma an excuse to start buying the imitation cardboard snotrags too. So she had started tossing her used Kleenexes into a paper sack to throw into the trash bins at school. (Touching the school garbage cans sent Lindy into a handwashing ritual befitting Marcus Welby, M.D.) Bottom line: Lindy was at a point in her life where she could not live without her Kleenex with a capital "K," and that's why she took pains to waste as few of the precious tissues as possible. Damn that Jo.

~

Lindy positioned the Kleenex to turn the knob to the back door where she found her father outside on the deck—"deck" being a fancy name for a slab of concrete big enough to hold two cheap lawn chairs or, presently, one dormant calf. The deck was enclosed in a wrought-iron fence, which kept unsuspecting sunbathers safe from cattle stampedes, but not from rattlesnake roundups. The good news was that it was a frigid early October and, while it was true no sunbathers would weather subpar temperatures to work on their tans, it was also true that the rattlesnakes had slinked into their dens, thus ending the threat of one of the slime mongers crawling through the gate and sinking its fangs into the helpless heifer. There was, however, a danger of the young cow freezing to death on the cold concrete. Father had laid the calf on a bed of old blankets, covered it with more of the same, and plugged in a beat-up space heater. He was attempting to force-feed the baby warm milk. A pinprick in a rubber glove provided its makeshift udder.

"How's he doing?" Lindy tiptoed out of the house, careful not to disturb the patient. Or the doctor.

"She's eating a little. Not enough." Lindy noticed how gently Father held the calf's head with his free hand.

"Is she gonna live?"

"Too soon to tell."

When the calf stopped suckling the fake teat, Father removed the glove from the animal's lips and tenderly placed her head on the bed. He pulled the blankets up around her neck then held the glove near the space heater to keep the milk warm.

Lindy had never seen her father so caring.

Father and daughter continued to sit in silence. They sat that way as the sun fell below the horizon. They sat that way as the sky turned to black, and the first star lit up the darkness. That sat that way without Lindy feeling awkward, without her feeling nervous, without her feeling frightened.

Finally, Father went inside for a cup of coffee and asked Lindy to watch the calf. Lindy did more than that. She asked God to save the calf. She also thanked God for this time with Father.

By the time Lindy went to bed, the patient had stabilized. The calf was gonna be OK, she was certain.

∾

That was the first question out of her mouth when Father knocked on the door for their 6:30 a.m. wake-up call. "Is the calf OK?"

Father hesitated, and for a moment, appeared as if he didn't hear the question. "She died. I woke up to find her tongue all swolled up."

"She died?" Lindy repeated in a sad sing-songy whine.

"Yeah. Well. It was just an animal." And with that, Father lowered his head and walked away.

That's when Lindy's conjured bond with her father broke. His reaction was practical, yes. Typical of a farmer, yes. Detached, oh yes. And she couldn't help but wonder if he'd say the same thing about her. Lindy, yeah, well, she died. But she was just a daughter.

CHAPTER THIRTEEN

Lindy heard the commotion on the playground that afternoon at recess. A crowd had gathered around the fight. She stopped out of curiosity, but could see nothing and was about to leave when one of the fighters yelled in a high-pitched but vicious voice, "Welcome to euphoria. I'm so happy I could choke you."

Lindy paused for a minute and, as if in slow-motion, flashed back to last night. *Weren't those Momma's words to Daddy?*

Lindy snapped back to attention and pressed her way through the circle of students in time to see Principal Murphy pulling Jo to her feet and off of the poor kid she was pummeling. Lindy had never seen Jo resort to physical violence and was feeling sorry for the poor little girl in Jo's class when she realized...the kid lying on the ground wasn't a girl at all. He wasn't even a fourth-grader. He was fifth-grader Brian Sloan.

"If this ain't hell, I don't know what is!" hissed the once cherubic pixie that was Lindy's sister. *The Exorcist*'s Linda Blair now possessed Jo's body. Lindy expected to see split pea soup come regurgitating out of Jo's mouth at any moment.

Lindy turned to Renee, the only other girl in Jo's class, and asked what had happened.

"Well," Renee said, flipping her curls and excitedly reporting, "Brian was teasing Jo about her invisible friend. Wendy, is it?"

"I don't know," Lindy said, feeling like she was talking to a Jo clone. All Renee's hair flipping was making her dizzy.

"Then your sister just went crazy, asking why she had to put up with this 'godforsaken wasteland'—for the record, I don't cuss, but I do believe in accurate reporting—and saying she needed more in her life than 'sandstorms and cotton.' Where did your sister learn such language?"

Lindy ignored this. "What happened next?"

"Brian looked at her like she was whacked...or maybe just a lot smarter than him. Anyway, he put up his dukes and dared her to do the same. That's when she decked him."

"No!" Lindy couldn't help her exclamation. She never suspected Jo had it in her.

"Yes!" Renee went on to explain that that first hit had laid Brian out on the ground at which point Jo pinned him and continued her slugfest. This attracted a large amount of schoolyard attention, mostly because every other elementary school kid dreamed of revenge on Brian Sloan.

"It was amazing," Renee said, caught up in the story, "like the Rumble in the Jungle, and Jo was Muhammad Ali."

"Wow," Lindy said. "That is amazing."

"Thanks. I work on conjuring up images with words," Renee said. "I'm going to be a television reporter one day." And with another flip of her hair, she walked away.

Principal Murphy led the Greatest and the Neanderthal to his office where he asked Nurse Berkley to call their parents. The nurse was delighted to do so, as she thoroughly relished any time she got to play Gestapo. She never rooted for one side in these brouhahas—all offenders must be punished equally—but this time she secretly triumphed in Jo's victory. (In fact, the entire administration would quietly celebrate little Ali taking the spin out of their fifth-grade Tasmanian devil.) But because she had personally discovered the duct tape abuse of the oldest Logan girl, Nurse Berkley took a special pride in the littlest Logan girl's ability to fight back against her assailant, to break the cycle of abuse. It was enough to make a school nurse cry with joy. Especially if she could finagle any credit for the child's breakthrough. It was, after all, almost time to vote for school employee of the month.

As Grady's grade school delinquents awaited the wrath of their parents, they were subjected to the monotony of Principal Murphy. He recited the standard "don't fight" speech, and blamed Brian for being the fight's instigator. The interesting thing, the only interesting point in his whole boring tirade, was that he referred to Jo as trying too hard to finish the fight. Principal Murphy was reprimanding Jo, yet there was a ring to it that made her beam with pride. Jo the Finisher. The biggest, baddest wrestler of them all. She pictured beating up on those ugly and unkempt professional wrestlers while she wore a frilly and fashionable costume of leather and lace. And carried a parasol. The parasol would be her gimmick. Principal Murphy rambled on, something about both kids being punished, a week of staying inside during recess, blah, blah, blah. *Who cared?* Jo the Finisher. The possibilities for fame were endless. Her own clothing line for the style-conscious wrestler. Her own sitcom with Wendy, the sidekick only she can see. Her own comic book superhero who gets to buddy around with those cute super hunks, Batman and the Green Lantern.

"I said, as a sign of good faith, I want you both to shake hands," Principal Murphy repeated loudly, interrupting Jo's fantasy.

The culprits grasped hands, and as they did, Jo stared down wrestling's Neanderthal Boy and imagined crushing the bones in his hand, doubling him to his knees in pain. All on national TV, of course, and with only the cutest wrestling costume ever. Jo the Finisher.

It didn't take Bus Driver Sloan long to arrive in the principal's office. He worked as the custodian/

repairman for the school and the nurse was able to locate him in minutes. He listened to the principal recite Brian's crime and punishment and promised to work on his child's behavior at home, which meant giving his child a good working over with his homemade leather strap complete with metal studs for memorable disciplinary emphasis.

Momma was cleaning a house in town and couldn't be reached, so Principal Murphy sent a note home with Jo to bring back signed.

Jo was unusually calm when showing Momma the note. "You woulda been proud of me. I gave it to that Brian jerk and he just rolled over and took it. Just like Father." Jo grinned.

But Momma did not grin back. "Don't you ever talk about your father like that. He doesn't just roll over and take it. He is not a wimp. And he is not a bully. He works hard and does his best and we do not beat him up for it. You hear me? You hear me?"

"Yes, ma'am."

"Now go tell your father how much you love him." Momma handed Jo the note. "And explain this to him."

Jo took the note and headed into the living room. Slowly. She knew from Momma's reaction that she had done something wrong. Something more than the fight. But she didn't know quite what. She had acted just like Momma.

~

The Sloans emerged from the Pounding on the Playground (Reporter Renee played with the phrase Rumble in the Jungle until she came up with her own alliterative and locale-specific spin) with a newfound respect for Jo (or at least for their dad's studded leather strap). No Sloan ever bothered Jo or her sister Lindy again. Jo knew why. Her reputation preceded her. Somebody else might start the fight, but she was Jo the Finisher.

CHAPTER FOURTEEN

The Harvest Festival was how Grady County welcomed the fall. It was held every year on the Saturday night before Halloween. But—and this was made very clear—it did not celebrate Halloween. It used to celebrate Halloween, but that was a few years ago before a handful of Grady mothers decided that Halloween was the Devil's holiday. Claiming they were sent by God, the mothers rallied to change the name of the festival and, in spite of anemic opposition from the citizens with common sense, the mothers won their holy war. The name Halloween Festival was never again to be heard in the Grady county limits (except from a few cantankerous and reminiscent old-timers).

Like the Halloween Festival, the Harvest Festival was still a big bash held in the new show barn near the school. It still had booths and festivities sponsored by each junior high and high school class to help make money for their senior class trip (an annual venture for which classes saved all twelve years so that graduates could skip the last week's minutiae of school and travel to remote and exotic places like Six Flags Over Texas). There were still cakewalks, dart throws, and a dunking booth (to the chagrin of each year's junior class who sponsored it and supplied their bodies to be dunked in it).

The difference was that anyone attending Grady's social function of the year would no longer see any signs that it coincided with Satan's day of folly. Streamers and decorations were inspected to ensure they gave no pictorial indication of Halloween. Likewise, the colors orange and black had no place in the Harvest Festival. But above all, no one was allowed to enter the saintly festival wearing any item of clothing remotely resembling a Halloween costume. For clarification, a sign awaited those deviants daring to defy the mothers of Grady: "Halloween costumes will be apprehended and discarded." Halloween costumes were found in hell. Not in the county of Grady.

The core of anti-Halloween mothers did not include the county's wealthy five. They were drawn to religion only for the social aspects. Who needed to be saved spiritually when you could afford to buy your way into heaven? The Lord knew they gave buckets full of money to their churches and charities, and like all good ranch bosses, He undoubtedly kept a financial ledger. Heaven awaited with plenty of gold stars in their crowns and just as many angels to polish them up. The clique liked their gold shiny.

But numbered among the original anti-Halloween mothers was Mrs. Airhart, mother of Darius. For some reason, this point of fact popped into Lindy's mind when Darius asked if she was going to the Harvest Festival Saturday night. Perhaps subconsciously she was trying to offset her guilt in being hit on by an older man with the knowledge that his mother was a Holy Roller. Perhaps reminding God that the older man had a mother for a saint made the situation less sinful. Perhaps Lindy was going to hell in a handbasket no matter what she did. All she knew was she had to keep replaying her moment with Darius as she now went through the motions in seventh period P.E.

She had closed her locker and there he stood.

"Going to the Harvest Festival Saturday night?"

Lindy had hesitated, not certain he was talking to her though he was standing only inches away in a near-empty hallway. In her pause, the seventh-period bell rang, and so she said what any eloquent and poised young woman would to a boy who had come a courtin': "I have P.E."

"Yeah, me too."

They walked their separate ways, she headed for the gym, he for the football field.

It had been magic.

~

Bing! The basketball conked Lindy on the side of her head, smushing her wire-framed glasses into her face and pounding its nose piece into her nasal cavity.

"Earth to L squared," Amber said.

They were in a circle passing the ball. Basketball drills. Amber had been the passer.

"Keep your head up," the coach instructed Lindy. "One eye always on the ball."

Lindy wondered what to do with the other eye.

The coach clapped his hands together to get everyone's attention. "Layups." Then he blew his whistle for effect. He liked effect. He was also the drama coach for the school's one-act play.

The junior high grunts lined up above the top of the key.

"And stand up straight." Amber dug her knuckle in between Lindy's slouched shoulder blades, and she snapped to attention with the efficiency of a human switchblade.

When it was Lindy's turn, she took her layup, shot off of the wrong foot and missed. She headed to the back of the line and encouraged her mind to wander out of the gym. She didn't want to think about basketball or Amber or posture. She wanted to daydream about Darius.

Seventh-period basketball held no magic.

~

In the car on the drive over to the Harvest Festival, Maggie vowed not to grace with her presence the elite five who had spurned her party. She had nothing to say to them.

Unless they spoke first.

"Maggie, put your pie on that table there," Sally said when Maggie walked up to the tic-tac-toe beanbag toss, the seventh-grade fund-raiser. Three Xs or

Os in a row won any number of goods baked by one of the seventh-grade mothers.

Maggie remembered her vow, but she decided there was no need to stoop to their level and be rude. Besides, Sally was technically her boss now, although Maggie hoped that would be forgotten in social circles. Maggie had been cleaning Reata for the last few weeks, and Sally had been easy to work for, cordial even.

"Lindy didn't tell me mothers were supposed to man the booth too," Maggie said.

"Amber's shooting free throws at the Freshman basketball throw. She was on a roll of eight straight when her shift came up," Sally explained. "I'm just working 'til she misses."

"You might have to work the whole shift." Barbara Breedlove stepped into the conversation. Her body language was that of a woman born with a silver spoon in her mouth and a stick up her butt, er, bottom. Only Sally's rigid smile gave away that her best friend had just made a joke.

"She is that good," Sally said.

"I've heard she is." Maggie tried to be part of the conversation. Again, no need to be rude.

"You don't come to basketball games, do you?" Barbara had Sally's same lacquered smile.

"No. Lindy doesn't play," Maggie said. "Yet." She felt the need to add that.

"Well, we need bench warmers as well," Barbara said.

Barbara was the mother of Holly, seventh-grade Fab Four member and Amber's best friend.

"See, Holly's over there rooting for Amber right now," Barbara said to emphasize the importance of bench warming cheerleaders. "Course, she is one of the junior high starters."

"They're both very talented," Sally said of their two daughters.

"Maybe I should have Joe put up a basketball hoop over the garage," Maggie said. "So Lindy can practice."

"Which one is Lindy?" Barbara whispered out of the side of her mouth.

"L squared," Sally answered just as covertly.

"Right," Barbara cooed, as Lindy's identity dawned on her. "I don't know if a hoop over the garage would do the trick."

Maggie did not like Barbara Breedlove. Did not like her one bit. And unless Barbara quickly indicated she liked Maggie, that was going to be her opinion.

Barbara stared at Maggie with detached disdain.

It was time to kill this highfalutin snotrag with kindness. "I don't believe we've met," Maggie said, knowing damn well who Barbara was. She was a party spurner. "I'm Maggie Logan."

Barbara shook Maggie's extended hand as if she was picking up a dead bug. "Barbara Breedlove."

"Right. B squared," Maggie said, mimicking Barbara's sing-songy sweetness. "It is so nice to meet you. I've heard what a pillar of the community you are. A true giver." That was harsh enough. There was no need to risk future inclusion into the clique.

"Sally's been telling me so many nice things about you too," Barbara said sincerely.

Maggie smiled. Maybe she had judged prematurely.

"I'm just sorry I can't hire you. But my Messkin has been with us so long, it wouldn't be right to let her go. But I tell you, it would be so nice to be able to communicate with the help in English." Touché. When it came to killing with kindness, B squared was a master.

Stunned, Maggie laid down her kindness killing sword. She opted to lick her wounds and say nothing else because, after all, she was the bigger person and also because, at that moment, Amber walked up with Holly.

"Hi, honey. Did you win?" Sally asked.

"Probably. Fifteen in a row. Puts me in the lead."

"And gets her a fondue pot," Holly said sarcastically.

"Yeah, big first prize, huh?" Amber said.

"It can go in the gift drawer, I guess," said Sally.

"You'd actually give that tacky thing away?" Barbara sounded horrified.

"Somebody still uses them. Right?" Sally got no answer from her supports so she turned to Margaret. "Right?"

"I have one and I love it." Maggie looked at these two women and their daughters, chips off the bitchy old blocks. "I think enjoyment of such a thing just requires the ability to have fun." She smiled. "Have a lovely evening."

Maggie smiled as she walked away. *Touché to you too, Mrs. Logan.*

~

Joe stood in a huddle near the concession stand with the county's other farmers and ranchers. A.J. Donovan was holding court.

"I need backers for this. We're talking gold mine," he said.

"Now, A., don't you think this one's a little risky?" Donald Breedlove was the only person besides Sally that could call A.J. by his first initial only. He was also the only person who could question his Midas touch in the financial market.

"No guts, no glory, my friend. Have I steered you wrong yet?"

"Let me get this straight: A cotton seed hybrid that holds up under all kinds of weather and produces twice as much crop?" Smiley reiterated. "Does sound almost too good to be true."

"Produces *up to* two times the crop," A.J. clarified. "I don't want to mislead anybody. But the bottom line is technology's changing faster than we can keep up. And if we don't jump on the bandwagon and reap the rewards, some other tycoons will." He nudged Joe, including him in the inside joke.

Joe salivated at the fantasy of making "tycoon" type money. But it was just that—a fantasy. Joe didn't believe what A.J. was selling was worth diddly squat. Granted he had always erred on the side of caution, a grave error if you asked his wife, but, come on, seed that *magically* doubles the size of your crop? *These men didn't really believe such a crock of horse manure, did they?*

"I'll buy some shares," Smiley said.

"There's a smart man," A.J. said. "Any other takers?"

"Like you said, you haven't steered me wrong yet," Donald said.

"Jump on the bandwagon, friends, before it's too late," A.J. said, sounding like a carnival barker. Several other men verbalized their interest. Then A.J. turned to Joe.

"How 'bout you, Logan? Interested?"

Joe felt all eyes on him. The new guy. Would he pass inspection? Would he survive initiation? Would he get into the fraternity? *Did he really want to?*

"Think I'm gonna pass. For now anyway." All eyes stayed on him. Was it pity they reflected? Or admiration? Maybe it was all in his imagination, but he suddenly felt like a rebel. A rebel without a cause maybe, but a rebel nonetheless. And he knew the answer to his question; he didn't really care about being part of the pack.

~

Maggie surveyed the show barn, concentrating on walking with her head up and making eye contact with passersby. She came upon the sophomore-sponsored petting zoo and spotted her Jo Bean, standing all by herself at the pen that contained two lambs. She occasionally held out her hand to one of the bleating babies. But mostly Jo Bean just stared.

Momma walked up beside her little lamb. "How 'bout some hot chocolate?"

Jo's face came to life. "OK."

"Then maybe we can win a cake at the cakewalk. I'm dying to see if any of these women can cook worth squat."

"Me too," Jo said, and off they went together. Best friends. Security blankets.

~

Lindy was walking aimlessly among the home-made arts and crafts tables when she felt a tap on her shoulder. She turned around and found herself face-to-pectoral muscles with Darius.

All at once she felt exposed, vulnerable, tingly. Bad Lindy was taking over.

"I saw you walking around here," Darius said.

"I was walking around looking at the arts and crafts."

"I saw you all by yourself."

"Yeah."

"So I decided to come over."

"Yeah." Lindy paused. "That's good."

"Good."

Pause.

"You wanna walk the cakewalk?" he asked.

"Sure."

The cakewalk was the premier event of the Harvest Festival and as such was always sponsored by the senior class. It cost a dollar a walk, and its concept was similar to musical chairs. When the music started to play, contestants walked in a circle following the cardboard numbers that had been taped to the floor. Contestants stopped walking when the music stopped. Then the announcer would draw a number out of a no-longer-used bingo shaker (the Grady handful had deemed that bingo was gambling and therefore also for heathens), and the person standing on the selected number won the cake.

"This here round we'll be giving away an oldie but a goodie," announced Horace Vandever over the cakewalk mike.

"Horace, you old coot. I just made that cake this afternoon," yelled back Wanda Hutchinson, the baker of the prize of the moment. She thought of her German chocolate and Italian cream cakes as exotic European delicacies. The rest of the county thought of them as darn good chocolate and white cakes. Regardless, Wanda's cakes were a famous staple of the cakewalk, although there were some whispers questioning their reputations as the best cakes ever. Still, it wouldn't be a cakewalk without at least two Wanda Hutchinson cakes, so each Harvest Festival the seniors begged her to bake. Wanda—a drama queen at heart—loved to be begged, and only after a sufficient amount of groveling would she give in to their demands. She also craved the recognition that came with being the cakewalk's most celebrated baker. All of this contributed to her good-natured needling of Horace as he announced her three-layered slice of heaven. It was all part of the famous Wanda Hutchinson Wild West show.

"Hold your horses, Wanda," said Horace into the mike. "I meant it's an old family recipe and it's everybody's favorite."

"That's OK then. I just don't want you calling anything old unless you're looking in a mirror. Now you be nice about my cakes or I'll sic my dogs on ya." Wanda settled back into the crowd, tickled at having elicited more accolades for her baking.

Horace addressed the crowd. "Once again Wanda's right. I'm old, her cake's fresh, and we're both better off than the other way around. Just ask my wife. As far as Wanda Hutchinson's famous chocolate cake, it is, as always, a three-layered chunk of culinary nirvana. I looked that up in the dictionary; it means it's a real good cake. By the way, I hope the winner won't mind that I helped myself to a piece."

"Horace, you old coot!" reprimanded Wanda. What an act they had. Just like *The Sonny and Cher Comedy Hour.*

"I'm kidding, Wanda. The cake is intact. But my getting a piece is a proposition I would like to discuss with the winner," said Horace. "So buy a ticket everyone and step onto a number."

Darius was heeding Horace's advice and standing in line to buy tickets when Lindy spotted Momma and Jo entering the circle and stepping on their numbers. She panicked. Momma could not see her with a boy. That would be worse than catching her with a *Cosmo.*

"Here's your ticket," Darius said as he walked up behind her.

Lindy quickly steered herself around Darius and used the football player to shield her body from Momma. "You wanna take a walk outside?"

"What about the cakewalk?"

"Later. I don't like chocolate cake." *And the Pope's not Catholic.*

"OK. Sure."

As soon as they opened the door to step outside, the biting wind slapped their faces and hands. It was colder than the North Pole.

"It's nice out," Lindy said, trying to be upbeat. "A little chilly."

"You wanna go inside the school?"

"I thought it was locked."

"I have a key."

"You have a key?"

"I'm friends with the equipment manager. He made me a key to the storage room where they, you know, store all the sports equipment."

It occurred to Lindy that she might soon have frost bite. "Let's go."

Darius opened the door to the pitch-black equipment room.

"Where're the lights?" Lindy asked.

"Don't turn 'em on. That way nobody'll know we're in here. Our eyes'll adjust in a second."

It wasn't long until the light from the parking lot and the many night stars began to illuminate the room through the single row of windows atop the side wall.

Darius grabbed her hand. "You wanna make out?"

"What?" Lindy's heart stopped. Frostbite and a heart attack all in one evening.

"You said you were cold."

"Chilly. I said I was chilly. That's not as cold as cold."

Darius was unfazed. "So you wanna make out?"

Lindy froze. She felt her body lock up on her, become a shell over which she had no control. And then the shell spoke. Its voice wasn't Lindy's. It belonged to curiosity. "OK."

Darius steered Lindy toward a stack of vinyl track and field mats used for the high jump event. The pile rose almost ten feet off the ground. He hoisted Lindy up by allowing her to step first onto his hands and then onto his shoulders. Darius made quite a sturdy step ladder, and, once at the top, Lindy found herself rolled into a hole in the top mat and cradled in a four-foot by four-foot make-out haven. The setting reminded Lindy of those playgrounds McDonald's had started building in front of their Lubbock restaurants, and for a second she felt more like a little kid awed by a fast-food fort instead of a slut about to succumb to the sins of the flesh. Then Darius landed beside Lindy in the hole.

"Comfy?"

"Yeah. This is kinda neat."

"It's private."

Darius put his arm around her. They sat in silence for an eternity of thirty seconds—anticipation igniting fireworks from Lindy's head to her toes—and then he leaned over and kissed her. Open mouth, slight tongue, whiskers scratching her chin.

And Lindy's fireworks fizzled.

She felt nothing.

Maybe after a few more kisses.

For a half hour, Lindy kissed—open mouth to partner's lips, slight tongue, more tongue, kiss neck, repeat. She was a quick learner. She had little trouble with the basic beginner stuff—no bumping noses or locking braces. She even thought to take off her glasses to avoid possible facial abrasions. She had to be doing something right; Darius was moaning and groaning like he was having a grand old time.

Lindy felt as if her cheeks were being grated with a Brillo pad.

Straddling the arm of the couch was more thrilling.

She felt so dirty. And so ripped off. For her sin—a sin she would pay for with guilt for probably the rest of her life—she had gotten nada. Zilch. Zero. No fireworks. No excitement. No passion. Detachment. She had gotten out-of-body detachment, a far cry from the women in all those *Cosmo* love stories; they got hotter than firecrackers on the Fourth of July. Lindy had to be the only woman in the world who didn't like making out. Well, her and Edith Bunker on *All in the Family*. She remembered some episode where Edith talked about not liking sex, only performing it as part of her wifely duty. So Lindy's sex drive was more Edith Bunker than *Cosmopolitan* woman. She was a twelve-year-old Edith Bunker. God help her.

Lindy couldn't stand this make-out session a moment longer. But she didn't know how to get out of it. She wished she could simply disappear, leave Darius kissing air and then never have to see him again. She didn't want to tell him the truth—that his touch was making her nauseous—and hurt his feelings. Momma taught her never to be rude. She was supposed to be a people pleaser.

"I need to go work my shift," she said between kisses. "At the, uh, tic-tac-toe throw. You know, the beanbag throw. For my class." The brillance of this excuse was that it was the almost the truth.

"Now?"

"Yeah. Now. I think I'm already late. So. Thanks." Lindy stuck her hand out for him to shake like she was sealing some business deal instead of behaving like slutty old Mrs. Robinson.

Darius climbed out of the make-out hole first then spotted Lindy on her descent. He locked up the equipment room and walked her back to the show barn. Lindy ditched Darius by feigning a need to go to the bathroom and hid in a stall for forty minutes until it really was her time to work the booth. He only stopped by once during her shift and had the decency to disguise his flirting by throwing a round of beanbags. After her hour of work, Lindy sneaked out of the barn. Momma, Father, and Jo found her lying in the back seat of the car, claiming to not be feeling well and ready to go home. The thing that convinced them of Lindy's illness was that she hadn't eaten a bite of Momma's cakewalk prize—Mrs. Hutchinson's famous chocolate cake.

~

Momma declined to pronounce Mrs. Hutchinson's chocolate cake famous, but she did find the charity within herself to declare it very good. And that was because she wanted to entice her eldest into eating a piece. She was worried about Lindy. The world's foremost connoisseur of chocolate cake had gone a whole night and day without taking a bite. This was more than a stomach bug.

Momma was right; Lindy did have more than a stomach bug. She was pregnant. Expecting. With child. She was positive. After all, she had kissed Darius repeatedly.

"I need to talk to you," Lindy said to her mother.

Finally, Momma thought, relieved. "OK."

They sat on Momma's bed. That's where all good talks took place.

The moment Lindy opened her mouth to confess her sin she started to cry. No words came out yet her mouth continued to open and close and the tears continued to flow, like some fish with a glandular problem.

"What is it, honey?"

"I'm very bad."

"What did you do?"

Tears flooded Lindy's face. May the good Lord—and Momma—have mercy on her soul. "I'm gonna have a baby."

"You're gonna *what?!*"

"I kissed a guy. I made out with him. And now I'm gonna have his baby."

"Wait a minute. You kissed him?"

Lindy nodded. "I'm soooo sooooorry, Momma." Her sobs left her gasping for breath.

"That's all you did?"

Sob. Gasp. Nod.

Momma sat for a moment. And then she started to laugh. "Don't you remember me teaching you about the birds and the bees?"

Sob. Gasp. "I dunno."

"Intercourse? To make a baby you have to have intercourse."

The gaps between Lindy's gasps widened. "That's not kissing?"

"Honey." Momma's voice was a mix of exasperation and sympathy. "Intercourse is when the man's penis enters the woman's vagina."

"*What?!*" It was Lindy's turn for disbelief.

"His sperm attaches to her egg and forms a baby."

"He comes in through here?" Lindy pointed to where her maxi pad nestled.

Momma nodded. "You have been so sheltered."

"Not sheltered enough. That is gross!" *If kissing was that bad...*Lindy shuddered, literally, at the thought.

"You just keep thinking that for a few more years." Momma smiled. "Who was the boy?"

Lindy's tears brimmed again. "Darius Airhart."

"Doesn't he play football?"

"Yes. And basketball. And track."

"A pretty good family from what I hear."

"I did it because all the other girls do."

"Kiss?"

"Um-hum. And have boyfriends."

"Really? Amber Donovan?"

"Um-hum."

"She and her friends have boyfriends?"

"New ones every couple of weeks."

"Hum. Well, if you want to have a boyfriend, that's OK."

The tears broke through again, and soon Lindy was engulfed. "I don't wanna have a boyfriend."

"Honey." Momma grabbed her daughter's hand and patted it. "Lighten up." She winked and got up to leave.

"Momma?"

She stopped at the door.

"Do you hate me?" Lindy asked.

"No, and your father won't hate you either."

Father! Father couldn't know about this! Lindy would never be able to face him again never, ever, ever. "Don't tell Father. Please, don't tell Father."

"Alright, alright. This'll be our little secret. Between best friends." Momma smiled again. "Now dry up before you prune."

Momma waited a whole hour until Lindy went to bed to tell Father about their daughter and her first kiss. She couldn't keep such important information from him. A father needed to know of his daughter's early sexual experiences, or at least that the boy was a good catch and Lindy was so scared of getting pregnant she wouldn't sleep with the catch until they were married. Father shrugged it off and figured it was all part of growing up. He hated when his wife interrupted him during *Kojak.*

~

At school the next day, Darius strolled by Lindy's locker.

"How ya doing?" he asked.

Finally, the moment Lindy had psyched herself up for. It was time to defend her honor and she was gonna sock it to him, just like Goldie Hawn on *Laugh-In.*

"What was that?" Darius asked after Lindy's inaudible mumble.

"I said I can't see you ever again," she repeated, her whisper slightly louder. "I'm not that kind of girl." *I am woman, hear me roar. Rrrrrr.*

With that, Lindy's trembling hand closed her locker door, and off she walked, stumbling over her feet only once, and proud that she was no longer a slut/victim.

Darius stood scratching his head in the hallway until well past the tardy bell. What the hell was that all about? He knew Lindy had a thing for him. He knew she liked making out. Amber had told him so.

There was only one thing to do: chalk it up to hormones and go take a nap in the equipment room before Principal Murphy caught him wandering the halls.

Women.

CHAPTER FIFTEEN

Holiday parties during the last hour of school were a tradition for the elementary and junior high classes at Grady County. High schoolers were deemed too near adulthood to deserve cookies and punch for the lesser holidays. They were allowed to partake only in the school's Christmas festivities. Actually, everybody took part in the school's Christmas festivities. Nobody in Grady County didn't celebrate Christmas.

But this holiday was Halloween and, Christmas being two months away, the only partying to be done at school would be done by the underclassmen (and Nurse Berkley and Superintendent Garrett after hours in his office...but that didn't involve cookies and punch).

Superintendent Garrett was more than a little put off by the zealousness with which the religious mothers demanded the school follow their lead with the Harvest Festival and ban Halloween. In fact, their fanaticism only made Garrett more determined that the Grady County Independent School District would celebrate Halloween, complete with hall decorations and end-of-the-day class parties.

But the mothers proved equally as stubborn. They filed a formal protest with the school board and a complaint against Garrett. Just last week, their protest had been denied and their complaint written off. (It didn't hurt Garrett that his brother-in-law was president of the school board.) So the handful of mothers simply refused to send their kids to school today, the day of Satan's birthday.

This meant that Mrs. Airhart wouldn't let Darius go to school today, an event that upset him so greatly he was barely able to contain his ear-piercing screams of joy.

This meant that Lindy wouldn't have to see Darius today, an event that disturbed her so enormously she could hardly squelch her side-splitting giggles of relief.

This meant that—dare she even think it—Lindy was on track for a Perfect Day.

Since it was a holiday and all, and since Lindy was less anxious, having discovered Darius wouldn't be at school, she chose to adhere to her *Bible of Perfect Days.* The night before, she had taken extra time blow-drying her hair and selecting her outfit and matching accessories, even bothering to polish up her tarnished silver-plated bracelet. During school today she had pushed herself to speak up loudly and clearly in class, to appear pleasant and approachable, and to look almost every passerby in the eye and greet them with a cheerful "Hello."

And as a result of following the rules today, Lindy had earned the right to fit in today. But the perfection of today would not naturally flow over into tomorrow, tomorrow she would have to walk the tightrope of perfection all over again, tomorrow and all the days that followed. But today, she had put in the work and it was paying off. She was accepted. She belonged. She had even made a joke under her breath in study hall, and Kari laughed. Kari the Kard had laughed. Lindy secretly hoped she could get Kari to like her enough to invite her to her birthday party even though it would be a last-minute invitation since the party was tomorrow night. Better late than never. But, regardless, Lindy had made Kari laugh. She couldn't remember the last time she had been so happy.

The topper to Lindy's day was Momma's presence at their class party. She was on the seventh-grade party committee for Halloween. Perfection, party, Momma, and a ride home in the car instead of on the bus. It didn't get much better than that.

The bell rang, signaling the end of Mr. Bristow's sixth-period math class. Lindy gathered her pencils and books, smiled at Mr. Bristow, and bade him a cheery "Good-bye," then headed to home room for the party.

She heard the commotion in the hall before she hit the door. A crowd of students and teachers stood peeking in at Mrs. Westmorland's room. The object of their attention—a giant ghost. A sheet-clad, sombrero-wearing ghost with a white Crisco grease-covered face and two saucer-sized blackened eyes.

Lindy politely worked her way through the crowd and into the room to see the ghost. The ghost was playing to a group of seventh-graders who were laughing hysterically. Lindy walked up and whispered to Kari, "Who's the Frito Bandito?"

"And here's my little pigeon-toed spook now." The Criscoed ghost was looking at Lindy, and Momma's voice was coming out of the greased beast. "Course I always walked with my toes out, like a duck. But I never tripped over my feet and fell into the Christmas tree. Remember that, honey? You were walking with your head down, looking at your feet like you always do, and next thing you know, boom. Came up with icicles in your hair and a Christmas ball in your mouth. Looked like a stuffed turkey in a discotheque."

The group of seventh-graders laughed, no one louder than Kari. "Your mom's a hoot. She must be so much fun to be around all the time."

"Um-hum." Lindy tried to conjure the old beauty contestant smile.

"But her walk's gotten much better since then," added Momma the friendly ghost.

"Now if she'd only learn to stand up straight," said Amber as she dug her knuckle into Lindy's spine.

"That is an improvement," said Momma of Lindy's erect posture. "But how are you gonna look at your feet?" Momma, the Don Rickles of ghosts.

"Your mom is so funny," reiterated Kari, and then added absentmindedly, "I wonder if she could come to my birthday party."

Lindy felt her insides wilt. "'Scuse me, I need some punch," she said to no one in particular.

She inconspicuously backed away, looking for a place to hide. All around her, Halloween-starved kids of all ages were loving this. Some of the little kids were frightened. Some of the big kids were aloofly cool.

But the only kid who wanted to vaporize into thin air like the travelers on *Star Trek* was Lindy. Her perfect day had fizzled as quickly as Pop Rocks candy. And all she had to show for it was a bad taste in her mouth and an ache in her stomach. *Beam me up, Scotty.*

Lindy stopped at the refreshment table for a cup of Kool-Aid. Barbara Breedlove worked the punch bowl. Beside her, Sally Donavan was in charge of cookie distribution.

"Why don't you take a cup to your mother. She must be parched from all that talking." Mrs. Breedlove handed Lindy another cup of the orange concoction.

Lindy walked away with her two cups, but she wasn't out of earshot when Sally said to her friend, "Maggie's never that chatty at my house. Thank God."

Beam me up, please.

∾

Momma knew that by going all out with her Halloween costume she was risking any chance she would ever have to break into the ranks of the county's elite. But that was part of what prompted her to do it. She knew deep down she didn't have a chance in hell of being accepted by those snobs, and, by jiggers, if they wouldn't accept her, then at least they'd notice her.

She told her girls as much in the car on the ride home from the class party. "Those school kids needed to have some fun. They couldn't possibly ever have any at home."

"My class thought you were great," Jo gushed.

"So did mine," Lindy said flatly.

"Did you see Barbara Breedlove's face when I walked in? I thought she was gonna have a heart attack. Too bad she didn't."

"She thinks you talk too much," Lindy said, wanting to hurt her mom. But as soon as the words left her mouth, she wanted to take them back.

Then Momma laughed, but too loudly and with anger underneath. "Well, I don't think she talks *enough.* She and Sally whispering in the corner. To hell with those uptight bitches." Ever since her failed "Welcome Me to the Community" luncheon, Momma had changed her rule against cussing. She seemed to like the change. "At least they noticed me."

They sure did, Lindy thought. *They noticed you were a freak.* And, by association, they noticed she was a freak. Or at least the freak's daughter. More than anything, Lindy wanted not to be noticed. She wanted to blend in. She wanted to be like everybody else. And now she had the mother everybody noticed. She hated her mother.

The crash landing of Lindy's guilt almost gave her whiplash. She felt transparent, afraid Momma could read her mind. *I hate my mother,* in flashing neon letters across her forehead. Immediately, she yanked the feeling back, buried it deep inside and covered it with shame. Who was she to hate her mother? She was nothing. Momma was everything. Lindy didn't hate her mother. Herself, maybe, but not her mother. She was nothing without her mother. Nothing. The thought of life without Momma stopped her heart and flushed tears to her eyes.

Momma couldn't help but notice her daughter's Rudolph red nose. "What's wrong, Lindy?"

"I love you."

And she did. She loved her mother more than anything in the whole world.

If there was a freak in this family, it was Lindy. OK, really it was Jo. But it was Lindy for not realizing at every moment what she had in her mother. Her mother was her life. Lindy was nothing without Momma.

CHAPTER SIXTEEN

There was only one anomaly that could halt Lindy's quest for a Perfect Day. A Magical Day.

Magical Days were rarer even than Perfect Days. On Magical Days, God shined upon Lindy. Magical Days were sprinkled with fairy dust. Everything enchantedly fell into place. Lindy didn't have to try to be perfect; she just *was.*

These days came about as often as an eclipse of the sun.

This had been one of those days.

It had started off ordinarily enough. Breakfast, bus ride. But during second-period music, the magic began. Mr. Barber, the band teacher, announced the hiring of a part-time music teacher, Mrs. Samson. She would take over his classes with the elementary kids, plus she would teach private piano and voice lessons for a nominal fee.

The clouds parted. The angels sang. Mrs. Samson was the catalyst that would turn Lindy the out-of-place geek into Lindy the famous pop singer.

Then Mr. Barber introduced the new music teacher, live and in the flesh. Mrs. Samson stood in front of the class looking a little like the Pillsbury dough boy, pale and puffy from her head to her toes. Lindy thought she was beautiful. Then Mrs. Samson said that any students interested in private lessons should see her after class. As soon as the bell rang, Lindy made a beeline to Mrs. Samson. She wanted to be the first one in line. She was. She was also the only one in line.

Students fled the band hall like it was on fire, leaving Mrs. Samson alone with her first student. She eagerly started playing scales.

"*La la la la la.* That's high C...the note, not the drink," Mrs. Samson said, chortling at her joke. "Can you hit that note? Sing out, my dear."

Mrs. Samson played the key again, and Lindy la-la-ed 'til she hit the note.

"Don't be afraid to sing loud. Sing proud." The music teacher demonstrated. Lindy worried Mrs. Samson's high C might break glass.

"You see? Never be timid."

She played a few more scales for Lindy. "You have a nice range. But your lower register is your sweet spot." A sweet spot. Lindy liked the sound of that.

Mrs. Samson rifled through a box full of sheet music. "I want to assign you a piece so we can get started." Lindy didn't have the heart to say she needed to OK this with her parents first.

Mrs. Samson pulled out the sheet music for the Eagles' "Desperado." Lindy knew the song from her Linda Ronstadt eight-track. "I love this song. You really think I can sing it?"

"I *know* you can sing it." Lindy was so happy, she wanted to lick this woman's shoes.

She set up a weekly time to meet for lessons, thanked Mrs. Samson, and headed straight for the nurse's office. In her excitement over inching ever closer to her life's calling, she had forgotten about health class, and was already fifteen minutes late. So she complained to Nurse Berkley about a non-existent stomach ache and lay on the office cot for the remainder of third period. That way she not only missed health, but was written an excused absence for the class. She did not, however, waste her time napping on the cot. She used the half hour wisely, pondering the best way to convince Father to let her take voice lessons. She knew Father would have the ultimate say in her voice lesson fate, but she also knew that by winning over Momma, she stood a better chance of winning over Father.

So during her after-school snack, Lindy mentioned the music teacher to Momma.

"I want to be a professional singer," Lindy said.

"Uh-huh," Momma said skeptically. "Well, just make sure you finish your homework first."

"I'm serious, Momma."

"I'm sure you are. Just like you were serious about playing the guitar and learning to paint." Lindy stuck with both of those callings for less than a month.

"This is different."

"I know. You're gonna be Karen Carpenter. Be loved and adored by fans everywhere." Momma made it sound so trivial. "You still have to ask your father for these lessons. He doesn't think you can stick with anything. Now go do your homework."

Lindy tried not to let Momma's lack of enthusiasm get to her. Momma might not believe in Lindy's talent now, but she soon would. Lindy was going to be a star. Momma loved stars.

Besides, today was her Magical Day.

~

Lindy sang her heart out during that night's shower:

Desperado...

After just four notes, Lindy knew that Mrs. Samson was right. Lindy *could* sing that song. A good thing because Lindy *had* to be able to sing that song. She had to have talent. If she had no talent, she would never be loved. Talent was the reason people would love her. Talent was her last great hope.

"Father?" Lindy approached him when *Hee Haw* broke for a commercial. Lindy never understood her father's attraction to the silly hillbillies on that stupid show. Her father was such a contradiction. He was always trying to educate himself by reading books on history or science or business. One minute, he would be sitting in his La-Z-Boy reading one of these books, and the next he'd be laughing his head off at *Hee Haw.*

"Yup?" Father looked up from his book.

Without taking a breath, Lindy regurgitated her spiel. "I want to take singing lessons from the new music teacher at school. It's not expensive. She thinks I have talent, and so do I. I'm serious about this. I'll stick with it. This isn't like the guitar lessons or the painting. I really want this."

Father thought for a second. "You'll stick with this?"

"Definitely."

Father paused. "OK, then."

"OK? Really?"

"If you help out around the house after school and help me on the farm on the weekends, I'll pay for the lessons."

"OK. Wow. Thanks." Lindy leaned in to give her father a kiss. He puffed out his cheek as a target for placement of her peck. "Good-night."

"Good-night."

A Magical Day.

CHAPTER SEVENTEEN

Jo loved her birthday. It was the best day of the year. She loved the attention. She craved the attention. She glowed with the attention.

And the presents didn't hurt either.

For every one of the girls' birthdays since they were born, Momma had made her famous cartoon cakes. Her cartoon cakes didn't have some lame plastic figurine slapped on top or that pathetic store-bought-tube-of-icing writing. Oh, no. When Momma's cakes were finished, they were actually three-dimensional cartoon characters. Lindy's *Looney Tunes* Roadrunner ("Beep! Beep!") birthday cake a couple of years ago had been nearly three feet long.

To aid in the assembly of her culinary creations, Momma sketched a cake blueprint to scale before she started baking, then cut the sheet cakes into shape and pieced the smaller parts together with toothpicks. The cakes were always chocolate with marshmallow icing. But what really brought the cake to life was the final touch. She would dye the white icing any number of hues and frost the character in animation-quality Technicolor.

Jo always requested a Tweety Bird cake for her birthday. Tweety was her favorite cartoon character. She used to follow Lindy around the house chirping, "I tawt I taw a puddy tat. I did! I did!"

The afternoon of her ninth birthday, Jo couldn't tear off the bus fast enough. She was out of breath by the time she reached the kitchen and saw Momma standing by her Tweety Bird cake, candles blazing.

"Make a wish," Momma said.

Jo wished for all of Momma's attention today.

She blew hard, extinguishing every candle in one breath so her wish would come true. She loved her birthday.

"I want his right foot," Jo said. She always wanted his right foot.

"OK," Momma said as she started to cut.

"And Lindy gets the leg," Jo said.

"What if I want the left foot?" asked Lindy.

"I get the feet. You get the legs."

"Whatever," Lindy shrugged and scowled.

Jo would never understand her sister. Jo gave and gave, was nice as pie, and still it was never good enough for her older grouch of a sibling.

"Grump," Jo said. It was *her* birthday after all.

"Geek," Lindy said back.

"Stop bickering, you two. I demand you love each other. Or at least fake it." Momma inhaled and exhaled slowly. "Now. Let's have a birthday party, dammit."

Jo had begged Momma not to invite any kids to her birthday party. She wouldn't dream of having that stuck-up Renee snob in her house. Momma joked about wanting to throw a party for all the kids she had entertained at Halloween. Jo knew it wasn't a joke. She toyed with the idea of letting Momma invite Wendy, but she didn't think Wendy would be enough of an audience for Momma. Momma finally stopped asking Jo if she wanted a big party when Jo answered in her little girl voice that all she wanted for her birthday was to spend the day with her mommy. Momma had rolled her eyes and let out a big sigh and said, "Why you kids are such introverts, I'll never know. Get it from your father, I guess." Jo didn't care that she was an introvert, whatever that was, she just cared that she didn't have to have a big birthday bash.

"How was your day, Jo Bean?" Momma asked as they ate their cake.

"Fine," she said.

"Did anybody sing you 'Happy Birthday'?"

"At lunch," Jo said. She caught Lindy's eye and dared her to tell Momma otherwise.

"How nice. I bet they don't do that for just anyone."

"Can I open my present now?" Jo asked, shoving her last bite of cake down her gullet.

"What makes you think you're getting a present?" Momma teased.

"'Cause I'm your Jo Bean." Jo batted her eyes, and watched Lindy make a "gag me" motion.

Then Momma presented Jo Bean with a gift-wrapped package the size of a large hat box. It shook riotously with rattles and clanks. Jo's insides rattled too with excitement, but not so much that she disregarded her routine of meticulously removing each piece of tape from the gift wrap, folding the paper and putting it aside. When it came to unwrapping gifts, Jo was no nine-year-old kid. She was an eighty-year-old grandmother.

Jo opened the box and started pulling out wads of toilet paper. She pulled and pulled and pulled. The amount of bathroom tissue coming out of that box went on and on and on, like hundreds of clowns climbing out of a tiny shoebox of a car. Soon, Jo and her party-goers were all giddy with laughter. Lindy even snorted one of her laughs. That made them all hysterical.

"We've never had this much toilet paper in the house in my life," Lindy said when she caught her breath.

"It's a twenty-four-pack," Momma said, wiping the laughter from her eyes. "I bought it to wrap Jo's gift. Now this is our TP for the next month. Don't tell your father, he'll flip."

"The bathroom's not big enough to fit it all," Jo said, viewing the mountain of toilet paper.

"Then it's a good thing I kept all the spools," Momma held up one of the little brown cyclinders.

That did it. They were all hysterical again.

"Hey, where's my present?" Jo asked when she finally reached the noisemakers at the bottom of the box. She knew full well her gift was more than a few pennies and nuts and bolts.

"Well, that's what your father said we could afford." Momma rolled her eyes for effect. "But I decided to splurge." She handed Jo Bean an envelope.

Jo opened it with a swoosh of one finger. When she saw what was inside, she gasped. "A day of modeling school. Oh, Momma." She threw her arms around Momma's neck. "This is my dream."

"Well, when you're getting just one present, it should be a doozy," said Momma.

"A whole Saturday in Lubbock," Jo said, reading the card. "This is the best gift ever."

"I'm glad, sweetie. Maybe you can grow up and have the career that I never had."

"Oh, Momma. Do you really think?"

"I don't see why not."

Jo would give her little toe to model housewares in Lubbock department stores like Momma did. Course if she were a model, she might need that little toe.

"Why don't you give us a show? Strut your stuff on this make- believe runway."

"Maybe I should take the class first."

"Why stop now? You primp all the time already," Lindy said. The Grinch Who Stole Birthdays.

Jo shot Lindy a "kill 'em with kindness smile" just like Momma had taught her and said, "OK, I will."

She stood up, brushed herself off, fluffed her hair and strutted, hips swinging. Momma couldn't stifle a giggle.

Jo stopped immediately. "What am I doing wrong?"

"Nothing, honey," Momma said, laughing. "It's just that, well...you're not a streetwalker."

"You mean, like on *Starsky and Hutch*?" Jo thought of those skanks that hung around Huggy Bear.

"*Starsky and Hutch*?" Momma said. "Who lets you watch *Starsky and Hutch*?"

Daddy, Jo started to say, but before she could get it out, Lindy blurted, "Aunt Birdy."

"Birdy?" Momma repeated.

Aunt Birdy was Momma's goody-goody sister who didn't let her kids watch anything but religious programming.

"Well, if Birdy let you watch it..."

Jo had to admit Lindy saved her on this one. She gave her big sis a nod of thanks. Lindy practically snarled.

"Walk again," Momma said to Jo.

Jo obliged, this time adding a swish of her head like she'd seen the professionals do.

Momma howled.

"What?" Jo looked down. Was her fly open?

"I'm sorry, I'm sorry. It's just that...well, don't flaunt it so much, sweetheart. You'll scare the people."

Jo Bean looked earnestly at her mother, her mentor. "I'm scary?"

"Subtlety is the key." Momma moved her arms in a flowing motion, gracefully demonstrating her imaginary cookware.

"I see," Jo said.

"Let me get my scrapbook. Maybe you can learn from my pictures," Momma said as she left the room.

"OK," Jo called after. Then she turned on her sister. "Don't make fun of me."

"I didn't do anything," Lindy said in defense of herself.

"You laughed at every step I took. Told me I was doing it all wrong."

"I didn't say anything."

"What do you know about modeling? You can't even walk except pigeon-toed."

Lindy threw up her hands and let out a frustrated growl. "Momma's right. You are scary."

"Momma wouldn't say that if you didn't make fun of me!"

"I did *nothing*!"

"Here we go." Momma walked in with two books more stuffed to the gills than a Thanksgiving Day turkey. "Jo, grab this top scrapbook, will you? One has pictures of Miss Texas and the other's the Lubbock pictures."

The moment Momma opened her books, Jo forgot about her grouchy-poo sister and all of her hurtful teasing. The day was now about Momma. Thank goodness. Jo hated when the day was about her. She hated the attention. She hated being under the magnifying glass. She felt the sun's rays hotter through the glass. She felt her dreams going up in flames.

~

"Happy birthday, Kiddo Beano," Father said to Jo as he handed her a cotton boll from his field when he came home later in the day.

"Thanks," Jo said, disappointed in his gift offering.

"What'd you get for your birthday?" Father asked.

Ah-choo, Jo sneezed. "You're making me sneezy."

"Joe, your dirty clothes and that filthy cotton boll are stirring up all our allergies. Now will you go jump in the shower?" Momma said.

Father started to trudge off just as Jo piped up. "Thanks for the day of modeling school in Lubbock."

Father stopped. He turned. He looked at Momma. He turned back. He walked silently out of the kitchen and into the bathroom.

"What'd I do wrong? I was just minding my manners," Jo said.

"He doesn't understand about modeling school, honey. He's a man." Momma heard the water pressure force the shower to life and said, "I'll go talk to him."

She knocked on the bathroom door and let herself in. Lindy was watching television in the living room. Jo joined her. From there, she could hear her parents' every word through the crepe paper walls.

"How dare you ruin her birthday," Momma shouted.

"I told you we couldn't afford modeling school," Father said, yelling over the shower.

"So we go a little deeper into debt," Momma replied.

"We can't get our money back, can we?"

"It's nonrefundable."

"It's a rip-off," Father answered back.

"It's not a rip-off to fuel her dream. People need to have hope to keep on going."

There was a pause. "This has nothing to do with Jo and you know it," Father said softly, but still detectable through the paper-thin walls.

"I was the best damn housewares demonstrator Lubbock ever saw. I could've traveled the world. They were gonna send me to New Jersey!"

The running water squeaked to a halt, and the shower curtain rolled back. "I fell in love with that housewares demonstrator, didn't I?"

"Well, if you still love me then let me give this to my daughter," Momma said. "She needs this. Just like Lindy needs to take voice lessons. You didn't have a problem with that."

"My problem is that one day of modeling school costs as much as three months of voice lessons."

"It was her birthday. She needed something special, something to look forward to, something to take her away from all of this." Momma's voice quivered like she was gonna burst into tears, like the pressure of the move, the clique, the debt was gonna break open her fuzzy orange head. "I could've been famous. The Paul Harvey of cast iron cookware."

Then there was quiet. What Jo didn't hear was Father wrapping his freshly toweled-off arms around Momma and holding her. Since Jo couldn't know what she didn't hear, she imagined the worst. At Wendy's suggestion, she let herself be mesmerized by the twenty-inch screen glowing in front of her face. Thank God *Donny & Marie* was on. It was Wendy's favorite show.

~

After supper, as Joe sat in his La-Z-Boy simultaneously watching *Hee Haw* and reading a book on the Civil War, Jo walked in from her bedroom, tears streaming down her face.

"I'm sorry modeling school costs so much," she said between intakes of breath.

Joe could handle focusing on Robert E. Lee and Buck Owens, but throw a crying child into the mix and he was clearly off balance.

He fumbled frantically for the box of Kleenex. "Don't cry. I don't want you to cry." He just knew his wife would lay into him for this any second.

"Here, wipe your eyes."

Jo took a Kleenex and wadded it up in her fist. She continued crying.

"You know what?" he said, fishing for something to say. "I'm sorry it cost so much too. But when you're a big, famous model, it won't matter one bit." That sounded pretty good, he thought. Maybe honesty was the best policy.

"You're lying. I'll never be a big, famous model."

Then again maybe honesty was a bunch of hooey.

"Jo Bean, why are you so upset?" Maggie came in from carrying the trash to the garage.

"I stink as a model!" Snot was now running out of her nose.

"Where did you get that idea? You do not stink. You are an excellent model." She shot her husband a look. "What did you tell her?"

Nothing, he mouthed soundlessly.

"You can be anything you want to be, Jo Bean. And don't let anyone, and I mean anyone, tell you otherwise." She held a Kleenex for Jo to blow her nose into, then kissed her youngest on the forehead.

"Happy birthday."

"Yes, happy birthday, Jo." Joe tried to follow his wife's lead.

"Good-night," Jo said as she kissed her father's puffed-out cheek.

"Good-night."

"'Night, Momma," Jo said, scurrying back to her bedroom.

Joe quickly ducked his head into his book, and Maggie padded back into the kitchen. Hard as he tried, he would never understand females and their mood swings as long as he lived. Just his luck that his sperm couldn't even yield him a son.

~

The next day, Momma's guilt had chipped away at her but good. She was determined to make up for the price of the modeling school. She was on a quest to save money.

"Lindy, why are you out of maxi pads again?" Momma asked as she looked over the grocery list.

Lindy said nothing. There was no need to answer. Momma's tone said this was a one-sided conversation.

"These adhesive kind are too expensive to go through so fast. How often are you changing pads?"

Lindy said nothing.

Momma headed straight for the bathroom. She dug into the trash basket and pulled out the first used feminine napkin she saw.

"Look at this," she said, aghast, as she unwrapped the toilet paper that covered the discarded maxi pad. "You're not supposed to use the whole twenty-four-pack to wrap these in." She unfolded the pad and brandished her evidence.

"This doesn't even look worn. There's barely a drop of blood on it. We are *broke.* Do you know that? You better make this next box of pads last. I mean bleed on each one and bleed good. You hear me?" And with that, Momma flew out of the room.

Lindy said nothing.

CHAPTER EIGHTEEN

Thanksgiving was Lindy's favorite holiday. Every American was obliged to gorge themselves on a variety of starches and carbohydrates, candied vegetables, and sweets. It was unpatriotic not to. God bless America. Lindy couldn't fathom those foreign countries who celebrated holidays by *fasting*. Those poor people. One taste of Momma's turkey and dressing and they'd see what holiness really meant.

The meal had taken Momma the better part of a week to prepare, starting with the dressing on Monday which she kept frozen until this morning. On Tuesday, she baked pumpkin and fresh apple pies. Wednesday, she snapped peas then peeled and mashed taters for the twice-baked potato casserole. And, starting Thursday morning at 5:00 a.m., she began cooking the turkey, kneading the dough for the rolls, candying the yams, and adding the finishing touches until every dish came out hot and perfectly seasoned at exactly 1:00 p.m.

The other three Logans devoured the meal in sixteen minutes.

"Oh, I'm so full," Lindy moaned in blissful agony from her perch on the floor. As was her habit on Thanksgiving Day, she had eaten herself into a tryptophan-induced coma. A few minutes ago, she had laid down her fork, successfully having conquered the twin mounds of dressing on her plate. Her goal had been to move from the table to the couch. She had set her goal too high.

Momma watched her daughter whining on the floor. "Lindy, could you at least move so those of us who have to clear the table can do so?" Momma's "us" was like the royal "we." She was the only one clearing the table.

"OK." Lindy painfully pulled herself to a sitting position. "When's dessert?"

Momma ignored the question and said, exhaustedly, "A week to cook, the rest of the afternoon to clean up, and fifteen whole minutes at the table. Next year, we're having TV dinners."

TV dinners! The words of a madwoman! Lindy had to nip this train of thought in the bud.

She rose to her feet. "That was a really good dinner, Momma. The best dressing ever. Nobody makes it like you."

Momma stopped. "I don't add as much sage as the recipe calls for. Merle always used too way much. Her taste buds were dead even when she was alive, poor thing." Merle was Father's momma.

"Well, yours is the best," Lindy added for good measure.

A smile crept across Momma's lips. "Dessert's whenever you no longer feel like you're gonna explode, gobble-gobble girl. Now why don't you go lay down in the living room while I clean up."

"You need help?"

"No, no. I have my own method for arranging it all in the fridge." Her sarcasm was gone.

Lindy rubbed her stomach. "Sure was good."

She walked away feeling so happy she could bust. And it wasn't just from her bloated gut. She had averted the threat to next year's Thanksgiving dinner. And she had made Momma feel appreciated in the process. While Father and Jo hurried from the table with barely a thank you, Lindy had literally fallen on the floor and shown her gratitude. She was a good daughter.

She could hear the Dallas Cowboys Thanksgiving Day battle over the TV as she neared the living room. She personally didn't care one way or the other about the Cowboys, but Father did, and Lindy wanted Father to care about her, so she pretended to care about the Cowboys. If she could care vicariously for the Cowboys, Father would care vicariously for her. It made sense in Lindy's mind anyway.

So every Sunday Lindy sat with Father after church and watched the Cowboys game. During the commercial breaks, she would try to make conversation:

"I like their away uniforms, don't you? Their blue jerseys don't show the blood and dirt as much as their white ones."

Or "Charlie Waters would be really cute if his neck weren't so thick. Why do they all have to have tree-trunk necks?"

Or "Do you think Tom Landry ever changes hats?"

Father always reciprocated with a grunt.

"What's the score?" Lindy asked now as she waddled to the couch.

"Ugghh, zzzzz." Father responded with a grunt plus a snore. A special response for the Thanksgiving Day game.

Lindy arrived at her destination and plopped onto the couch. Father dozed in his La-Z-Boy. On TV, the Cowboys were threatening to score against the St. Louis Cardinals.

Jo walked in and made a move toward the TV channel.

"What are you doing?" Lindy hissed.

"Changing the channel," Jo whispered back.

"No."

"I don't like football."

"Father's watching it." Lindy took her role as Father's television guard dog very seriously. Plus, she knew from experience never to change the channel when Father was watching TV. Especially when he was asleep.

"He's asleep." Jo glanced at Father, and he confirmed her proclamation with a snore. Jo stuck her tongue out at her sister as if to say "see," and reached for the knob on the TV. She flipped to the next channel and seemed content with its program—Julia Child cooking (what else?) turkey and dressing. Jo didn't care what she watched as long as it wasn't football.

"Turn it back to the game," Father growled from his chair. He didn't move, he didn't stir, he didn't even open his eyes. Jo snapped to attention and quickly changed the channel. Her father never ceased to scare the bejesus out of her. She tiptoed toward her room, hoping not to wake the man who really did have eyes in the back of his head. Lindy stuck her tongue out at her sister, "See."

She stayed on the couch; what little volume emanated from the TV was annihilated by the snores of her father. Truth be told, she was scared of the man too. She had just learned to weather his storms. The key was he liked his children to be seen and not heard. OK, she often got the feeling he would prefer she not be seen either, but when it came to living together they had worked out a compromise—do it Father's way. As long as that criterion was met, Lindy and her father got along just fine.

So Lindy sat with her father on this Thanksgiving afternoon listening to the music of his adenoids, watching his Cowboys game, and being grateful for their time together.

~

While most Americans spent the day after Thanksgiving partaking in the busiest shopping day of the year, the Logan girls did their partaking elsewhere—in the cotton field. It was stripping season for Father. That meant it was tromping season for the girls.

When Lindy first heard about tromping cotton it sounded like so much fun, like jumping on a big old cotton-filled trampoline. It was her first lesson in things not always being as they seem.

"Aahhh blooey!!!" Lindy sneezed with the velocity of a teamster because now, on day three of their Thanksgiving Weekend Tromping Extravaganza, her sinuses were ablaze.

"Move over," Jo yelled, "Father's about to dump another load."

Lindy lumbered across the mounds of cotton and joined Jo at one end of the trailer, then leaned over the metal rail and waved to signal they were out of harm's way. And then she convulsed another sneeze.

Receiving his cue that his daughters were safe from being buried alive, Father manuevered his John Deere beside the trailer. Seconds later, the gigantic basket atop the tractor rose mechanically and cotton, stickers, stalks, and dust spilled into the trailer. It was a cloud of allergens.

The girls tromped their way across the trailer, smushing the cotton as best they could. It was their job to compact the cotton so as much of the crop as possible could fit into one trailer before being driven to the gin.

"Fall on it harder," Jo called out. She could be so bossy.

"I'm already scratched up as all get out," Lindy said. No matter how much she bundled up, the burrs and bolls always worked their way inside her clothes. It was hard to believe that this filthy crop became the clean, fluffy balls she bought in stores to *remove* dirt from her face.

As Father drove off into the sunset with his lone compadre, the Deere, the girls dramatically tapered off their fevered tromping.

"Bet I can make a better snow angel that you," Jo said.

"In your dreams," Lindy said, ignoring her allergies to accept the dare.

Each girl lay on her back in the trailer high above the ground, waving her arms and legs, competing to make the best snow angel in the snowless cotton. Neither angel turned out for squat, but Jo came up covered with the most stickers and burrs, which she took as an indication that she had worked harder, and therefore declared herself the snow angel champion. Lindy didn't put up a fight; her sinuses were too inflamed from all the flailing around for her to give a darn.

She did stop wheezing long enough to notice Smiley's pickup pull up.

"Hi, girls," he said.

"Hi."

Lindy saw her sister not make eye contact with Smiley. She saw because she didn't make eye contact either. It was hard to look adults in the eye. Adults were too intimidating. Even nice adults like Smiley. Come to think of it everybody was too intimidating, no matter what their age.

"I wanted to show your daddy my new purchase," Smiley said, gesturing to Father's incoming tractor. "You girls might wanna see this too. Come on down."

Lindy climbed down first because Jo refused to get out unless somebody spotted her so she had a safety net. Like Lindy would really risk her own life to catch Jo.

The three of them stood at Smiley's pickup as Father poured another full basket of cotton into the trailer. He turned off the engine and climbed down from the cab of the tractor.

"Had to show you my latest purchase," Smiley said, pointing to the horse trailer that brought up the rear of his pickup.

"Bought yourself a Thanksgiving present?" Father asked.

"Bought myself a present for every occasion for the rest of my life. And that's no joke."

Then he led his audience to the doors of the trailer and revealed what did look to Lindy like a joke—two jokes to be exact.

"Ostriches," Smiley beamed. "One female and one male. Gertrude and Hank. Gonna breed 'em. Supposed to be the next booming market."

"Why?" Jo asked what Lindy was wondering.

"People may not know it yet, but this bird has what they want," Smiley replied.

Lindy stared into the bulging eyes of this dinosaur-sized bird and couldn't imagine what it possibly had that anybody would want.

"Ostrich skin boots," Smiley said, "ostrich meat steaks, even ostrich feather hats. The sky's the limit."

"How much do these birds go for?" Father was dying to know, but tried not to sound too eager.

"Well, now, they're a pretty penny. But, ah, you gotta spend money to make money, I figure. I slapped down $5,000 apiece for 'em. Pretty near all my savings."

Lindy thought her father was going to choke.

"Easy there, Joe," Smiley said, offering up his packet of Red Man snuff. "You want a pinch between your cheek and gum?"

"Naw, thanks," Father said, taking a drink from his Thermos.

"You think I'm crazy as a loon, don't ya?" Smiley asked.

"Well, they sure are funny-looking things. But I've never been a trendsetter, so what do I know. They probably have nice-looking skin and good-tasting meat."

"Melt in your mouth. One of these days, when they got lots of youngins running around, we'll keep one for ourselves and fry up some steaks. Heck, maybe we'll even stitch us up some boots."

Lindy heard the growl a split second before Lulu hurled herself at the horse trailer. Lindy had seen Lulu move, but never with the speed of light. Her sausage legs were a blur. Luckily, Smiley was facing the blitz and closed the trailer doors in time for Lulu to get a taste of metal instead of bird leg. But Lulu was not deterred. She erupted into a staccato of barking frenzy. The ostriches fluttered wildly in their enclosed quarters.

"Settle down, Gert. It's OK, Hank," Smiley cooed to his new treasures.

"Get that dog outta here," Father yelled, lunging for the hound. He scooped the dog up in his arms, which only served to make her bark louder.

"Wow, guess you got more of a bird dog there than I do," Smiley said. "Bart didn't bat an eye when I brought his new siblings home." Bart was Smiley's purebred Scottish deerhound, the closest thing to offspring Smiley had. 'Til now, anyway.

"Guess I'll be going," Smiley said, ducking into the cab of his pickup. "Catch y'all later."

As Smiley drove away, Father was finally able to grab Lulu's mouth and stifle her bark.

Lindy watched her father's eyes blaze. "I want you to keep this dog tied up and away from those $5,000 birds. You hear me?"

"But she wouldn't hurt 'em. She just thinks she's a bird dog."

Father was already halfway to the pickup. "We'll take her home and tie her up now."

"Please don't tie her up. I'll watch her. She won't hurt those dumb birds, I promise."

Father started the pickup.

"Please?" Lindy was ready to fall on her knees if it would help.

Father looked out the truck window. "Get in and hold the dog."

Lindy followed Jo into the pickup cab. Father jerked to a halt in front of the house, went straight to the backyard and tied Lindy's dog to a post.

Every time Lindy looked at Lulu tied to that post, she felt sick to her stomach. It was ridiculous, she knew, but it got so she couldn't look at her dog at all. Lulu was a captive in her own backyard. She could no longer run free, or see her friends, or have adventures. Lindy knew exactly how she felt.

CHAPTER NINETEEN

The voice recital was only two weeks away, and Lindy took that as a sign she should start practicing her song. Mrs. Samson had recorded her piano accompaniment of "Desperado" on a cassette tape so she could practice at home. Mrs. Samson had strongly suggested that she practice at home. Lindy could tell from the urgency in her teacher's voice that she wanted her star pupil to be perfect.

She practiced by first crooning to the eight-track with Linda Ronstadt and then by herself to Mrs. Samson's cassette. Lindy could not tell the difference between her voice and Linda's. Funny how their names had just one letter different.

Her plan was to record a tape of her singing during rehearsals to give Momma for Christmas. She was going to be a singing star, and she wanted Momma to have her first-ever recording. Momma would treasure it, she knew. Momma loved stars.

"Lindy, could you take a break?" Momma yelled from the kitchen.

"I've only rehearsed ten minutes."

"I think it's been closer to forty-five."

Lindy looked at the clock. "Nope. Ten."

"Well, go to your room to rehearse. I've got a headache."

Lindy stepped into the kitchen. "I'm trying to get used to an audience."

"Lucky us," Jo said from her perch at the kitchen table. *Jealous brat.*

"Jo, that's enough," Momma said, purposely not adding the "Bean." That meant she was serious. "You've been working all afternoon, Lindy. Why don't you sit down and have a snack?"

"I'm on a diet. So I'll look good for the recital." Lindy knew it was important for divas to look the part as well.

"You're just hoping people won't notice what you sound like," Jo said smugly.

"You better shut up before I shut you up," Lindy said.

"Both of you shut up," Momma said. "Lindy, stop threatening your sister. And, Jo, stop making fun of Lindy."

Jo looked to Momma. "You were laughing at her before."

Lindy's head whipped around, and she met Momma's gaze. Her eyes begged to know if this was true.

"You just need to practice. Which you're doing," Momma said. "That's all." She patted Lindy's shoulder. "And maybe support your breath a little more from your diaphragm." She smiled. "And maybe listen to the notes a little more carefully."

"Why don't you show her?" Jo said.

"Would you mind if I did?" Momma asked Lindy.

"No, that'd be great." Lindy said, sincerely. She adored Momma's singing voice.

Lindy pushed the button and the accompaniment tape began to play. Momma read the words off the sheet music. She didn't sound anything like Linda Ronstadt.

She sounded better.

Momma sang the heck out of that song, and when she finished, one thought ran through Lindy's mind—she would never be a singing star.

Compared to Momma, Lindy was simply a background-singing Supreme. Momma was Diana Ross.

~

Mrs. Samson had printed up a program that listed each of the performers in the recital. "Desperado" sung by Lindy Logan was number six, over halfway into the program. Lindy saw no need to get nervous. She had all the time in the world.

The first five songs were over in a beat of her heart.

Lindy stepped onto the stage of the school auditorium and dragged her stomach along by a string. The stage lights blinded her from seeing the audience, but she could hear them. Tittering. Shuffling. Waiting. *For her.*

Mrs. Samson played the first keys of Lindy's song. Lindy wasn't ready. Mrs. Samson was supposed to wait for Lindy to nod when she was ready. She wasn't ready. Not near ready.

Desperado...

The first word of the song which had sounded so strong, so rich when she sang it in front of her mirror warbled timidly into the microphone.

Lindy watched her hand shake like she had Kate Hepburn's Parkinson's disease. Suddenly, she was the one who was desperate. Desperate to get off the stage.

Two and a half minutes passed like an eternity, but Lindy woke from her torture to audience applause. Applause. Not just polite, but sincere. What was a torturous eternity in the moment was now over in what seemed like the blink of an eye.

"There's the little songbird," said Wanda Hutchinson in the lobby after the recital. "Such a pretty little voice."

"Thank you," Lindy said.

"You sound just like that girl on the radio," Horace Vandever said. "That one with the three names."

"Olivia Newton-John?" Lindy asked, amazed. That was even better than sounding like Linda Ronstadt.

"That's the one, I think. You sound just like her."

Lindy almost hugged Horace.

Maybe she was a singer after all.

Lindy waited for Momma to say something about her performance.

"Mrs. Samson could really use a rinse on her hair," Momma said on the drive home. "It'd take years off her age."

By the time Lindy kissed Momma good-night, she was about to burst.

"Horace Vandever said I sing like Olivia Newton-John," she blurted.

Momma surveyed her daughter. "Really?"

Lindy nodded excitedly.

"Well, he's much too kind."

Lindy nodded slowly.

~

That night after everyone was in bed, Lindy bundled up in her long johns and winter coat and snuck outside. She crept into Father's pickup truck and gently closed the door. There, shielded from the freezing wind, she could conduct her business without anyone in the house being the wiser. She clicked the button on her portable cassette recorder and replayed her recital performance.

Momma was right.

Horace Vandever *was* much too kind.

She rewound the tape. Her rehearsals had to sound better. She was nervous in the recital. That's why she stunk. She could conquer stage fright, a common affliction for performers. Even superstars like Barbra Streisand got stage fright.

Lindy pushed play again and said a little prayer. She had a lot riding on this song.

She stopped the tape before the end of the first verse.

She placed the cassette under the heel of her boot and crunched the plastic into shards. Then she pulled out the tape and ripped the resulting magnetic spider web to smithereens. Lastly, she slithered out of the truck and tiptoed to the garbage cans, skulking around like the Grinch as Whoville's fake Santa. She lifted the lid to the fullest can and buried the evidence of her singing career deep inside weeks of sour food and decaying rubbish. Her main concern was that the tape never be found nor used to blackmail her someday.

The next morning, she thumbed through the Monkey Wards catalog in search of a Christmas gift for Momma that wouldn't embarrass either one of them. And she told Mrs. Samson that she was quitting voice lessons. The teacher actually seemed upset that Lindy was going to ignore her talent, and she kept trying to talk her into continuing the lessons. *Oh, just shut up and dye your hair*, Lindy wanted to shout.

But Momma accepted her daughter's decision to quit without question. She simply comforted her eldest with the best medicine she could supply—homemade cherry cobbler.

Lindy decisively stopped listening to music. There would be no more movie musicals. No more Linda or Olivia. No more Carpenters or Captain and Tennille.

Like her mother a decade and a half ago, Lindy felt that if she couldn't be a part of this world, she wanted nothing to do with it at all. She would squelch her love for music until it was extinguished. It was too painful to pine for what could never be.

So instead of practicing her singing, Lindy went back to watching TV every afternoon. Thankfully, she still had the program listings memorized from *TV Guide.*

CHAPTER TWENTY

Maggie knew her husband was not having the best of birthdays. He had just come from the cotton buyers where he had sold off his crop to the highest bidder. Unfortunately, this year's overabundance of cotton meant the highest bid was still far too low. Almost as low as Joe's mood.

"I've got chicken fried steak for the birthday boy," she called to the living room as she set the table.

"Um, hum. Finger-licking good," Jo said, trying to sell it. For the life of her, Momma could not figure out where her daughters got their flair for the dramatic.

"It's almost ready, Joe. You wanna wash up?"

"Sure. Smells good, honey." He absentmindedly patted his wife's tush en route to the bathroom. He just wasn't right. Maggie could tell.

"Keep stirring the gravy, Lindy," Maggie said. "Turn it to low when all the lumps are out."

Maggie knocked lightly on the bathroom door, then entered.

"I'm coming," Joe said, sounding like he was expecting a lecture.

"I didn't come to get you. Well, I did come to get you, but not like that." She put her arms seductively around his neck. "Happy birthday."

She kissed him tenderly, gently.

He lifted her arms off his shoulders. "Isn't the steak gonna burn?"

She pulled away from his neck, ready to ring it.

"Dinner'll be on the table, master," she said, acerbically. *Go ahead and have a rotten goddamn birthday. And a frigid one.*

~

Momma threw Father's chicken fried steak onto his plate as if it were a Frisbee. She lit a candle atop it, and the wax was dripping onto the meat by the time Father arrived at the table.

Lindy could only shake her head. Her two parents alone in the bathroom always ended in disaster. She swore never to even consider marriage unless guaranteed separate bathrooms.

The bummer about Father's birthday was that since he didn't eat sweets there was no birthday cake. Which was a shame because dinner could desperately have used a little sweetening.

"Don't worry, I didn't spend much," Momma said as she handed Father his gift. She always said that when she gave Father a gift.

He opened the box to reveal a bolo tie adorned with plastic turquoise. "Thanks, honey. I love it," he said. It was obvious to Lindy that he was just trying to butter Momma up, but Momma seemed to take him at his word.

"It's the latest thing," Momma said. "I bought it from Joseph Minsky." Mr. Minsky's house was one of the ones that Momma cleaned in Jessip. He was the only Jew in Jessip, and the only lawyer. Lindy's only concept of a Jew was Barbra Streisand. She loved Barbra. Or she had while she was still allowing herself to dream of a career in music.

"He's making them as a hobby," Momma went on. "I was his first customer."

"You're kidding?" Father said. From his tone, Lindy could tell he knew Momma wasn't kidding.

Lindy was about to offer up her present when Jo butted in, whining, "Open *mine* next. Open *mine*."

Fine. Save the best for last.

Lindy felt the thrill of victory when she saw Jo's homemade gift: a clay ashtray for Father's occasional pipe smoking. The stupid thing looked like a cow patty. Lindy was in like Flynn.

"My turn," Lindy said, unable to conceal her excitement.

Father tore open the wrapping paper and his eyes sparked for the first time since he pried the wax off his chicken fried steak. This was indeed his favorite birthday gift.

"I thought Henry Mancini over Beethoven," Lindy said, explaining her album choice.

"Thank you, Lindy. I love it." This time he meant it. Lindy could tell the difference.

"I broke open my piggy bank. I wanted to make up for disappointing you after quitting voice."

Father looked up from the album. "You quit voice?"

"I thought Momma told you," Lindy said. Damn, if she didn't know when to shut up.

"I thought we made a deal."

"We did, but..."

"Joe," Momma said, "Lindy realized after the recital that she's not a singer. The whole thing was a nerve-wracking experience for her. Now she's looking elsewhere to find her talent."

Momma ran her palm alongside Lindy's face and said, "Don't be so hard on her."

Momma to the rescue. Only Lindy didn't feel her usual sense of relief.

"Why don't you put on your new record while I clean up?" Momma said to Father even though Sunday morning was still twelve hours away.

"I think I will," Father said, pulling the album from its jacket and rising from the table.

"Here, take my ashtray with ya," Jo begged as she plopped the concrete turd into Father's arms.

"Jo, I can't carry..." Father juggled the two gifts, saved them from crashing to the ground, and ended up with both in his arms.

Only the ashtray was enveloped like a giant taco by two dark half-moon circles that were once a whole black vinyl disk.

Father lifted the broken record as a hush deafened the room. This was the calm. Lindy prepared for the storm.

Well, one good thing's gonna come of this, she thought. *Father's finally gonna kill Jo.*

And then the unthinkable happened.

Without another word, a homicide, or even a scene, Father turned and left the house.

He came back in a few hours after a long drive. He never laid a hand on Jo.

~

In the middle of the night, Lindy got up to use the bathroom and saw Father sitting at the kitchen table, applying Elmer's glue to the two broken pieces of black vinyl. His movements were small, cautious, painstaking. Like those of a child.

He then married the two halves, holding them as tight as kissing cousins to begin the bonding process. But when he turned his left wrist to look at his watch, the delicate balance shot out of his hands like a house of cards.

This was too painful to watch.

Lindy tiptoed back to her room, grateful for Father's frustration only in that it allowed her an easy escape.

She burrowed under the covers, but couldn't hide her embarrassment. It was as if she had walked in on him in the shower. And she might as well have. Seeing Father that vulnerable was like seeing him naked.

∾

The next morning, the whole house awoke to the strains of Father's birthday album. Or rather the first two seconds of the album. Then the needle jumped the crevice of dried glue and began the album's first two seconds all over again. The needle never once made it past two seconds on its own. But that didn't keep Father from trying. Time and again, he placed the needle on a new song, and, time and again, after two seconds it hurdled the crack and started the song all over again. Father tried to play that record all morning long. Not one song made it past two seconds.

Father was determined, but his determination couldn't make the record whole again. So, just in time to salvage the sanity of the remaining Logans, a defeated Father surrendered and tossed the album into the trash. He turned off the stereo and turned on the Cowboys game.

Usually when the Cowboys played the Redskins, Father joked that "It's the Cowboys and the Indians on TV, the Cowboys versus the Indians, the Cowboys and Indians are playing." Bang, bang, shoot 'em up. Ha, ha, ha. Not this time. This time there were no jokes.

In their last regular season game, the Cowboys got trounced by the Redskins, 27-14. It was a lousy birthday weekend.

CHAPTER TWENTY-ONE

Lindy didn't think a thing about it at first. After all, Momma always had mood swings.

But then she noticed that Momma's stomach seemed puffier. Her appetite was strange. She craved dill pickle and peanut butter sandwiches. And that was just wrong. Oh, make no mistake, Lindy loved peanut butter and pickle sandwiches. But she was a kid. Kids were supposed to like weird food. Momma was an adult. Adults were supposed to make fun of weird foods that kids like. It was just wrong.

So maybe it was little wonder that with a diet high in weirdness, Momma was getting sick every morning. Momma herself waved it off as a little stomach bug. But she did not stop with the peanut butter and pickle sandwiches. They made her stomach feel better, she said. Yet they weren't the cure-all. After several days, Momma was still throwing up every morning. So much for the twenty-four-hour flu.

Then in the week before Christmas, Mrs. Turner, the kindergarten teacher who had just announced she was having her first child, visited Mrs. Westmorland during her class's lunch break. Lindy was diagramming her sentences with lightning speed when she overheard Mrs. Turner—whose stomach was nothing but a little pooch, so tiny it appeared she had merely overeaten—say something about throwing up every morning and how she'd be so glad when this morning sickness was a thing of the past. And then she joked about craving pickles with peanut butter like there was no tomorrow. Suddenly, Lindy could not remember how to diagram a sentence to save her life.

Momma was expecting a baby.

Like Superman when faced with kryptonite, Lindy began to shut down, the energy quickly draining from her body. *Can't live without Momma's love.* After all, Momma only had so much love to give. She couldn't share it with yet another addition to the family. Jo and Father already took up a lot.

Must throw up. The bile rose in Lindy's throat as a new thought hit. The only thing worse than another Jo would be a baby brother. A BOY. *Gonna be sick.* A BOY. Father had always wanted A BOY. A BOY would be a disaster. A BOY would suck all the love away from Lindy. Father wouldn't need a tomboy daughter; he'd have a real son. Momma wouldn't need her either; she'd have her frilly daughter, Jo, and her BOY. Momma's BOY. A BOY would take away Lindy's place. A BOY would take away Lindy's love. A BOY was a nauseating idea.

Must get out. Go to Nurse Berkley's. Lindy walked up to Mrs. Westmorland's desk and asked for a hall pass to the nurse's office. There, she took some Pepto, threw it up, and lay down for half an hour. *Can't think about baby.* And she didn't. She forced herself to look at the possibility that she might be jumping the gun. Momma might, just might, have the flu after all.

Sated by Pepto and having pushed the kryptonite from her mind, a regenerated Lindy used her fifth-period study hall to do some personal research. She copped the "P" book from the school library's Encyclopedia Britannica, hid in the corner behind the tallest set of stacks and poured over the page on pregnancy. There, in black and white, were listed the symptoms of the dreaded affliction—morning sickness, gradual expansion of the abdomen, unusual appetite, mood swings.

Screw the flu. Momma was pregnant.

∾

Lindy nursed Mrs. Berkley's bottle of Pepto for the rest of that afternoon, too distraught over the impending birth of her baby brother to even enjoy missing seventh-period basketball practice. Lindy had to know what was going on. When was the baby due? Did Momma know for sure it was a boy? When exactly did she plan to stop loving Lindy altogether? After the baby was born or right away?

But these were not easy subjects to broach. Lindy shuddered at the thought of her second birds and bees discussion in less than two months.

At home, for once, Jo was actually, albeit unknowingly, helpful. She was in the midst of a modeling session when she ran across something of interest in Momma's sewing cabinet.

"Momma, why do you have all these patterns for fat ladies?" Jo held the picture to her face ala *Let's Make a Deal*'s Carol Merrill.

"Those are my maternity patterns," Momma answered.

Lindy seized the moment. "Are you expecting?" she asked with all the finesse of a bull in a china shop.

"What? A baby?" Momma laughed. "I hope not. Your father was fixed after Jo was born. Unless it's the milkman's."

"The milkman's?" Lindy repeated, mortified.

"Lighten up, Mary Sunshine. It's a joke." Momma shook her head in frustration. "Good grief."

"So why do you have these?" Lindy asked, thumbing through the Vogue and McCall's maternity patterns.

"They're from when I was expecting Jo. Remember how I sewed maternity clothes for myself and matching dresses for Soft Baby?"

"So why are you keeping them?"

"I'm not. I'm giving them to Goodwill."

"Oh." Only then did Lindy start to laugh. "'Cause you don't need them? Right?"

Momma shook her head again, tiredly this time. "I'm gonna go lay down before I start dinner. Keep the TV low, OK?"

"OK." Lindy watched her mother retreat into her bedroom and shut the door behind her. She didn't know why—call it a sixth sense, call it woman's intuition, call it the curse of being so damned smart—but she knew. Without a doubt, she knew. Momma was lying.

She was expecting a baby.

Lindy watched Jo flit around the living room pretending to be one of *Charlie's Angels.* She let out a big sigh and for the only time in her life wished—desperately, direly wished—that she were more like Jo. Born without the sense that God gave a gnat.

~

Unless Momma was napping, she and Father never shut their bedroom door during the day. So when Lindy saw them enter their room and close the door, their unspoken request for privacy begged for eavesdropping.

She stood outside their door in the hallway, pretending to study the family pictures on the wall, stiff portraits of generations of Logans and Franklins—people whose identities Lindy wasn't even sure of—plus the mandatory baby pictures of Lindy and Jo: Lindy wearing her father's cowboy hat and Jo picking her nose. Jo hated that snapshot of herself. Lindy loved it.

At the sound of Father's voice, Lindy refocused on the task at hand. He was talking about "Dr. Ted's test results...seeing the gynecologist..." *The baby.*

Then Momma said something that sounded like she was talking in the same deep and muffled voice as Charlie Brown's teacher. "Waaa, waaa. Waaa, waaa, waaa, waaa." Probably the most important part. Something about *our beloved baby BOY.*

Lindy watched the photographs begin to spin and held onto the wall to steady herself as Father went on about "...doctor's bills...dropped our health insurance...didn't see this coming...need a hospital stay... borrow from the bank...if they'll let me." *Stupid baby.*

There was a lull. Then the knob to the bedroom door turned and Lindy realized the conversation was over. Panicked, she darted into the bathroom and found herself closing the door on her parents as they entered the hallway. "Emergency," she said to explain her hurry.

But once inside the porcelain paradise, she found that she wasn't in a hurry at all. Exactly the opposite. She wanted time to slow down. Go in reverse, if possible. She would revert back to infancy if God would let her. She would savor her mother's love at a time when she had it all to herself. She would not make the mistake again of taking that love for granted. Never again for granted.

Ah, she sighed as she crouched on the commode. To be young. To be naïve. To be Jo.

CHAPTER TWENTY-TWO

The day before Christmas break, in the time-honored tradition of the Grady County Independent School District, all those associated with the institute of learning—educators, students, janitors, even some parents gathered in the auditorium after lunch to watch a film—not an educational film, but a real Hollywood movie. Afternoon classes were canceled in lieu of whatever festive holiday film had been selected to honor the joyful birth of our Lord baby Jesus. Last year it was the maudlin *Brian's Song*.

Only morning classes were mandatory. That's where Secret Santas exchanged gifts. Each member of each grade, kindergartners through seniors, had drawn the name of one classmate and become his or her Secret Santa, the secret yuletide pal obligated to buy a surprise gift for ten dollars or less. Only in Lindy's class there were no surprises. Everybody knew their Secret Santas on the day names were drawn. Some traded up names and some flat out told their Santa what they wanted to get. None of the gifts Lindy heard bantered around cost close to ten dollars—more like twenty or thirty—yet no authority figure said a word about the preteen mafia. Evidently, the Holy Roller mothers had no problem with extortion.

Lindy had drawn Jenna's name. Every evening she poured over the three big Christmas catalogs—Sears, J.C. Penney's, and Monkey Wards—for ideas. And every night she dreamt about what was on page 647 of the girls' clothing section or page 203 of the toy section. In the end, she settled on an all-leather basketball for the basketball star that she bought for forty bucks at the K-Mart in town. Lindy spent more on this gift than she had spent on Father's birthday album. She spent more on this gift than she could ever imagine spending on any gift, ever. She had borrowed a little money from Father, saying she was buying a special Christmas gift for Momma. She had borrowed a little money from Momma, saying she was doing the same for Father. Sort of a "Gift of the Magi" con artist.

Lindy knew the basketball was way too much, but, dammit, she wanted to get Jenna a good gift. Lindy's Secret Santa was Amber, and she couldn't bear to be sitting there with an expensive gift from Amber having given a cheap gift to Jenna. Lindy's gift was a representation of herself. It was nice to feel good about herself for a change.

The seventh-grade class exchanged gifts in homeroom English. Mrs. Westmorland instructed her students when it was time to reveal all Secret Santas. Lindy set her large square package on Jenna's desk and stood there waiting for Jenna to return from delivering her Secret Santa gift. Amber tapped Lindy on the shoulder.

"I'm your Secret Santa," Amber said, offering her present. "I know you don't already have one."

"Thanks," Lindy said, almost embarrassed by how excited she was to be getting a gift from a Fab. The head Fab.

Jenna returned to her desk. "For moi?" she said, rattling the square box. In one fluid move, she tore off the wrapping paper and exposed the basketball in the box. "Cool. Thank you," she said to Lindy. "I have one at home just like it. Except that one's signed by Dr. J."

The life blew out of Lindy like a Macy's Thanksgiving Day balloon punctured by a Central Park tree branch. "Dr. J. That's neat."

"Open mine." Amber rattled her gift in front of Lindy's face. "I put a lot of thought into it."

This will cheer me up, Lindy thought. She opened it. She examined it. She had no idea what it was.

"It's a back brace, goober," Amber said. "To correct your posture." She grabbed the brace and began undoing the buckles. "Let me fit it to you."

"Not now." Lindy had dressed up today, wearing her favorite sweater and even accessorizing. Today was designated Perfect.

"I wanna try it on," Jenna said, throwing her basketball on the floor.

"Hey, Jenna, what'd ya get? A training bra?" asked cocky boy Trent. Lindy cringed at the "B" word. Didn't these people know *lungholder*?

"It's not mine," Jenna answered. "It's Lindy's."

"Ohhh," sang Trent. "Lindy got a training bra. Lindy got a training bra."

By this time Jenna's expensive leather basketball had bounced across the room and was being used as a kick ball by the guys.

The curious crowd that gathered around the back brace grew until Lindy could no longer see Amber's "thoughtful" Christmas gift. They all seemed to think it was funny, cool, neat. Everyone tried it on, even Mrs. Westmorland. Everyone except the hunchback that it was meant for.

Later, when Lindy returned the brace to its box, she noticed the price tag had fallen under the tissue paper. $8.95 it read. $8.95.

~

Lindy ate lunch that day at the geek table with geeks ranging in age from fifth- to ninth-graders. The facade was over. She was not a Fab, would never be a Fab. She would have to settle for being a geek, albeit a perfect one.

Momma would call this a pity party. Well, pity parties were all Lindy expected to ever have again and she was gonna be the life of them. What did catch her by surprise was that she still had room to feel sorry for the ninth-grade geek, perhaps because she so feared that would eventually be the ninth-grade *her.*

When everyone packed into the auditorium for the movie, Lindy snuck away from her class and sat in the back with the teachers where she continued her sympathy soiree for one. She was a freak. She was the Hunchback of Notre Dame. With her luck that was probably the movie scheduled for today.

Actually, the movie was *With Six You Get Eggroll* starring one of Momma's perennial favorites, Doris Day. It was a nice family film about a husband and wife adding on to their existing family with a new baby.

It made Lindy wish for *The Hunchback of Notre Dame.*

It reminded her that she wasn't just a freak; she was a freak whose mother was expecting a baby. Nobody else her age had a mother expecting a baby. Their families were all done. They already had all of their brothers and sisters. Nobody could see the evidence of their parents having had sex, at least recent sex. Lindy's classmates could all giggle at her mother as her stomach grew larger. They could laugh that the hump on her mother's stomach looked like the hump on Lindy's back.

Lindy was certain she would be sitting with teachers and geeks for the rest of her life.

CHAPTER TWENTY-THREE

Momma's dreamlife proved much more tantalizing than her real life. Her dreamlife allowed her to float above depression. Her real life dragged her down into the mire. Her dreamlife consisted of romantic dinners that Father would instigate, romantic gifts he would lavish. Her real life consisted of a bucket of Kentucky Fried Chicken and a spaghetti western on TV. That was Father's idea of romance.

Every Christmas, Momma dreamed of a tennis bracelet. She wanted the real thing, of course, but only ever truly hoped for the rhinestone version. Every Christmas, she dropped hints. Every Christmas, Father dropped the ball.

Father's biggest turkey landed not on Thanksgiving, but on Christmas morning in 1971 when he proudly gave Momma a home haircutting kit, complete with plastic smock and barbershop quality scissors. The Logans no longer spoke of that Christmas.

This Christmas, Momma was going to get more than a dream of a tennis bracelet. Father was going to give her the real thing. She had made up her mind. Now she was going to get Father to make up his.

Lindy assisted Momma in her plan like Santa's devious little elf. She wanted that tennis bracelet for Momma more than she wanted anything for herself. With the exception of the new Bay City Rollers album. And a silver bracelet Seiko watch.

In the weeks leading up to Christmas, Momma had dropped more hints than a pigeon drops shit.

Father found one note on his nightstand: "Dear Santa, Please bring Momma a tennis bracelet. Ask the lady in the jewelry store in the mall what it is. XXX & OOOs, Your Little Helper."

But with Father, it was no good being subtle. That's how one ended up with a home haircutting kit.

Taped inside the windshield of his pickup truck was a page torn out of a newspaper supplement: "Pre-Christmas Sale on Our Entire Stock including Tennis Bracelets! Run, don't walk to Jewelry Emporium!"

But Lindy's favorite was when she got to play accomplice.

"Lindy, have you seen my tennis bracelet?" Momma yelled from the bedroom.

Lindy sat by Father on the couch.

"No, I haven't Momma because you don't have one," Lindy hollered back. She sounded casual, relaxed, spontaneous. Academy Award stuff.

"That's right. It's not Christmas yet. Do you think your father knows that's what I want?"

Lindy looked at her father. He was reading the Sunday paper he always picked up in town after church, oblivious to their conversation. Then Father turned to the sports page where under the caption "Sports" there were no pictures, no stories, but a full-page letter from the editor to Mr. Joe Logan. "Dear Mr. Logan," it began, "It has come to our attention that your wife desires a tennis bracelet for Christmas. We are withholding your sports page today in order to bring this to your attention. Thanks for your patronage. Signed, Mr. Editor and concerned citizens for Mrs. Logan's Christmas present." Momma had hidden the paper from Father when they got home and dummied the whole thing up, pasting it over the regular sports page.

"Where's my sports page?" Father said, looking straight at Lindy.

"I think he knows now, Momma," Lindy yelled back. She swelled with pride. Momma was brilliant. And, just think, this gift of manipulation was in Lindy's genes.

~

But with only a few days left until Christmas, Momma had stopped dropping hints completely. She wasn't nudging. She wasn't nagging. She wasn't nitpicking. Something was wrong. Maybe she had changed techniques. Maybe she was leaving it up to fate. Or maybe she thought the money should go toward the new baby.

Regardless, when the Logans sat down to open presents on Christmas Eve night, Momma made nary a reference to a tennis bracelet.

It had been Momma's family's tradition to exchange gifts on Christmas Eve night and for Santa to come the next morning. But Father had been raised opening all gifts on Christmas morning. So to be fair, each year the Logans alternated the opening of gifts between Christmas Eve and Christmas morning. This year it was Christmas Eve's turn, which Lindy and Jo liked better because they got presents two days in a row instead of on just one. Of course, there was nothing wrong with getting all the goods in one lump sum on Christmas morning either. That's why the years they opened on Christmas morning, Lindy and Jo liked that better. It was a win/win situation.

This Christmas, the giving was even more practical than usual. Instead of the Bay City Rollers and a Seiko, Lindy got a blank cassette tape and a Timex. A takes-a-licking-and-keeps-on-ticking Timex. The band wasn't even silver. It was vinyl.

Jo wanted the new Malibu Barbie and a silk dressing gown (she had been watching way too many movies from the '30s and '40s with Momma). She got a generic rip-off Barbie and a terry cloth robe. Thrift was the theme. It wasn't looking good for Momma's tennis bracelet.

Momma shook her present. It was in a box too large for a piece of jewelry and made the sound of tissue paper and clothing. Lindy knew that sound all too well from when her grandmothers were alive and gave her presents. It wasn't a pretty sound.

Momma tried to keep her chin up as she opened the box and pulled from it a very large flannel nightgown.

"It's an extra large," Father said, gently. "I didn't want it to bind you anywhere."

Father was proud of his thoughtfulness. Momma looked defeated. *Why doesn't she just deck him?* Lindy thought.

"Why is it so big?" asked Jo.

Lindy could take it no more. "Because she's expecting a baby, you dork."

Everyone stopped. "Really, Mommy?" Jo was practically bouncing off the walls. "I'm gonna have a little sister to be mean to?"

Momma couldn't prevent a tear from trickling down her cheek. *Mood swings.*

"Come here. Both of you," Momma said.

Jo skipped to Momma's side. Lindy didn't budge. She only said, "I figured it out forever ago."

"Will you come here?" Momma said to Lindy, not hiding her exhaustion.

"There's nothing you can say to make me feel better."

"I'm not having a baby."

"Oh." *That certainly doesn't make me feel worse.*

"Now will you come sit by me?" Momma patted the couch.

Lindy sat on the indicated spot, careful not to let go too quickly of the defensive chip on her shoulder.

"I don't know how to tell you this, so I'll just say it." The words caught in Momma's throat before a gust of air forced them out. "I have a tumor in one of my ovaries."

Momma looked at her girls. Lindy stared back, a fragile porcelain doll with a million fresh hairline fractures.

"That's female parts," Momma rattled on. "Ovaries."

Then she spoke quickly, her words rat-a-tat-tatting like a World War II fighter pilot. Perhaps that was her theory—get in, inflict pain, get out. "I have a tumor the doctor wants to remove it I'm going into the hospital the day after Christmas they'll do surgery to get rid of the tumor."

She forced herself to draw a breath and lighten her tone. "Don't worry. I'm gonna be fine. I'm sure it's nothing." She hugged her girls simultaneously, then kissed them one at a time. "Now you girls go enjoy your Christmas presents. I'm gonna go lay down."

The three remaining Logans sat in silence, two of them shell-shocked. *I'm not going to make it,* Lindy thought.

Panic washed over her from toe to head, like mercury speeding to the top of a boiling thermometer. Was Momma gonna die? Was this her family from now on? The people in this room? She couldn't stand one of them and couldn't talk to the other. *This silence is deafening.* Lindy had thought of that phrase so many times in the last months it had taken on the hokeyness of an overused cliché, and yet she couldn't help but let out a nervous chuckle. Momma was right. She was overly dramatic.

"Does Momma have cancer?" she blurted out.

Father had spent his entire fatherhood having no idea how to talk to his daughters. Now he had to. His words came slowly and with pauses aplenty. "The doctor. Is going. To remove. Her ovary. Then do. A biopsy." He exhaled. That wasn't so bad.

"What does that mean?" Lindy's tone was harsher than she intended.

Father inhaled and tried to remain patient. "It means. We don't. Know."

"How can you not know?" Lindy had no idea why she was so mad. She only knew she wanted to take it out on someone.

"The doctor. Will know. After. The biopsy."

"I wanna know now."

"We all do." Father's words came faster.

"Tell me if Momma's gonna die!"

"Goddamn it, Lindy, I don't know!"

"Stop it!!!" Jo screamed at the top of her lungs.

Instantly, time stood still. In all of Jo's nine years, she had never come remotely close to challenging Father.

"Wendy is here," she said, quietly. "It's rude to argue in front of company."

"Who?" Poor Father had no clue.

"It's her 'friend,'" Lindy whispered out of the corner of her mouth and whirled her finger around her ear to indicate that Jo was loco.

Father didn't know what was going on. Unruly daughters, imaginary friends. The *How-to-Talk-to-Your-Daughters Handbook* had said nothing about this.

Lindy looked at her father. "Are you telling us everything you know?" Her tone had lost its defensiveness.

"I am. And I will. I promise."

"OK." Lindy wanted to hug her father, but instead she held out her hand for him to shake. Father's awkwardness was contagious.

Still, he tried. "Do you want to come sit with me?" he asked the girls, trying to imitate Momma's nurturing.

The girls walked over obligatorily and sat at the foot of his La-Z-Boy. The three of them formed a perfect triangle. Not one angle dared touch another.

Despite what was known or not known about Momma's tumor, Lindy had a pit-of-her-stomach feeling about it. She looked at her new watch. Fifteen minutes had passed since she had opened her gift and set the time. Fifteen minutes ago, Momma was only having a baby. An innocuous little baby boy. Now she was almost dead.

Not for the last time, Lindy thought *I'm not going to make it.*

~

"Knock, knock." Lindy strained to listen for any indication of movement, but finally she couldn't stand it anymore. Besides, the mug of hot apple cider was beginning to blister her hands.

She quietly stepped inside. Momma lay on top of the bedspread, propped up by pillows, her eyes open.

"I brought you some hot apple cider," Lindy said timidly.

"That sounds good." Momma sat up.

"I put red hots in it like you like."

"Thank you." Momma took the mug, blew on the steaming liquid, and attempted a sip. "Woo. You got it hot." She set it on her nightstand. "I need to let it cool a bit."

"You want me to put a piece of ice in it?" Lindy asked, halfway to the door.

"No, it's fine."

"OK." Lindy stood in the middle of the room, wanting to stay, but afraid she should leave. "How are you feeling?"

"Tired."

"I guess that's why you're laying down."

Momma smiled. "How are you feeling?"

Lost. Alone. Like I want to die with you. "I always hoped we'd die together. Like in a car wreck."

"Lindy," Momma said in that wilting way of wistfulness. "Come here." She scooted over to make room.

"Look at me." She raised her daughter's chin until their eyes met. "I'm not gonna die."

"I can't believe you this time."

"I haven't lied to you yet."

"That's not funny. Don't leave me. I can't live without you."

"Stop it." Momma grabbed Lindy by the shoulders, desperate to shake some sense into her. "You're stronger than this. Stop being so maudlin. I need you to be upbeat. Please."

I can't. Not that. Anything but that. "OK, I can be upbeat."

To prove her point, she plastered on a smile faker than a Barnum & Bailey's clown.

"You want some more cider?" she asked with a perkiness that would make Dorothy Hamill proud.

"I'll finish this first," Momma said, quickly adding, "thanks though" as if to mirror Lindy's attempt at optimism.

"OK. Holler if you need anything."

"Thanks, sweetie."

Lindy squeezed out another smile and closed the door behind her. Mentally, she was psyching herself up. If Momma wanted her to be upbeat, she would be upbeat. She would. She would. She would. No matter how miserable it made her.

CHAPTER TWENTY-FOUR

I'm dreaming of a brown Christmas, la, la, la. Lindy couldn't get the song out of her head. She could see Bing Crosby singing in his crisp Christmas colors while being pelted with brown sand gusting across the plains of West Texas. Then Rosemary Clooney blowing by, a human tumbleweed.

Lindy couldn't imagine anyone having a white Christmas. The sandstorm raging outside seemed so very appropriate for Christmas Day 1976.

The mood inside the Logan house reflected the gritty external darkness. Santa had come, virtually by rote, and delivered the annual one-box-each allowance of Pop-Tarts to Lindy and Jo. It used to be the high point of the year. *Hey, God, trade you a year's worth of Pop-Tarts for Momma's life.*

After a breakfast, which nobody ate, the Logans loaded themselves into the car and headed to Birdy's house in Crosbyton for Christmas dinner. They might not have even made the trek had Momma's oldest sister, Lolly, and her family not driven all the way from Dallas to celebrate with their small-town West Texas relatives.

A house full of weirdoes and more food. *Yuck,* Lindy thought. Usually the abundance of food at such a gathering would make up for the abundance of weirdoes. *But not when your stomach's on a strict diet of acid and bile.* Lindy couldn't fathom eating a bite. But aloud she said merrily, "I can't wait to taste Aunt Birdy's apple pie." You see, Lindy had become Cheery Lindy on a mission to uplift Momma. If Cheery Lindy was cheery enough, maybe Momma wouldn't die. On the drive over, Lindy even tried to put a positive spin on the sandstorm.

"It may not be snow," she lilted like a cheerleader at a pep rally, "but at least we have something flying through the air on Christmas."

"Yeah, a lot of hooey." Momma's sarcasm sliced through Lindy's phony enthusiasm. Father and Jo laughed. Lindy felt like a horse's patoot. But their laughter caught on and Momma joined in. That's when Cheery Lindy did too. She had made Momma smile.

~

"Eww, come in out of that sand. My word, it's awful." Birdy opened the door, decked out in her new aqua polyester pantsuit.

The Logans trudged in, desert nomads arriving at an oasis. Birdy greeted her sister with a kiss on the cheek. "Let me take your coats. There you go, girls. Hi, Joe. Now...Wait!" Birdy stopped Lindy before she stepped beyond the linoleum foyer. "I just had my new baby blue carpet laid down so I'm asking everyone to take off their shoes at the door. Y'all don't mind, do you?"

Birdy's house was Mr. Clean pristine with the antiseptic feel of a doctor's waiting room. A doctor's waiting room that had been regurgitated in powder blue. The monotony of her baby blue color scheme was reinforced by her baby blue floral accents, her baby blue knickknacks, and even her baby blue furniture. And despite Birdy having two teenage daughters, every inch of her baby blue house was spotless. Birdy claimed to be easygoing and carefree, but her house was a museum of analness and she was the curator.

"Of course we don't mind," Maggie said although she did mind, especially with the pain that shot through her belly when she bent over to remove her shoes. But Maggie's priority had always been to make her older sisters happy. As a child she yearned for their approval, longed for their love. It was a need that had never gone away.

Each Logan added a pair of shoes to the extensive row in the foyer then Maggie led her brood onto the newly laid shag carpet to greet the rest of her barefooted family. *Lord,* she prayed as she watched all those naked toes digging into blue shag. *Please help their hearts to be as resilient as their feet.*

~

"Did I mention my first hip replacement was in '68? Well, they were so much more advanced in '74 when I got my second hip replaced. But I was battling the gout that year and—Lord a mercy—that was a booger..."

Bud had picked up Aunt Edna that morning from the nursing home in Floydada. Forty-five minutes ago Lindy had walked up to Momma's great aunt to say hi. She still hadn't gotten that little word in.

Aunt Edna had a lot to say. A lot about gout, hip replacements, cataracts, dentures, and arthritis. Lindy was sure the list went on and on.

That's why she had to escape.

She looked around, desperate to spot someone to come to her rescue. From across the room, she made eye contact with Jo and mouthed the word, "Help."

Jo wrinkled her brow. She didn't get it.

"Help." Lindy exaggerated the word. Then she nodded subtly in the direction of Aunt Edna.

The whites of Jo's eyes enlarged and she shook her head abruptly, then looked away. *Classic.* Lindy wanted to bean the weanie.

"Thought I was having a heart attack. Called the attendant, scared to death. Rushed me to the hospital. Turned out to just be pleurisy. We laughed and laughed about that. Oh, mercy." Edna chortled to herself.

Lindy smiled politely, but Aunt Edna didn't notice; her conversation had room enough only for one. So she tuned Edna out and let her focus wander across the rest of the house. She settled on the kitchen.

There, Birdy was basting the bird. Lolly was wresting the Jell-O from its mold. Maggie was refereeing her sisters. Silently.

"What do ya mean, what does it mean? I don't know what it means." Lolly was on a tirade. "That's the point. It's whatever you see in it. The eye of the beholder."

"Well, I see blasphemy," Birdy said. "They did not serve hot dogs on paper plates at the Last Supper."

"Of course they didn't. The hot dog wasn't invented until the 1800s."

"Then why frame a hot dog inside a picture of the Last Supper?"

"It's art."

"It's doggy do."

"Oh, Birdy, get your panties out of a knot."

Momma was unable to muffle a snicker.

"What are you laughing at?" Birdy snapped at her little sister.

"She's laughing at the fact that you have no sense of humor," Lolly shot back.

"I have a sense of humor. Just not when it involves our Lord Jesus Christ."

"God has a sense of humor. How do you think you got here?" Lolly added.

Maggie jumped in. Maggie the peacemaker. "So when are you gonna create a masterpiece for me?"

"Oh, please. Don't encourage her," Birdy said, rolling her eyes.

Lolly's eyes narrowed at Birdy. "Just because one of my sisters appreciates art."

"The art of kissing up," Birdy said, prudishly.

"That's the best kind of art. You should try it sometime," Lolly said, swiping a finger full of Birdy's turkey dressing. Birdy swatted at her sister's retreating hand.

"Yum, Birdy, that turkey smells wonderful." Maggie knew a compliment of Birdy would level the delicate balance of egos.

"See?" Lolly said. "That baby sister of ours is a true artist."

"The art of survival," Maggie said. "It comes from being the youngest in a family of Franklins."

Lolly chuckled. "You should have seen Memaw and Papaw in their youth. Of course, Daddy had the same rascally streak. A lineage of ornery old coots."

Birdy sneered at her eldest sibling. "So that's where you get it from?"

"Same as you, my dear."

Maggie cleared her throat, placing a hand on each sister. "And I was an adoring little sister who wanted to grow up to be just like my sisters, Esther Williams and Loretta Young."

Lolly said to Birdy, "I'll never understand where she got that from."

"I did sort of resemble Loretta Young."

"As a fetus."

"Isn't it almost time for dinner?" Maggie asked.

"I'm not serving a thing until that abomination's out of my kitchen," Birdy said, referring to Lolly's artwork.

Maggie looked at the piece and smiled. "I'm just surprised Shorty didn't eat it before you got it framed."

"Oh, he tried to sneak a bite, but I'd already shellacked it. If you look close you can see his teeth marks in the wiener." Lolly pointed them out.

"I'll be. How'd he like the taste of shellac?"

"It's now his condiment of choice."

At that, the three sisters howled as they could only when in each other's company.

Personally, Lindy couldn't see how Lolly and Birdy ever resembled Esther Williams and Loretta Young. Lolly wore Coke bottle glasses over skin that was tough as boot leather. Her motto was "Brown fat is prettier than white fat," so she made sure she had a tan every day of her life. If she wasn't tanning herself in the sun, she was tanning herself in one of those newfangled tanning beds. The thing was, Lolly wasn't fat, in fact, she was thin as a rail, but you couldn't convince her of that. So whatever fat she thought she had was forever tan, and as a result her hide was the texture of lizard. Years of weekly facials did nothing to minimize the crevices around her eyes, lips, and neck, nor did her one face-lift. Her new face only served to pull her skin so tautly that her eyes bulged. Add to that the magnification of her Coke bottle lenses, and Aunt Lolly looked like a frog. Maybe that's what reminded Momma of Esther Williams. Both were amphibious.

None of this deterred the girls from loving Aunt Lolly, comparatively speaking anyway. If Lolly was one thing, she was fun, considering that eccentric equaled fun. And it did to Lindy and Jo; after all, they didn't know a single other forty-seven-year-old woman who owned every color patent leather go-go boot ever made. The woman always wore go-go boots. Always. Except apparently when she was sunbathing, a fact the girls might never have known if not for the fact that, after a heated argument, Birdy had finally coerced Lolly into taking off her go-go boots at the door. Seeing Lolly stripped of the flash of her go-go boots was almost like seeing the emperor without any clothes; an illusion was shattered. And a reality set in: her feet were fat. At least it was brown fat.

Birdy was Lolly's opposite—as rigid and stiff as the bun on her head. In private, Momma would call her middle sister a Mennonite and it always got a chuckle. Everybody knew the Mennonites as that strange religious sect that lived just outside of Jessip. They wore plain black clothes and didn't shave or cut their hair and the women always wore their manes yanked into severe buns. That bun fetish, plus a tendency toward religious zealousness, is why Momma likened Birdy to the Mennonites.

Birdy eschewed vanity—it was a sin—yet succumbed enough to dye her hair jet-black and claim it was still natural. The idea of letting her strands go gray like Lolly's appalled her. It just emphasized her sister's screwed-up priorities—that she would get a face lift and blab about it to the world, yet not have the sense to color her hair a shade that would make her look years younger. What Birdy failed to see was that her obvious dye job only made her look like a woman trying to look years younger.

Whereas Lolly and go-go boots were freely associated, to her nieces and nephew Aunt Birdy would forever be linked to one trait: she stocked her candy dish with cough drops. The mediciney kind. They were individually wrapped so an innocent first-timer couldn't tell the difference between them and candy (which Birdy labeled a useless indulgence) until the drop was popped into a mouth and the neophyte's sinuses were flushed open with menthol. This horrified every child ever to dive into her dish. No kid made the same mistake twice. To sum up, Birdy was simply no fun.

In fact, the only thing Lolly and Birdy had in common besides their DNA was their dark and weathered skin. Birdy wasn't a sun goddess; her tinting came more from a martyr's tan, a distant cousin to the farmer's tan which came from working outdoors (and left its recipient red-necked and brown-armed, but ghost white where shirt sleeves met torso). Birdy worked outside habitually in the garden and yard, but only because they didn't waste their money on such frivolousness as hired help, a virtue she never let anyone forget. Hence, martyr's tan. But the same pigment of Lolly's and Birdy's skin clearly linked them as sisters; in dim light, they could even have been mistaken for Indians, albeit a Bible-beating Cherokee and a go-go dancing Apache.

Now, as Lindy looked at the three sisters, she wondered how Momma ended up with such creamy white, baby-soft skin. Momma always said that as kids Lolly teased that her real father was the milkman. Maybe that was true.

~

"I'm here to tell you a bladder infection is so much worse than a urine infection." Lindy was abruptly aware of Edna's rambling. "Burn. I mean. Lordy. I don't even want to talk about it. *Bur-ern.* What I really hate is having to pee in that Dixie cup. Talk about a mess. Doctor made me promise to drink cranberry juice every day for the rest of my life, and I hate cranberry juice. Tastes like battery acid..."

Listening to Aunt Edna was akin to watching a car crash, it was morbidly fascinating to gaze at the wreckage. Still, Lindy's attention drifted elsewhere. Her eyes followed Birdy as she set out two replenished plates on the coffee table in front of the men. Dinner would be ready soon, she announced, so don't overdo the appetizers.

Shorty, Lolly's wide-bodied blowhard of a husband, immediately inhaled two deviled eggs and began annihilating a pimento-cheese-filled celery stick. "I'd never tell her, but that Last Supper number stinks worse than a freshly-laid cow patty. Although I do like the food theme." He swallowed a third deviled egg. "For Christmas I bought her art lessons. She didn't see why she needed them." Second celery stick. "I told her I didn't mean anything by it. Ended up promising to build her an art studio to prove I believe in her talent." Fourth deviled egg. "Too bad you're not closer to Big D, Joe. I'd pay you to build the damn studio. Keep the money in the family."

Joe smiled tightly, biting his tongue so as not to say what he really thought of the arrogant son of a bitch.

Shorty was the stereotypical Texas cattleman. Big ranch, big money, big belly. In fact, everything in Shorty's life was big including the town he lived in—Big D.

Shorty wasn't born into wealth; he lucked into money late in life. But he had always talked like a big shot, like money was just around the corner. And, eventually, one year, it was. Lucky, arrogant, *rich* son of a bitch.

Birdy's husband, Bud, sat next to Shorty. Behind his back, Bud's nickname was "Brownie" in honor of the brown hair paint he sprayed to cover his rapidly balding scalp.

Joe liked Brownie, found him to be a bit of a kindred spirit. Brownie was a working man, a cotton farmer like Joe, and he was also the overwhelmed male in a family of three females.

"What'd you get for Birdy, Bud?" Only Shorty would ask such a question, wanting to hold his gift up as better than anybody else's. *If he tries to ask me,* Joe's smile seemed to say, *I hope he chokes on a celery stick.*

"For Christmas?" Bud asked.

"Well, now, that is the holiday we're celebrating," Shorty replied.

"Uh, I got her a diamond tennis bracelet. Fourteen carat gold, uh, band," Bud said, meekly avoiding Shorty's gaze.

Shorty made a whistling sound, the kind that meant he knew that cost an arm and a leg. Joe almost laughed out loud; that should shut Shorty up.

"Birdy, uh, told me what to get her."

"Well, good for you, Bud," Shorty said. Then a smile eclipsed his lips. "You got a little of that shoe polish running down your ear there, Buddy boy."

~

The snoring trickled into Lindy's consciousness as she watched the colored perspiration run into Bud's shirt collar. Edna was sound asleep. Lindy seized the moment, slithering out of her chair and gingerly treading hot coals on her way out of Edna's range.

Once in the clear, she headed down the hall to the bathroom. She wanted to beat the pre-meal bathroom rush. She was too late. The door was closed and the bathroom occupied. She waited in the hallway.

Lindy felt a tap on her shoulder and turned around. It was Fay; at 16, she was Birdy's oldest girl. "The line forms here? And I'm in the rear. I can't breathe, 'cause I gotta relieve. That's why I'm a grump. Gotta take a dump."

Lindy cringed. Fay loved bathroom humor. Birdy blamed Fay's streak on Bud who tended toward a "blue" sense of humor. This was a revelation. Nobody knew Brownie even had a sense of humor.

"I'm a poet and I know it," said Fay. And she was. She was the author of the "Beanie, Weanie, the Fartin' Meanie" poem that taunted Jo for years. The problem with Fay was that while all around her matured, she never did.

Lindy tried to ignore her rhyming cousin and breathed a sigh of thank-the-Lord when Donnie came out of the bathroom at that moment.

"Hey," thirteen-year-old Donnie said to his cousin Lindy.

"Hey," Lindy said back. Donnie, Lolly's youngest, was her favorite cousin, probably because he was the only one who didn't talk much.

"I brought my yo-yo," Donnie said. He had taught Lindy to yo-yo last Christmas.

"Excuse me-ee, but are you gonna chat or pee?" interrupted Fay.

Lindy, who didn't much like the pressure of using the bathroom while someone else was waiting, said, "You know, if you wanna go before me, I can wait."

"You may can wait. But if I go first, you'll have to fum-i-gate." Fay held her nose and waved away imaginary fumes. Lindy went in first.

Lindy's fear of being ridiculed for staying in the bathroom too long was compounded by the fact that she had her period. Changing maxi pads not only took time, but meant that anyone could look in the trash and see the evidence of her period. She couldn't wrap the pad in enough tissue paper to disguise it; shoot, there wasn't enough tissue paper to disguise the king-sized mattress that she wore between her legs. And she was certain Birdy's and Lolly's daughters used tampons. So everyone would know that the maxi pad in the trash was Lindy's. Her name might as well be branded on the bloody thing.

The thought closed in on Lindy that, at this moment, Fay was probably outside the door writing a limerick on the amount of time cousin Lindy took in the bathroom, and this pending embarrassment spurred a brainstorm. Instead of disposing of her pad in the trash, she would flush the clod of cotton down the commode. And that's just what she did.

Lindy passed Fay on the way out of the bathroom. Fay wiggled through the door with her thighs pressed exaggeratedly together, but she didn't rhyme a lick.

~

"I told him I didn't know which was bigger. His heart or his soul." Birdy's fifteen-year-old girl, Mary, had cornered Jo. "He said his faith. Isn't that beautiful?"

Jo caught Lindy's eye and jerked her head, indicating that she should come over and bail her out. Lindy smiled and stayed where she was, watching Jo squirm. Sweet revenge.

"Have I told you we are going to become missionaries? We are so in love with each other and with God. It's like our own Holy Trinity. We are already husband and wife spiritually. But not physically, of course. We will remain models of virginity until God brings us into the fold of his most scared and prestigious of agencies..."

"Ford Modeling?" Jo said, her ears perking up.

"No, silly...matrimony," Mary said.

"Oh yeah, that," Jo said. She glanced again at Lindy, eyes pleading for help. Lindy smiled and waved.

"In keeping with that spirit of purity, I only allow Zeke to give me one peck on the cheek per date." To emphasize her point, Mary held up a single finger, then turned that finger toward her neck. "I've told Zeke never to touch me below the neck except to hold hands, and that's only to see me safely across the street."

Jo sighed and with her exhalation slumped even further into her misery. Lindy walked away. Her work here was done.

~

"Will you stop whizzing that thing by my head?" hissed seventeen-year-old Kate to her younger brother Donnie. He was whirling his yo-yo in vertical circles by his side. "You're gonna knock me in the skull, dipshit."

"Potty mouth," he replied.

"Prick." Kate saw Lindy approach. "Go play with your hillbilly cousins, dipshit." Kate returned to her book. *The Catcher in the Rye.*

Lindy sensed the tension. But, then again, Kate had always been intense. As the oldest cousin, she seemed to feel she was better than the rest of them, a feeling made stronger in this, her senior year.

"Nice 'Round the Worlds," Lindy said to Donnie, commenting on his yo-yo trick.

"Thanks."

"You had 'em going a long time."

"Yeah."

Kate rolled her eyes at her brother's inability to make conversation. Children.

"I've gotten pretty good at yo-yoing since you taught me. Wanna see?"

"Sure."

Donnie handed Lindy his yo-yo. Lindy consciously backed away from Kate and carefully worked the yo-yo straight up and down. On a down yo, she let it rest for a second, then skitter a foot across the shag carpet.

"Great Walk the Dog," Donnie said. "Do some more."

"Sure," Lindy said. She began whirling the yo-yo as Fay bopped into the room with this spontaneous rhyme: "We oughta sue, for what was flushed down the loo. The commode is backed up with all sorts of goo. It's flowing and flowing and flowing some more. Soon water's gonna be all over the floor."

Immediately, Lindy knew her flushing had done this. The yo-yo was in the middle of an Around the World when Lindy lost her concentration. The Duncan Butterfly fluttered within an inch of Kate's ear.

Kate shot up, livid. "Dammit. I should take that thing and jam it..."

"Hey, you rhymed," said Fay.

Kate's look told Fay what she could do with her rhyming.

"Fay, sit down and be quiet." Her Mennonite Momma was taking control. "Dinner's ready. Everyone fix your plates. Bud, go check on the commode."

Suddenly, the room was buzzing with activity. Barefoot people everywhere doing as they were told.

Lindy wanted nothing to eat, now more than before. She wanted to escape. To flush herself down the toilet with her feminine hygiene product. To be far away when Bud resurrected the commode-clogging culprit. To be dead.

She should have Momma's tumor. It would only be fair.

~

"Don't tell me you're dieting, Mags," Lolly said when she saw how little Maggie had dished onto her plate.

"You do look like you've gained a little weight," Birdy said, patting her own stomach to indicate Maggie's pooch.

"It's just that I've been bloated."

"Water retention," said Birdy. "You eat too much salt."

"I don't eat too much salt." *Don't push me,* her thin smile indicated, *the peacemaker's getting tired of making peace.*

"Well, if you're retaining water, there's clearly too much sodium in your diet."

"I'm not retaining water."

"Drop it, Birdy. She's not retaining water, and she's not eating too much salt." Lolly stared at Maggie's plate. "She's just eating a plateful of bread and butter pickles."

"Oh, my Lord, you're pregnant," Birdy said. Both she and Lolly gasped, so certain were they of this revelation.

The whole table stopped and looked at Maggie. The kids' table even turned its attention to her. Maggie couldn't believe she had to confront this accusation for the second time in two days. *Talk about bad deja vu.*

"I'm not pregnant," said Maggie, and it appeared to her that her sisters sighed with relief. *Of course,* she could hear them thinking, *the last thing baby sister needs is another kid she can't afford to feed.* "I have a tumor in my ovary."

The room froze. Nobody said a word. But their questions flew through Maggie's head. *Is it cancer? Will she die? Will she live? If so, for how long?*

"It's no big deal," Maggie said, sorry she'd opened the can of worms. "They're removing it in the morning."

"They?" Lolly raised her eyebrow.

"The doctors at Methodist hospital," Maggie answered.

"You're having surgery, and you weren't even going to tell us?" Birdy looked physically wounded.

"Are they any good?" Lolly demanded. "These doctors at Methodist hospital? 'Cause I'll fly you up to Dallas and pay for the finest medical care money can buy."

"They're fine," Maggie said. "I promise it's no big deal."

"We're family," Lolly said. "Everything's a big deal."

"Crises are what I do," Birdy said. "They're my calling."

Maggie could see her middle sister salivating at the thought of a funeral. Birdy was never happier than when death was pending.

"We know who to call in a crisis," Maggie said. "But right now, it's really no big deal."

"Nonsense. We are coming to the hospital to sit with Joe," Lolly said.

"No," Joe said, quickly. Too quickly. "I'm fine," he said. "I'm bringing crossword puzzles."

"Nothing is keeping me away from that hospital," Birdy said. "I'll be there at sunrise." *Oh great,* Maggie thought, *a candlelight vigil.*

"And if you think I'm hightailing it back to Big D 'til I know my baby sister's OK, you can bark up another tree," Lolly added.

"I can't believe you didn't tell us," Birdy said, mortally, or martyrly, wounded.

"It's no big deal," Maggie said one last time. But she could see that no one was really listening.

CHAPTER TWENTY-FIVE

So it was settled. Birdy and Lolly would share a hotel room in Lubbock and spend every waking moment at the hospital. Lindy and Jo would stay with Smiley and Vernice. Nobody was happy about any of it.

Cheery Lindy had been Chatty Lindy on the ride home. The family had ignored them both.

Now the family was in the living room watching old movies, and Lindy, alone in her room, was neither cheery nor chatty. She was mad. She wanted to throw something, so she did. Her Christmas presents. Not the Timex, but the book of daily Bible verses from Birdy and the pierced earrings from Lolly. Birdy wanted to salvage her soul. Lolly wanted to salvage her sense of fashion. Lindy wanted to salvage neither.

Thawck! The book of Bible verses hit with a force Lindy didn't know she possessed. She raged with both power and embarrassment at the same time. *Please don't let anybody come looking for the cause of the crash.* She was sick to death of playing Cheery Lindy. Let 'em watch Shirley Temple. *On the good ship Lolly puke...*

Lindy was spiraling down...down...like Alice through the rabbit hole. The demons were coming and fast. She needed a distraction. *Now.*

She would clean.

Her focus landed on a box of junk in her closet that, despite Momma's admonitions, she hadn't cleared out before the move.

The box consisted of everything from old report cards to doodlings from her artist days to her record album from *The Sound of Music.* Lindy so loved Julie Andrews in that movie that every time it got to the part where Maria married the Captain, Lindy felt a pang of betrayal. This jealousy was illustrated in the picture of Christopher Plummer on the album's inside jacket. A four-year-old Lindy had taken a pencil and gotten revenge by pockmarking the actor's face with dozens of holes. Julie Andrews' face remained pristine. Lindy still loved Julie Andrews.

At the bottom of her box of junk was Raggedy Ann, the doll that Momma had sewn years ago to replace Soft Baby. The rag doll very much looked like she had been at the bottom of the pile for years. Her face and body were squished flat and one button eye was dangling from a thread while the other pierced through her socket of flesh-colored material.

Lindy had forgotten all about her Raggedy Ann.

She picked up the neglected doll and tried to reshape her form. Raggedy Ann kneaded back to shape rather quickly, virtually resembling her old self. It was Lindy that had fallen to pieces.

This was the doll her mother had made with her own hands. This doll didn't deserve to be buried at the bottom of some immaterial pile of trash. Even if it was below Julie Andrews. This doll deserved to be placed upon a pedestal.

Lindy chided herself for being so thoughtless. She had taken the doll's love for granted in her earlier years, combing her hair, dragging her through the sandbox. She had assumed Raggedy Ann would be around forever. And now she looked so old, so worn, so ill. Raggedy Ann deserved better. She wasn't durable enough for such harsh treatment. The years of abuse showed in her stained skin and frayed hair. Lindy would have to preserve her now, hoard her love, not be so wasteful.

She sat Raggedy Ann upright at eye level on the bookshelf in her room. She wanted to look upon her with reverence. Look, but not touch. The doll was too precious to touch. She wouldn't love the stuffing out of her anymore. She would cherish her from below. Raggedy Ann would remain on a pedestal forevermore.

∾

The next day the doctors at Methodist hospital removed Maggie's ovary. Because the Logans had no health insurance, Maggie was relegated to one of the hospital's first-year surgeons. (Behind his back, Lolly called him "Dr. Diapers" because he looked like he was all of twelve years old.) Another doctor, a pathologist, examined tissue from the ovary and diagnosed Maggie as being in the later stages of ovarian cancer. The disease had most certainly spread throughout her body.

The doctors deemed further surgery futile. The patient was going to die soon and only an act of God could change that.

Lolly insisted Maggie's ovary be flown to an oncologist friend in Dallas who was "tops in his field." She would pick up the tab for the shipping charges and the second opinion.

The doctors at the hospital referred Maggie to a clinic that would administer chemotherapy on an outpatient basis for a nominal fee. This might gain her a few nausea-filled months of life, but given the mountain of cancer in her body, the doctors agreed that this too would ultimately be pointless. They were certain that the Dallas oncologist, who was indeed tops in his field, would concur.

∾

"I'll have to drive her up to Lubbock for treatment," Father said when he called from Methodist hospital. Jo was on the phone in Vernice's kitchen. Lindy was on the extension in the bedroom.

Considering this was a long distance call, Father spoke with the speed of a house afire so as not to run up those expensive minutes. "Your Momma and

I need you girls to help out; Lindy, I want you to watch over your sister every day after school and I want you both to get along with each other; you need to do this for your Momma."

"How is she?" Lindy asked.

"She's fine fine, just fine and dandy," he answered, sounding suspiously chipper. "We'll probably be home the day after tomorrow."

"I thought she was staying for a week?" Lindy asked.

"Well, that's the good news," Father said. "The doctor isn't gonna do anymore surgery."

That should be good news, Lindy thought. *Why doesn't it feel like good news?*

"They are taking good care of her right, Father?" she couldn't help but ask.

"Of course they are and Aunt Lolly's paying for a second opinion, to be sure."

To be sure? "To be sure of what?" she asked. "That they're taking care of her like they're supposed to?"

"I have to go, girls; visiting hours are almost over."

And the long distance bill is running up. Was that why they weren't staying longer? Father didn't want to pay for more hospital time?

"Give her a hug," Jo said.

"I will," he said. "See you soon."

Lindy hesitated. How could she think such thoughts about her father? *What a creep I am.*

"I love you," she said.

The only reply was a dial tone.

CHAPTER TWENTY-SIX

Vernice suggested that she and the girls clean Momma's house for her homecoming. Lindy agreed that was a wonderful idea and berated herself because she hadn't thought of it first. She had been so busy trying to think of clever ways to cheer Momma up—Cheery Lindy—that she missed this obvious one. Still, it wouldn't be as flashy as the dozen bottle rockets she planned to set off at the precise moment Momma and Father drove up to the house.

So at 9:00 a.m., Vernice loaded Lindy and Jo into her '68 Impala and drove the quarter mile across the white caliche road to the Logan house to scrub, scour, and sweep for the next three hours. Vernice divided the work load unevenly, giving herself most of the tasks. Jo set about her chores by pretending Vernice was the evil stepmother, Lindy the wicked stepsister, and she Cinderella. Amazingly, as Cinderella, she managed to finish all of her chores, a feat never before accomplished by Jo.

Lindy was a different matter entirely. She couldn't finish a chore to save her life. Her crazy-as-a-loon life. The voices were raging.

It all started when Lindy was dusting Momma's knickknacks and unexpectedly burst into tears. She distracted herself the only way she knew how—by polishing her eight-track tapes, S.O.S.ing all of Momma's already clean pots and pans, and soaking several white T-shirts in enough Clorox to bleach a whale—tasks all performed meticulously, but unnecessarily. Why? Because the voices told her to.

Vernice couldn't understand Lindy's odd behavior; hell, nobody could. Lindy didn't really know what went on in her head herself. She was a slave. A slave to the voices. She was their puppet. They, her puppetmaster.

And when they said dance, she did.

But no matter how fast she danced, she still felt *it*, whatever *it* was: sorrow, depression, insecurity. She felt *it* to her bones. *It* made her keep running. *It* made her want to sleep forever.

~

Vernice expected Momma and Father to arrive at around three in the afternoon. Lindy talked Vernice into letting her wait at her own home, saying she wanted to surprise her folks. Of course, Jo immediately presented the same argument, which was just as well because Lindy would need help lighting the fireworks. Vernice had no clue about Lindy's sparkling surprise and left the girls around a quarter to three so they could have their private reunion with their parents. For heaven's sake, their mother was dying. It was the least she could do.

Lindy quickly lined up her twelve Coke bottles in front of the house, each stocked with its own mini-rocket. She sat below the self-made "Welcome Home" banner on the porch and watched the long and unwinding road for any sign of life. The sun was hiding behind a cloud when she saw Momma's old yellow Ford emerge from a chalky puff of dust miles away on the flat horizon. She ran inside to get Jo, thrusting into her sister's hand one of the Bic lighters she had "borrowed" from Vernice's purse.

"Here. You light the bottle rockets from that end."

Jo stood there. "Bottle rockets? It's not the Fourth of July."

"Just go," Lindy said, and shoved her sister to the other end.

The first bottle rocket ignited just as the car pulled up.

"Welcome home," Lindy shouted, waving her arms and jumping up and down.

The rocket flew into the sky and exploded into clear sparks, quickly followed by the second, and then the third. This was spectacular, and Lindy paused to glimpse her parents' faces so she could forever remember their joy.

"What the hell are you doing?" Father yelled as he snatched the Bic lighter from her hand.

Words stuck in her throat. Father's eyes blazed. And a deep, guttural howl filled the air. *He's going to kill me,* Lindy thought. But the sound didn't come from Father. It emanated from Lulu, who was tied to her usual rope. She tipped her nose up to the sky and wailed. Lindy had never heard such a noise from her dog. Then the hound ran in a series of zigzags as fast as her stubby basset legs would take her and built momentum until she broke free of her tether.

Both generations of Logans watched as Lulu sprinted like a greyhound across the dusty cotton field, heading straight for Smiley's house—specifically for Smiley's ostrich pen.

Lindy ran full out after her. Father followed. But their weight drove their feet into the loose dirt like it was Texas quicksand while lithe, little Lulu sailed across the newly stripped cotton field. She roared up to the ostrich pen, barking to wake the dead. Hank and Gertrude flapped wildly, their gangly legs moving up and down in fast slow-motion, like Lucy and Ethel stomping winery grapes.

Gert especially didn't care for Lulu's presence. She ran from her predator, berserk, hightailing it across the pen. Her short journey ended when she collided headfirst with the brick wall of the house. Then the large, misproportioned bird fell to the ground and stopped flapping.

Father lunged for Lulu. He scooped her up and clamped her mouth shut to stop her barking. Smiley was already there, having sprung from his easy chair and arrived just in time to witness the disaster. He calmed Hank then eased his way into the pen to examine the motionless Gert.

"Gert. Honey?" Smiley stood over his two-hundred pound princess, searching for any sign of life.

Lindy knew the diagnosis before Smiley even said it. "She has a broken neck," Smiley confirmed. *A $5,000 broken neck,* Lindy thought. *I'm dead meat.*

Out of her peripheral vision Lindy saw Father's eyes close and his head shake in disbelief. Did he almost chuckle to himself?

Finally, he opened his eyes and said aloud, "I'll pay you back, Smiley. With interest."

"Don't you worry about it now," Smiley said, his voice cracking. "You're going through enough." He inhaled deeply and exhaled through gritted teeth. Though his breath was measured and steady, he was no longer living up to his nickname. Smiley was now Frowny.

"I'll take care of this dog so it doesn't happen again," Father said.

"You can't shoot her!" Lindy shouted.

"Don't do away with the girl's dog," Smiley said, almost reluctantly. Inhale, exhale. "I'm gonna move my pen away from the house."

"We can work out a payment plan," Father assured.

"Later," Smiley insisted. "Go take care of your family."

Father turned and walked away. Lindy knew she should apologize to Smiley, but she was too embarrassed to get the words out. She ducked her head and followed Father.

As she trekked through the naked cotton stalks, a porcupine blossomed to life in her gut. Its quills teased her insides and snaked her skin. Father didn't say a word to Lindy on the walk across the field. That only intensified the porcupine needles in her stomach. He said nothing to her during dinner either. Or while watching TV. Lindy didn't challenge her father to speak; she shrank like a dog who knows he's been bad, very, very bad. Father's silence was harsher than anything he could say or any punishment he could dish out. When he went into that quiet place that was beyond mad all other beings tiptoed around him, afraid to trigger the storm that followed the calm. Only one other situation in Lindy's lifetime had been dire enough to send Father into this eerie land of tranquility—when she and Jo wouldn't stop fighting on the way back from a disastrous Logan family reunion in ancestral Georgia. Father had been antsy to leave the gathering of relatives he barely even knew and the traveling Bicker & Whine show of Lindy and Jo sent him over the edge. He turned around to slap both girls' hands and ended up in a fender bender with the car in front of him. This fiasco quieted Father for a few hours, but by the time they hit the Louisiana border he had recouped enough to resume talking. This time there wasn't an end in sight. Father didn't say a word all night, and Lindy's porcupine continued prickling its way through her stomach lining.

∾

The next day, Father finally punished Lindy. All of her future allowances and cotton-hoeing proceeds would go toward helping pay Smiley back—a goal that would probably take the rest of her natural born life, but to which Lindy readily agreed. Father also reprimanded her for digging out last year's Fourth of July fireworks and using them without an adult around, although he blamed himself for not throwing away the bottle rockets in the first place. He wouldn't make that mistake again. If only he could say that for all the other mistakes he'd made in life. Then maybe he wouldn't be the failure he now was.

He wondered if he had ever truly held promise as a husband, father, human being, or if he had just deluded himself into thinking so. He wondered how, why, and when he had fallen so far or if he had always been the disappointment his father declared him to be. He wondered a lot and held answers for little. Whatever he used to be, whatever he might have been, he was now a man who couldn't support his family financially, emotionally, or in any other way. This was the truth, and he knew it once he sorted through all the dissonance that infiltrated his head—the questions, the doubts, the cobwebs—and got to the bottom of things. He got to the bottom of things once a day because the clamor in his head wouldn't clear out and leave him alone until he did. Once the bottom was reached, his mind would go numb, and he no longer dwelled on how he had let down everyone he had ever loved. He just accepted it. His brain then clicked over to automatic pilot, and he robotically went through the motions for yet another day.

But sure as clockwork, the next day when his guard was down, usually in the pre-dawn glow when he had finally fallen asleep and was ripe for attack, his brain turned on, discord rang between his ears, and he had to get to the bottom of things all over again. He spent most nights on the couch in front of the TV, the picture tube illuminating his silhouette. He slept less and less. He spent more and more time getting to the bottom of things. And he lived for the numbness to come.

CHAPTER TWENTY-SEVEN

Dick Clark's New Year's Rockin' Eve was Lindy's holiday television tradition. It was the one late-night show she was allowed to watch because there was never any school the next day. She had been allowed to watch *Saturday Night Live* until the night Momma decided to watch with her; that was also the night that Al Franken, during his Weekend Update monologue, said the word "penis" over and over and over again. Lindy was never allowed to watch *Saturday Night Live* again.

But she was allowed to watch *Dick Clark's New Year's Rockin' Eve* because Dick Clark would never say "penis" on TV.

Jo always begged to stay up and watch *Rockin' Eve* too and, since Momma always said yes, there was nothing Lindy could do about it. Fortunately, Jo also always wimped out and fell asleep well before midnight. This year was no exception. Jo was snoring on the couch by 10:05. Lindy gladly sleepwalked her into their bedroom at 10:15. *Here's to rocking solo on* rockin' Eve.

One reason Lindy loved the show is because Dick Clark always broadcast right in the middle of Times Square in New York. To Lindy, New York was a giant city of therapeutic neon calling to misfits from the sticks like her. And Broadway was its pulsating heart. As a kid, Lindy had staged mini-musicals with her malleable Johnny West dolls as stars and her beaded Mexican sombrero as the set on which they danced. It was the biggest Broadway hit ever to play in the Logan living room. But Lindy knew it was puny compared to the boards of the Big Apple.

Even the eve's drunk and disorderly masses didn't dim the glittering lights of Times Square. Lindy had never been to the city, but she somehow felt at home there, and watching the hoards celebrate the birth of each New Year in the midst of her city made her happy.

But as she watched the festivities now, she didn't feel at home. She felt in limbo. Lost. Lonely. *How can those people on TV be so happy?* All those people cheering, whistling, hooping, and hollering. *What was there to be happy about?*

Momma had been home a few days, and it was clear to Lindy that she felt like death warmed over. After she went to her first chemotherapy treatment, Lindy hoped Momma would feel human again and return to the Momma of old. She came back from chemo looking even worse than before. And instead of spending time with her girls, Momma was spending most of her time with the commode. Lindy was even jealous of the commode.

As for Father, he was moody and temperamental, snapping when he spoke. It made Lindy wish for the old awkward silence, silence that she now got from everyone else because of Father's new hard-and-fast rule: don't speak unless spoken to. Jo miraculously adhered to this, now having telekinetic conversations with her invisible friends whenever Father was around.

As for her part, Lindy was trying her best to be cheery, to lighten things up. It's just that nobody was cooperating.

So as Lindy watched Times Square countdown to the new year she wondered what this smiling swarm would do to make Momma happy. She sure had no clue. She had been trying all evening to write a happy fairy tale or some funny jokes to uplift Momma. She had even attempted a poem, but it was so bad it made Cousin Fay look like Elizabeth Parrot Brown, or whoever that famous poet was. *Pretty bad when Fay's poems beat the heck outta your stuff,* Lindy thought as she clicked off the TV only minutes before midnight. It may be New Year's Eve, but she didn't feel like rockin'.

~

Joe had been waiting for the right time to tell the girls about their mother's fate, and he knew that time had come when he walked into the living room on New Year's Day and saw both of his daughters amicably watching the end of the Rose Bowl parade. That they were harmonious was a miracle in itself, and he prayed this phenomenon would continue as he broke the news to them. It suddenly didn't matter that the Cotton Bowl started in five minutes, and he would now miss at least the kickoff if not the first half. The stress of this talk was just one more jackhammer destroying the lining of his stomach. He swigged from the bottle of Maalox he now carried with him as religiously as a gunslinger carries his six-shooter. Then he turned the volume down on the TV.

"I need to talk to you girls." He didn't snap like he knew he had been doing the last few days, but looked directly at both of them and smiled affectionately, even paternally. It seemed to scare the hell of them.

"What's wrong?" asked Lindy, cutting to the chase.

He took a deep breath. "You know your mother hasn't been feeling well since she got home from the hospital."

He glanced quickly at his daughters to gage their reactions. Jo sat, literally transparent, like a ghost. Lindy reminded him of a rock. A mad rock.

"She's gonna die, isn't she?" Lindy asked.

He froze like a deer in the headlights.

"I knew it." Lindy's bottom lip quivered and water surfaced in her mad rock eyes.

Joe panicked. "Don't cry. There's nothing to cry about. The doctor doesn't know anything for sure."

"Then what did you want to talk to us about?" Lindy asked. Jo, as was her MO the last few days, said nothing.

"Chemotherapy is gonna make Momma's hair fall out." Joe tried to steady his voice. "I thought I'd give you girls some money to buy her a wig."

"I love to shop," Jo said, her budding tears evaporating.

Joe released his breath for the first time in minutes.

"When can we go shopping?" Jo asked.

"I'll ask Vernice to take you soon."

Jo smiled. "I'm going outside to play with Wendy."

She hurried out and Joe turned to Lindy, "Who's Wendy again? A doll or a Fruit Loop person?"

Lindy ignored the question. "Look, you can be honest with me. I'm practically a teenager and that's almost an adult. Is Momma gonna die?"

"Lindy. Let's just take this one day at a time, OK?"

Lindy nodded, her eyes burning a hole through him. After a minute of her searing stare, Joe said, "Well, I guess it's time for the Cotton Bowl." Lindy got up to leave. "Wanna watch with me?" he asked.

Lindy sat back down. It was just after kickoff. At the first commercial, she said softly, as if to no one in particular, "You don't have to say it, but I know the answer to my question."

Joe took another swig of Maalox and turned his eyes toward the TV. He said nothing and neither did Lindy for the rest of the game. Both watched the entire contest without seeing a thing.

~

It took two weeks of chemotherapy for Momma's hair to fall out. Two weeks after a lifetime spent in the quest for perfect hair. A lifetime spent cutting, coloring, perming, and then salvaging what she had cut, colored, permed. Now most of her self-frosted mane was gone, and each Logan felt the loss.

But Vernice had gone shopping with the girls just like Father promised. And in that sense, at least, they were hair prepared.

Lindy had insisted the wig to purchase was a tall, swirling beehive. She fondly remembered Momma's topknot from the '60s and early '70s—much preferring it over her obsessive haircutting trend. A topknot had style, finesse, and height—a quality with which Lindy had never lost her childhood fascination. In fact, the higher the hair, the better. So despite serious doubts from Jo and Vernice, they bought the beehive. Just in case, Vernice made sure she understood the saleslady's return policy.

Lindy was certain an exchange wouldn't be necessary. Momma was gonna love it.

"What the heck is it?" Momma asked as she pulled the hair piece out of the box. "A raccoon's tail?"

"It's a wig. Just like Diana Ross wore in the Supremes," Lindy said.

"A decade ago, honey. Don't you think I'm more with-it than that?"

"I told her it was too out-of-date," Jo added, helpfully.

"I thought it looked like the topknots you used to wear," Lindy said in her defense.

"My topknots were braided."

"We can exchange it," Jo interjected. "Vernice said we could."

"Sure we can," chimed Cheery Lindy. "We can get any wig you want, Momma. Any wig at all."

"I'd like something that matched my own hairstyle." Momma's voice cracked. "When I had hair."

Lindy had no idea which of Momma's myriad of hairstyles she wanted to match. "Something curly and silver?"

"No. Something frosted and wavy."

OK.

"Jo Bean'll know. Let her choose."

"That's a good idea," Cheery Lindy said with ultra enthusiasm. Usually she hated to defer to her sister, but in this case she was glad to do it.

"Maybe Vernice can take me into town tomorrow," Jo said.

"I'll just wear this lovely scarf in the meantime." Momma loved the stupid scarf that Jo had chosen. It was multicolored with the look of a stained-glass window. "It reminds me of church."

"Sorry about the old-fashioned hair, Momma," Lindy said, embarrassed about her faux pas. "I think you're beautiful with any hair...or scarf."

Lindy didn't know what she had said to make Momma cry, but, suddenly, there it was—the motherload of gushing geysers. Momma hugged her girls like she'd never let them go.

"You know what," Momma said between gasps, "I do think I'll keep this wig. After all, I've already got my two Supremes." She held her offspring even closer, and, in that moment, they truly felt like they were the stars.

CHAPTER TWENTY-EIGHT

When school began again after the Christmas break it brought upon one of the most dreaded times of the year—class photos. Actually, only Lindy dreaded it. Jo anticipated it. Of course, Jo was photogenic.

With her thin, straight hair and wire-rimmed glasses, Lindy's class picture had a tendency to look like a John Lennon album cover. This phenomenon happened year after year, and Lindy had begun to assume she couldn't blame the photographer. She must look like John Lennon.

The subject in Jo's class photo resembled a porcelain Precious Moments doll—a cherubic face imbued with goodness and innocence. On second thought, maybe it *was* the photography. Lindy never saw Jo look like anything close to an angel.

The morning of the big photo day both girls primped anxiously. Momma helped with hair and tried to add body to Lindy's lifeless do. Mostly she aimed to calm the nerves of her preteen. Lindy was determined not to turn out another class photo that would make Yoko Ono swoon.

"What do you think of this shirt?" Lindy asked.

"It makes you look like a boy," Jo said.

"I wasn't asking you," Lindy said with a smile while imagining popping her sister's head like it was a pimple.

"If it makes you comfortable then wear it," Momma said.

"It makes you look like a boy."

"Jo Bean, let me do your hair now," Momma said as she positioned Jo's head.

Lindy slid into her favorite shirt, a wide-collared, loudly patterned ditty just like David Cassidy wore on *The Partridge Family.* Momma hadn't let Lindy watch that show in the last year before it went off the air. "You're acting too much like Keith Partridge," she'd said. *Like that's a bad thing?* Lindy had thought at the time. *He's the coolest thing on feet.* But that was three years ago, when she was a child. Now she was a teenager. Almost. Now she wanted to look like a girl. Not girl-y, but female. Well, maybe not female exactly, but at least not like a boy.

Lindy posed for herself in the mirror. This shirt didn't make her look like a boy. It made her look cool. Well, Jo sure knew nothing about that. Lindy ran the comb through her hair one more time, loosening Momma's curls a bit. Once she got her bangs to feather satisfactorily, she lacquered them with hairspray, gagging in the fumes. Still, she had to smile. *Hairspray was something girls used.* Maybe she'd even spray on some of that Love's Baby Soft perfume that Momma bought her last year. She felt so feminine she could burst. But, mostly, she felt like she didn't remotely resemble that famous former Beatle.

The pictures came back a week later, and Lindy looked eagerly into her envelope. She was horrified to see John Lennon staring back at her.

"Imagine all the people..." Jo sang somewhere in the background.

"Shut up," Lindy snapped. Jo's picture could have landed her a Life cereal commercial. "I mean it. Shut up."

"Jo, stop it." And, finally, because Momma said it, Jo stopped singing.

"Tell you what," Momma continued to Lindy. "How 'bout if I cut your hair into that Dorothy Hamill cut?"

"Really?" Lindy's jaw almost dropped at the thought of a new hairstyle. "But you like my hair long."

"Lindy, it's your hair. You should have it the way you want."

She couldn't believe her ears. Was this reverse psychology? She didn't know how to respond. Then Lindy finally said, "I don't wanna cut it unless you want me to."

Momma smiled. "I think I'd like it very much."

Momma got out her barber scissors and had Lindy set up the official haircutting stool on top of an old sheet to catch the trimmings. Momma clipped a towel over Lindy's shoulders, wet her hair with a spray bottle and began to snip.

"Thank you, Momma," Lindy said as the tufts began to fall. Later, alone in her room, she took off her glasses and squinted into the mirror at her new do. As long as she never put on ice skates, she might just pass for Dorothy Hamill. Regardless, it was a definite upgrade from John Lennon.

~

The rumor was that Mrs. Westmorland's body had twitched like a piece of frying bacon.

Lindy hadn't seen the actual seizure, but heard about the commotion in the cafeteria. Mrs. Westmorland's epileptic seizure happened during the school's rush hour—just after the bell declaring lunchtime—and smack dab in the middle of the crowded hallway. When she started jerking and twisting, students jumped back like oil recoiling from vinegar. Principal Murphy and Nurse Berkley held her down until the seizure ended and then rushed her into town in the school ambulance, which happened to be sparkling because Bus Driver Sloan had just finished washing the vehicle in anticipation of Friday's big basketball playoff game with McAdoo.

Mrs. Westmorland was the hot topic during lunch.

"Her eyes rolled to the back of her head, and she tried to swallow her tongue," Jenna was saying.

"Is that possible? To swallow your tongue?" asked Holly.

"It is if you're a circus freak," Kari said.

"Then," continued Jenna, "Berkley held her tongue down with a cafeteria spoon."

"Gross!" said Holly, spitting out her cafeteria spoon and some chocolate pudding with it. "Please tell me it wasn't this spoon."

Amber ignored Holly. "What Jenna said is true. Berkley kept Westmorland from swallowing her tongue by holding onto it with a spoon. And that's not easy to do seeing as how her tongue is forked."

"Good one," Kari said, laughing.

"I'm just glad we won't be having our English test this afternoon," said Holly after wiping her tongue clean. "I swear this is the last time I forget to bring a spoon from home."

"It's all so creepy," said Jenna. "Seeing her freak out like that."

"And sad," Lindy said as she played with the food on her tray. She looked up, afraid she had said that out loud.

Amber's sneer confirmed her fear. "This whole thing must be pretty upsetting to you, L squared."

"Yeah," Lindy said, wary of Amber's compassion. "It is."

"I figured. Being Mrs. Westmorland's long lost daughter and all."

"You know, it is uncanny. I can't tell them apart," said Kari.

"She doesn't look like Mrs. Westmorland," said Jenna. The other Fab Three shot her a look. She quickly corrected her mistake. "But she kinda looks like Rick."

"I heard his dad's taking him out of school today," said Holly.

"Why? Does he foam at the mouth too?" asked Kari, laughing.

"Yeah, it's a family trait," Amber said.

"Mad dog Westmorlands," Kari added.

"Do you foam too, L squared?" Amber asked.

Amber and Kari were so enamored of their so-called humor that they barely noticed Lindy pick up her tray and leave.

"Where you going, L squared?" asked Amber, feigning innocence.

Kari waved. "Good-bye, Mrs. Westmorland, Jr."

Lindy desperately needed air. She handed her tray to the dishwasher and focused only on reaching the door that led outside. With each step her breath drew quicker, and all because she couldn't shake the image from her head. The image of Momma writhing on the floor in spasms, her cancer-ridden body rejecting the chemo. Who was to say it couldn't happen? Momma upchucked her insides out after every treatment until she started to shake. What if her body tired of upchucking and went straight to the shaking? What if the shaking turned into seizures? What if she had one of these seizures in public? *Stupid Fab Four.* They were bitches. Plain and simple. Stuck-up snobs.

~

"Denny Anderson said your teacher had a fit of spasms bigger than any prisoner electrocuted on death row," Jo said later that afternoon. "Said you could see her hair standing on end."

Since Father had taken Momma into Lubbock for a chemo treatment, Lindy had no reason to censor herself. No need for Cheery Lindy. So she wheeled on her sister. "Shut up, you idiot."

"You're the idiot," Jo yelled back.

"You're such an idiot, you have no idea what an idiot you are."

"I know I hate you."

"Well, I hate you too!" So there it was. Out in the open. They hated each other equally. No, wait. Lindy hated Jo *more.* "I've hated you ever since you were born. This was my family and you invaded it. I never wanted you to be a part of it, and I don't want you to be a part of it now!"

"I don't want to be part of anything that has to do with you either! You're mean. Meaner than a junkyard dog!"

Lindy gasped. "You've been into my Jim Croce tapes again! I told you keep your hands off my stuff!"

"Why? 'Cause I have fingerprints?" Jo wiggled her fingers in Lindy's face. "That's 'cause I'm *human*!"

Lindy wordlessly walked over to the cabinet and pulled out a box of Fruit Loops.

"NOOOO!" Jo screamed.

But Lindy threw the box on the floor and stomped on it anyway.

"YOU'RE KILLING THEM!"

Jo pummeled at Lindy with her fists. But it did nothing to stop Lindy from continuing to crush the Fruit Loop people.

The next thing Lindy knew, Momma's butcher knife was in her face. "Stop it or I'll kill you," Jo said, her voice ice cold.

Lindy stopped. The cereal box was flat as a pancake. Fruit Loop dust blanketed the lineoleum. Jo took out the broom and dustpan and ceremoniously began cleaning up the mess. Her heart beating a mile a minute, Lindy backed out of the kitchen, but not before she heard Jo add, "I wish you would die instead of Momma."

Thoughts ricocheted off Lindy's brain. *How does Jo know Momma's dying?* This somehow made Momma seem even more vulnerable. Lindy's solo perception could be wrong, but add a second opinion and... *Wait a second, this is Jo I'm talking about. She thinks Fruit Loops are alive. She's a freak of nature! And she's the one who should die instead of Momma.* But Lindy would never threaten to kill Jo like Jo had just done to her. She didn't know whether to be afraid of the little retard or make fun of her. Well, better leave her alone right now because one thing was for sure: the child was not right in the head. Never had been. *Jeez oh Pete.*

Lindy steadied herself along the couch, and her eyes settled on the cluster of family photos resting on the shelves of the entertainment center. She focused on one picture in particular, one of just her and Jo in which they were hugging each other, obviously too young to know better. Lindy couldn't kill Jo, but she could put a curse on her. A curse of her own making. *Who knows? Maybe it would work.* She grabbed the photo, frame and all, and headed for Momma's sewing machine.

She searched the drawers of the sewing machine cabinet only to find the scissors on top in plain sight. She opened and closed them repeatedly, the whir of the sharpened metal sounding like it came from the laboratory of a mad scientist. Or a butcher shop.

Next stop—the backyard.

Lindy sat beside Lulu's doghouse. Her canine friend rose from her patch of matted grass and waddled over to her master. There, she plopped.

Lindy petted the mound of dog. She loved her basset hound's lethargy. She wished she could shoot Jo up with some of it.

She held the photo over Lulu's food bowl and began cutting Jo's image up into small, bite-sized pieces. Then she retrieved Lulu's bag of dried food from the garage, loaded up the bowl, and added water to soften the kernels and make palatable the remnants of Jo. As if that was possible.

Lulu ate heartily, as always, and Lindy watched. She couldn't help but smile at the thought of her sister ending up a big pile of dog stinky.

CHAPTER TWENTY-NINE

To the untrained eye, it would appear that Maggie's chemo had worked. She no longer upchucked, her hair grew back, the color returned to her cheeks. For all intents and purposes, she was cured.

But Maggie knew better.

The truth was that the doctors—the first-year surgeon and Lolly's oncologist—had been right all along. A month and a half of chemo had not kept the cancer from spreading, just as the doctors had known it wouldn't. It had only served to prevent Maggie from enjoying the short remainder of her life. The doctors had dangled chemo as false hope, and Maggie had taken the bait. Well, no more. Margaret Franklin Logan was determined to savor and cherish her last days. She would stop and smell every rose she could get her nose on.

The first rose was one of the sweetest. On Valentine's Day, Joe presented Maggie with a record album, Ronnie Milsap's *It Was Almost Like A Song*. On the back cover, he wrote, "On Valentine's Day, this song is from me to you. Love Ya, Joe," and drew an arrow that pointed to the song "What A Difference You've Made In My Life."

Joe had never been so romantic. Maggie had never been so touched.

He played the record the next Sunday morning instead of his classical music. Nobody complained.

~

The day Joe opened the door to find Smiley standing there holding Lulu, he could hear the sound of cash registers ringing in his head—again. $5,000, ka-ching. $5,000, ka-ching.

"Don't tell me she killed the other ostrich?"

"No," Smiley said. "Hank's alive and kicking. And very amorous. Unfortunately."

Joe took Lulu, and Smiley followed to the backyard. "Uh, about Gert..." Did Smiley want his money now? $5,000, ka-ching. Joe reached into his shirt pocket for his Maalox.

"It's not fair to ask you to pay the whole amount for the bird. In fact, Vernice says we're not gonna ask you for any of it," Smiley said.

"I can't let you do that. It's my fault you're out that five...grand." Joe could barely say the amount.

"I checked with the guy I bought 'em from. Turns out since I hadn't quite had 'em a month, they were still insured under his plan. I'll get back better than half the money, after his cut, of course."

For the first time in months, the vise that had ahold of Joe's stomach loosened a millimeter. "I'll make up the difference."

Smiley waved his hand, "Nah."

"Well, this dog ain't going anywhere near Hank no more." Joe hooked the dog to her new tether—a thick metal link chain.

Smiley chuckled. "Well, it's kinda too late for the other amorous animal on my land. Hell, maybe it's early spring fever. You know how I been trying to breed Bart with another deerhound?"

Joe nodded.

"Well, Bart only has eyes for little Lulu. My damn dog won't even sniff those champions I been penning him up with, but it was all I could do to drag him off this basset. Maybe I caught 'em before we have puppies. Maybe not. Guess it's not my year for breeding."

Joe smiled to himself. He understood. Hell, it wasn't his year for anything.

Which is why, of course, it turned out that Lulu was indeed going to have a litter of puppies. When Joe told Lindy, she laughed and said something about it being so funny that Bart chose Lulu as his mate instead of all those snooty, rich, blueblood dogs. *Ha-ha.* Joe didn't see what was so funny about more mouths to feed.

~

St. Patrick's Day was one of those pure-fun, low-maintenance holidays. The Logans may have been of Irish blood, but none of them knew exactly why it was a holiday. At least there was no stress over the cooking of a big meal or the last-minute wrapping of gifts, and the day's only requirement of wearing green made for an attainable challenge.

Lindy relished her self-designated role of happy-go-lucky leprechaun. Cheery Lindy.

She had told everyone the night before to be sure and wear green or risk getting pinched. This morning she had gotten up first and started preparing Irish pancakes with Bisquick mix and the green food coloring that was usually reserved for Christmas cookies. Never mind that Lindy had added so much green dye that the pancakes now resembled cow patties, this was going to be the perfect St. Patty's Day for Momma.

Momma hadn't even remembered it was St. Patrick's Day, in spite of Lindy's warning of the night before. She was working three half-days a week in an attempt to maintain some sense of normalcy and was late for this morning's appointment. Plus, she was caught off guard by the stack of cow shit sitting in the middle of the kitchen table. So naturally when Lindy nailed Momma with a pinch on her Merm, she yelped.

"Lindy, don't. That's gonna bruise." The chemo had left Momma's body sensitive to everything.

"I'm sorry, Momma." Lindy regurgitated her apology as if saying it quickly made it mean more. "Are you OK? I didn't mean to hurt you, it's St. Patrick's Day, and you weren't wearing green, I made pancakes." She ended with a toothy smile. Cheery Lindy.

"Lindy, stop it," Momma snapped. "Stop being so...fake."

Lindy visibly wilted.

"Don't pout. Miss Overly Dramatic." Momma stopped and exhaled. "Just because you're not a good actress doesn't mean I don't love you. I'm sick of this cheerleader act, and I want to see my real Lindy. I miss her." Momma squeezed her eldest's arm affectionately and then, even though Lindy wore the mandatory green, broke off with a pinch. "Happy St. Patrick's Day."

Later in the day when Momma was at work and Lindy at school, Lindy replayed her momma's plea in her head. She couldn't hear the overtones of love because the volume was cranked on her shortcomings. She was fake. She was overly dramatic. She was a bad actress. *A bad actress? Momma doesn't know how good I've been lately.*

Still, she was a failure at winning Momma's love.

CHAPTER THIRTY

Word spread through the county like wildfire.

Women ignited the blaze via telephone lines. Men fanned the flames at the diner or post office. Half the county knew before school was out. The other half knew as soon as their children brought the news home from school.

A.J. Donovan had tried to commit suicide last night.

Lindy stood up and walked to the front of the bus before it stopped so she would beat her sister into the house. She was determined to be the first to announce the gossip to Momma.

"Slow down," Momma said. "I can't understand either one of you."

"Amber's dad...," Lindy blurted.

"...killed himself," Jo shouted.

"He didn't die, but he wanted to," Lindy finished.

"Suicide?" Momma asked, shocked.

Lindy felt her adrenaline pump. There was nothing like being the first to break such news to the unsuspecting. You had scoop, they wanted it. You were needed.

"He ate rat poison, then threw it up all over the house." Lindy was certain she had the more accurate facts. After all, Amber was in her class. "Amber's mom found him."

"She had to clean it all up," Jo said.

"You don't know that," Lindy said.

"I overheard Mrs. McEachron say it at recess," Jo added.

"That's how Aunt Eurlene killed herself. Rat poison puked up from one end of her house to the other. Birdy found her." Momma shook her head. "Horrible. Just horrible." She paused. "I should do something for Sally. I'll bake a pie." For a West Texas woman, baking a pie was the automatic solution to an array of neighborhood tragedies.

"But, Momma," Lindy said, "he'd been caught embezzling money. From his friends. That's why he tried to kill himself. Word is he's gonna wish he'd been more successful."

Lindy's information was indeed accurate.

A.J. Donovan's ruse was revealed when the cotton seed hybrid became a booming success. Its stock skyrocketed and A.J.'s group voted to quickly sell their shares and make a profit. The only problem was that A.J. had never invested in the cotton seed. He sold his friends on what he was certain to be the biggest sure-fire bust ever in the stock market, and had used their money to repay his own gambling debts. Unbeknownst to everyone except his bookie, A.J. had been addicted to the ponies for years and spent the family fortune long ago waiting to cash in on a golden trifecta. Alas, his winner's circle never came, and his bookie was ready to retire. The bookie wanted either the money he was owed with interest, or a full-length leather coat made with A.J.'s hide. A.J. had no choice but to swindle his friends.

Thus the county proceeded to shun the Donovans. At that night's junior high school basketball games, the court of public opinion had already sentenced the Donovans to the worst sentence imaginable: ostracism. Venerable ranch family or not, this was a scandal the likes of which had never been seen in these parts. Worse, it was a scandal that sucked an immense hole in the bank accounts of many of A.J.'s now former friends. The Donovans became instant lepers.

Maggie heard all of this firsthand when Barbara Breedlove sauntered up to her at the concession stand during halftime of the girls' game. "I hear the coach is gonna put Lindy in the game in the second half," she said. "Since they're so far ahead."

"How are you, Barbara?" Maggie asked flatly.

"I am devastated. Repulsed. Betrayed. And just plain pissed. By my best friend, no less. Make that former best friend."

Maggie fought hard to suppress a smile. Maybe there was justice afterall.

"Your husband didn't go in on *A.J.'s deal?*" Barbara spat the last two words out like it was a deal with the Devil.

"No, Joe didn't."

"Good for you," Barbara said, then changing the subject: "Sally Donovan must have been holy hell to work for. Excuse my language. I'm just so damned p.o.'d." She perked up an eyebrow, waiting for a response.

"Well..."

Barbara took that as a sign that Maggie was on her side and continued her tirade. She told Maggie how her husband, Donald, was the leading plaintiff in the lawsuit against the Donovans. "Money is not our priority; humiliation is," she said. "And I consider it my personal crusade to run the bastards—excuse my language—out of the county."

Maggie nodded noncommittally.

"I need a new friend," Barbara continued. "Someone not involved in this mess. Someone with simpler values. Someone who hates Sally Donovan as much as I do." She smiled. "Can I buy you a cup of coffee?"

Maggie had her long-awaited invitation to join the ranks of the county elite. And all she had to do was spurn Sally Donovan.

"Thank you. I would love a cup of coffee," she said.

~

The next morning was Tuesday, Maggie's usual day to clean for Sally. But when Sally opened the door, she stared at Maggie with dead eyes.

"What are you doing here?" Sally asked.

"This is my day to clean."

"I can't afford to pay you. I'm sorry you came all the way over. I thought you knew."

The truth was Maggie hadn't been sure why she had decided to come to the Donovans'. Partly out of responsibility. Partly out of curiosity. Partly out of compassion. But at this moment she only felt the latter.

"I wanted to come," Maggie said. "To help if I can. Cleaning...or listening."

Sally looked at Maggie skeptically. "I'm only here to get a change of clothes." But she stepped back and opened the door for Maggie to come in.

Maggie easily detected the stench. Her years of cleaning houses had opened up her senses to the aromas of ammonia and its cleaning cousins, but no solution could cover the gruesome stench of regurgitated poison.

"I was sorry to hear about A.J."

"Obviously you didn't lose money in my husband's deal. A.J.'s in the hospital half dead and the nicest phone calls I've gotten are to threaten me with lawsuits." Sally paused. "I'm sorry; I've got to get back to the hospital."

"If you need anything..."

Sally let out a bitter smirk. "I need everything. Everything I had two days ago that I don't have now. My house, my friends, my husband. I appreciate your kindness, but you couldn't possibly understand."

"Oh, I understand more than you know. I never had the big house or important friends or fancy car or rich husband, but I'm losing plenty."

"Maggie, I appreciate your attempt at empathy, I really do, but you can't lose plenty if you don't have plenty to lose."

"Sally, you may be losing the life you've *known*, but I'm losing my *life*."

Sally remained silent, her face blank more than questioning. Maggie explained anyway. "I have ovarian cancer."

Sally blinked and seemed to waken from a self-imposed coma. "I'm so sorry, Maggie. I had no idea you were sick."

"The thing is I'd give anything to have my life back. *My* life. Not the life you had two days ago. Not Barbara Breedlove's life. Not the life of my sisters or Princess Grace or Elizabeth Taylor."

It was true. In saying the words out loud, Maggie realized for the first time the wisdom of the old cliché: You don't appreciate what you have until you lose it. "I'd give anything to be able to have the energy to clean houses every day and see my kid sit on the bench at basketball games. I'd give anything to see next Christmas come and go."

Sally paused. Finally she said, “I guess none of us are fully content with our own lives. I always wanted to be Joan Fontaine.”

Maggie smiled, and Sally said, “Thank you for coming over. You have a way of putting things in perspective.” She glanced at her watch and then, just as quickly as it had landed, her flirtation with lightheartedness passed. “I have to get back to A.J.”

Maggie said, “If there’s anything I can do to help...”

“That’s kind, but you have enough troubles of your own...”

“And dealing with someone else’s somehow keeps my mind off of them.”

Sally looked up. “I’ll be packing up the house tomorrow. The bank repossessed it so we’re moving.” She sounded casual, but the tears brimming her eyelids gave her away.

“I’ll be here at... ten?”

Sally smiled at Maggie and for once there was no condescension behind it, no smug superiority. “Only if you’re up to it.”

“I can probably put in a couple of hours.” Maggie returned the expression—smiling as much at herself—then walked back to her dependable old Ford Fairlane.

Maggie was never accepted into Barbara Breedlove’s clique. Once word leaked out of Maggie’s goodwill toward the Donovans, she was equally ostracized.

Maggie got a kick out of that. She thought it hysterical that a clique of grown women had nothing better to do with their time than cackle about her. Poor insecure, desperate things. Needing the approval of others to validate themselves. Such low self-esteem. Such a waste of living. She felt sorry for them. Sorry because she understood them. She empathized with them. And she prayed that they would see the pointlessness of it all before it was too late.

~

Just like her mother, Holly Breedlove rallied the troops against the Donovans. Unlike her mother, she was not on a recruiting mission to add members to the existing Fab Three. In fact, despite their new leadership in the younger Breedlove, the Fab Three hadn't quite recovered from the devastating loss of their previous chief. They seemed a little out of kilter. Like the Beatles without Paul.

"Did they really take Amber out of school?" Jenna asked. Amber hadn't been to school since the scandal broke two days ago, and the rumor was that she wasn't coming back at all.

"Yep. Too bad, huh? Now we don't have anybody to talk about." Holly smirked to prove she was unaffected by Amber's betrayal.

Lindy walked up and set her tray down on the table.

"Who said we don't have somebody to talk about?" Kari sang under her breath.

"Anybody sitting here?" Lindy asked.

"You are," Holly said generously.

"Thanks." Lindy sat. She stirred the Frito pie on her tray, self-conscious that she was the only girl at the table without a homemade lunch. The Fabs always brought their lunch. Lindy always paid a quarter for the school slop. Just looking at the Fabs' fancy Tupperware lunch boxes with their lovingly prepared homemade sandwiches and cookies made Lindy jealous as all get out.

"So what were you guys talking about?" Lindy asked in an attempt to break the uncomfortable silence.

"That person who used to be in our class," said Holly.

"Amber?" Lindy asked, knowing good and well that's who they meant.

"You mean *Scamber*, the scam artist," Kari said sarcastically.

"Is she coming back?" Lindy asked.

"Why, do you miss her?" Holly wanted to know.

"No," Lindy said, unsure how to answer. "I just didn't know if she was gone for good."

"For good." Jenna threw in her two bits.

"Why don't you go with her?" Holly asked. "Then you and her and your momma and her momma could all be best friends."

"What are you talking about?" Lindy asked.

"You are so lame. You know exactly what I'm talking about," Holly said.

"I swear I don't," Lindy replied.

"Your momma's helping Sally Donovan, acting like she's her new best friend," Holly said. "My momma says she probably even got a cut of 'the sting.'"

"The movie?" Lindy asked, genuinely confused.

"No, dum-dum. We're not talking about Newman and Redford. We're talking about the Donavan crime...con...caper," Kari said.

"Our parents' stolen money," Jenna said.

A thousand thoughts raced through Lindy's mind. She should defend her momma. She should punch each Fab in the nose. She should get home and ask Momma if this was true.

Lindy was about to rise from the table and take her tray away before she encountered any further disgrace. But the Fabs beat her to it.

"Come on. Let's find another table," Holly said to her cronies as they grabbed their quality lunches and walked away.

∾

"Momma, did you go and be nice to Sally Donovan?" Lindy confronted her mother the moment she got home from school, her voice teetering with the anger that had been boiling inside her all day.

"If I *ever* talked to my mother with that tone of voice, I would have been disowned," Momma answered.

"Oh, you're in trouble," Jo taunted.

"Jo Bean, go take your snack and watch TV in the living room," Momma said.

"I'm fine here," Jo replied. But Momma's look told her that she, in fact, was not fine here, so Jo did as she was told.

Lindy knew if she persisted with this topic, she treaded thin ice; still, she asked, "Is it true?"

"You drop that chip on your shoulder and we'll talk," Momma said.

"I'm sorry. I didn't mean to yell at you, but the girls at school say you're friends with Sally Donovan and now they won't have anything to do with me."

Momma looked at her eldest. "And how does that feel?"

"Terrible."

"Uh-huh. That's why I went to see Sally. Because she needed a friend, and nobody wanted anything to do with her."

"But she's a thief," Lindy said.

"She's a person," Momma replied.

"Who's married to a thief!" Lindy said heatedly.

"So?" Momma asked. "Didn't Jesus have compassion for the robbers and thieves?"

"I'm never gonna have compassion for Amber," Lindy answered. "I'm glad I don't ever have to see her again."

Momma looked down her nose at Lindy. "You're gonna learn one day not to be so stubborn. That all we have is love and the ability to show that love to other people. I suggest you start practicing as soon as possible. You hear me?"

Lindy nodded.

"Now get out and let me cook supper."

Lindy got out and let Momma cook supper. She went outside and sat with Lulu and pondered. Life, death, Jesus, Momma. They were all enigmas.

But Momma was the puzzle she needed to figure out first. *Show your love,* Momma had said.

And then it hit her. An idea flashed in her brain like a lightbulb coming to life. She knew how to make Momma love her. She would *show* Momma her love. She would buy Momma a tennis bracelet.

CHAPTER THIRTY-ONE

Momma knew this Easter Sunday would be her last. She also knew it should be spent at church; she just couldn't muster the energy to get there.

So she requested that her family have their own church service at home. She wanted to see her girls in their Easter finest, even if they were only squeezing into last year's Easter dresses. Jo spiced up her ensemble by pinning on daintily-tied pastel ribbons. She even talked Lindy into letting her pin a bow on her. For Momma.

Momma tried hard to look presentable, knowing that this Easter, like all holidays before it, would be set in the stone that was family photographs. She revived her colorless complexion with makeup. She styled her hair with a curling iron until her arms tired from the lifting. That's when Father finished curling her hair and helped her into the evening dress he had bought for her on their honeymoon in Dallas. She had only ever worn the dress once before, to Big D's Old San Francisco Steakhouse during that honeymoon trip. There had not been an occasion to wear it since and the fact that over the years Maggie had grown four dress sizes made fitting into it impossible anyway. But she had never given up hope and now, with weight falling off her frame faster than leaves off trees in autumn, she once again fit into the dress of her dreams.

Jo gasped when Momma walked into the living room, and Lindy's jaw actually dropped.

"You look beautiful, Momma," Lindy said.

"Like a movie star," Jo said.

Every Logan participated in their homemade church service. Jo led the Lord's Prayer. Lindy directed a rendition of "Holy, Holy, Holy." And Father read from Matthew 28 in the Bible about Jesus being crucified and then rising from the dead. Lindy liked the audience participation aspect of their church service, and—unlike regular church—she didn't catch herself nodding off to sleep once. For her part, Jo adopted her standard ladylike church pose—upright posture, legs crossed at the ankles, hands folded one over the other. Always stiff, never moving. Lindy called it the body language of Birdy and the dead.

Joe asked Maggie to say the closing prayer. Momma nodded and asked if everyone would join hands and bow their heads.

"Lord God. On this, Your most miraculous of days, we give thanks for the miracle of life. May we use the days You give us to the fullest, enjoy them to the highest, and cherish them as they become memories. Thank You for our time together, however short. Or *long*." Maggie opened one eye and looked up to the heavens. "Just proving that I haven't lost my sense of humor, God. But You can ease up on the testing of me now. This is not to say I don't thank You for the stamina, strength, and determination You've given to me and my family. I *do* thank You. As we say, 'What does not kill us makes us stronger.' And as You say, 'God has not promised skies always blue, but strength for the journey all the day through.' And on that note, give us all strength, Lord God, and help my family to know I love them. Always and forever. Even when I'm a bitch on wheels. Amen."

Silence greeted the end of Momma's prayer. Reflection hung in the air. Lindy thought, *this is the perfect time for a group hug and a series of "I love yous."*

"So, what's for dinner?" Father said with a silly lilt that ended any opportunity for a display of real emotion.

"I could make omelets," Lindy said, desperately wanting to please. "Sort of Easter brunch."

"I'll help!" Jo said.

"I don't need your help," Lindy said cheerfully before remembering that being cheerful was now taboo.

"Lindy," Momma said. "Remember what we talked about: loving other people."

"Oh, yeah," Lindy's voice trailed off. She turned to Jo. "You can clean up."

"Lindy," Momma warned.

"I'm kidding," Lindy said. "Just showing God I still have a sense of humor too." Momma bristled, and Lindy instantly regretted her remark. She was just trying to be funny like Momma, but her smart-ass comment belittled her mother's situation, as if to deny that the woman had indeed been to hell and back in the last few months. The retort reeked of flippancy, like she was making fun of Momma's prayer, and she didn't know how to remedy the situation. To apologize might point up her attempt at ridicule, even though that wasn't her intention at all. She loved Momma's prayer. She loved Momma. She hated herself. *Oh, God—gosh,* she meant—it was wrong to take the Lord's name in vain—*I'm an idiot.* Her stomach liquefied and dropped to her toes. Her innards turned to mush and began to ooze out her pores. She was melting. Just like the Wicked Witch of the West at the end of *The Wizard of Oz—I'm melting, I'm melting.* She forced her rubbery legs into the kitchen, where she prayed to God she would not end up a Technicolored puddle of Lindy goo. *Keep me from melting, God. Also, help me not to stick my foot in my mouth again today. And please, one last thing, God, if You never do anything else for me ever in my whole life, please, as I stand before this stove, show me how in the world to make an omelet.*

~

Long after the Easter omelets had become scrambled eggs, and shortly after the kitchen had been returned to an acceptable level of cleanliness, Lindy checked in on her napping momma. As it turned out, Lindy hadn't melted, but remained solid—physically if not mentally. Standing in the doorway of the master bedroom, she cleared her throat to see if Momma was sound asleep. There was no sign of stirring, so she tiptoed lightly into the room and shut the door behind her. She was more afraid of Momma being awakened by the thunder of Father's snores from the couch than by her small footsteps.

She slithered through the room like a camouflaged commando and quickly spotted her target—the closet where Momma kept her sacks of Green Stamps. Lindy had soon realized she would need help in her quest to purchase a tennis bracelet. A lot of help. The price of such a bauble was far too steep to be covered by the twenty dollars she had stashed away in her sock drawer from Aunt Edna's Christmas gift. What she wouldn't give to have the money back from Jenna's stupid leather basketball. She had actually contemplated stealing the stupid thing back since Jenna had a closet full of them, but that would only taint Momma's gift because "Thou shalt not steal." Damn those Ten Commandments. So moving on with her plan, Lindy had called up the lady at the Green Stamps store and struck a bargain. If she could fill 175 Green Stamps books, then her twenty dollars plus those books would buy the crème de la crème of the Green Stamps inventory—a rhinestone-studded tennis bracelet. Lindy was prepared to lick her tongue green.

She floated toward the closet, pausing for a creak underfoot. Momma didn't move, immersed as she was in a tranquilized sleep. But she was at peace, and it had been a long time since Lindy had seen her momma at peace. Lindy couldn't help but fall under her spell. She changed her course and gently came to a halt beside the bed.

She lowered herself onto the floor and pulled her knees up to her chest. She watched as Momma's breath moved methodically in and out, in and out. It lulled her into a trance, and she relished this quiet togetherness. Calm blanketed the room, isolating its occupants from the world, and numbing the turbulence in Lindy's soul. And for a moment, Lindy felt no guilt, no stupidity, no shame. For a moment, she felt loved.

CHAPTER THIRTY-TWO

Lindy did finally sneak the sacks of Green Stamps out of Momma's closet, and she holed up in the bathroom for hours each afternoon slapping the things into their books. When questioned about the time she was spending in the bathroom, she blamed it on her blossoming vanity as a soon-to-be teenager.

But, really, if she was going to pull off this vanity excuse, she would have to stop licking the stamps. With each slurp her tongue grew greener than Kermit the Frog and, if one of her family members didn't notice that, they might catch on when the residual stamp glue welded her tongue to the roof of her mouth like a piece of scrap metal. So she started dampening the stamps with a wet washcloth. Soon she had an assembly line routine—running a long strip of stamps across the wet washcloth, sticking the required number of stamps within their block on a page, then ripping the perforation. Sticking, ripping, sticking, ripping, until it was time to wet another long strip of stamps. It was a heck of a lot faster, plus her tongue was salvaged. Only now her fingertips looked stricken with fluorescent gangrene.

Lindy's Green Stamps duty had escalated dramatically in the last two days. Momma was back in the hospital. Lindy worked at a fever pitch, certain that her little stamps held Momma's big cure.

The girls were again staying with Smiley and Vernice, sharing the small guest bedroom where Vernice housed her collection of antique dolls. Her collection was massive, the lifelike creations littering every nook and cranny of the bedroom. Antique dolls and mannequins gave Lindy the willies. Their eyes followed wherever she moved. She was positive they were alive and evil. Seeing Vincent Price in *House of Wax* on the afternoon matinee as child had eliminated any doubt of that. And now she had to sleep with the creepy things. As if her nightmares weren't bad enough without them.

Lindy wanted to be alone, but couldn't stomach the thought of spending time in the Doll House of Horrors. Still, she needed a place to sulk. It was her birthday, and no one had remembered.

They got clued in when the telephone rang.

"Happy birthday, Lindy," Momma said. "I'm sorry I didn't get you a cake made. I'd planned to do it in the shape of a crown this year. For my queen teen."

Lindy's memory sent the flavor of chocolate cake and white icing to her taste buds. "That's OK, Momma. I'll still be a queen teen next year."

Momma said nothing.

"How are you feeling?" Lindy asked.

"Like an old fart," Momma replied.

"Momma!" Lindy was shocked. Momma *never* said fart.

"I'm loosening up in my old age," Momma said with a chuckle.

"You're not old."

Momma paused. "Let me talk to Vernice, OK, sweetie?"

"OK."

"Happy birthday, teenager," Momma said.

Lindy handed the receiver to Vernice and continued to brood, but before she could finish her pity party, Vernice had returned from town with a store-bought cake and all the birthday trimmings—birthday hats, balloons, and noisemakers. It was a nice thing for Vernice to do, but these symbols of happiness only served to irritate Lindy more. She didn't feel like celebrating, and she didn't feel like eating that pathetic excuse of a birthday cake. She was supposed to get a homemade crown. *Queen teen.* Piggly Wiggly's version of a cartoon cake was to stick a puny plastic figurine on top of the icing. And, worst of all, the cake wasn't even chocolate.

Still, she blew out her thirteen candles like a real trooper to a less than rousing rendition of "Happy Birthday." Vernice pulled the candles out of the cake as Lindy said aloud the one thing that she knew would make her feel better. "I want to take a piece of cake to Lulu. Since it's not chocolate, it won't hurt her."

"Sure," Vernice said. "I'll get my keys and drive you over."

"Want to give a piece to Bart?" Lindy asked Smiley.

"Why the heck not?" Smiley replied. "He hasn't been too sweet since Lulu's been locked up."

"I want a piece for Wendy," Jo said, bouncing in her chair like she had to go to the bathroom.

"Who's Wendy?" Vernice asked.

"I'm sorry, I thought you had met." Jo turned to the air beside her. "Wendy, this is Vernice and her husband, Smiley. This is Wendy."

"Nice to meet you, Wendy," Vernice said, playing along.

"You're a skinny little thing," Smiley added. "I hardly noticed you."

Jo leaned over to Smiley and whispered, "That's nice. She's self-conscious about being chunky."

Was Lindy the only one who realized her sister was a nutcase? She had to stop this lunacy. So she said out loud, but judiciously, "Um, nobody's there," and waved her hand in the air beside Jo to prove it. "There is no Wendy. There are no Fruit Loop people." But, much to her surprise, no one said anything. Vernice just kept cutting the cake. Smiley just kept smiling. Even Jo just kept drinking her milk. So Lindy said out loud, but much less prudently than before, "Good Honk, can't anyone see she's out of her ever-loving mind?!?"

There was a pause, and, for a split second, complete silence.

Then Vernice looked up and asked, "Would you girls like ice cream with your cake?"

"Just cake for me," Jo said. "Both for Wendy."

"And Lulu?" Vernice inquired. "Would she like both?"

Lindy felt herself slump. "Yes, please."

Perhaps, Lindy thought as she observed the serenity around her, *Jo isn't the sister who's out of her ever-loving mind.*

CHAPTER THIRTY-THREE

The next day after school, Vernice drove Lindy and Jo up to Lubbock to visit Momma in the hospital. It seemed like a good idea at three o'clock in the morning after Jo woke up the whole house crying for Momma. But now, as they walked the halls amongst doctors and nurses and life and death, it didn't seem like a good idea at all. The bright lights illuminated the grown-up world of sterilized medicine. Inside these walls, everyone spoke quietly, reverently, like in church. And the atmosphere gave Lindy the same eerie feeling. It was all so serious. And real. And it brought home her true fear—people you love really do die.

Lindy had never had anyone close to her die. She barely knew her grandparents when they died, and every other death had been a really distant and old relative or a really distant and old friend of the family. She had given death a lot of thought though. What happened after you died? Did you really go to heaven? Or was heaven just a fairy tale to appease the living? If heaven did exist, was it the mainstream vision of angels with wings or Lindy's fantasy of twenty-four-hour all-you-can-eat buffets? (Known on earth as Vegas.)

Was death a kind of a sleep like before you were born, where it didn't hurt, it was just nothing? Or was your spirit reincarnated as a Scandinavian, or a jackrabbit, or, god forbid, a Washington Redskins fan?

Lindy didn't know the answers to any of these questions about death, but she had given the issue a lot of thought. Especially when it came to Momma dying.

As Vernice led the girls down the hallway, Lindy couldn't take her eyes off a woman standing outside one of the rooms, discreetly sobbing. She was being comforted by her husband or brother, who was saying how Daddy feels no pain now because he's in heaven. Flying around with angels. Or bellying up to the Wild West buffet. Or making his way back to this world as a little Swedish girl. Lindy may not have known a thing about what happened to the dead after death, but this distraught woman reawakened her fears of what happened to the living after death. The living had to go on living. In an empty world without their father. Or mother. That had to be a fate worse than death.

Vernice slowly pushed open the door to Room 1022. The girls saw Father first, sitting in the chair beside the bed. Momma was partially hidden by the curtain that divided the room in two, but as far as Lindy could see the other bed was empty. When Momma came into full view, her appearance shocked the girls more than the first time they had laid eyes on one of her self-imposed crew cuts. Tubes stuck out of each arm, dark circles rimmed her eyes, and despite an attempt at lipstick and rouge, her skin mirrored the whiteness of the bed sheets.

"Howdy, girls. I tried to get real purty for y'all," declared Momma in her yuckety-yuck hick voice that was meant to defeat the heaviness in the room. In a knockout, heaviness won.

"Hi, Momma," both girls said in unison.

"Joe," Momma said, "why don't you go treat Vernice to a cup of coffee."

"Sounds good to me," said Vernice.

"Push this button if you need a nurse," Joe said anxiously.

"I'm fine. Go on," Momma said.

Vernice steered Joe by the shoulders, throwing a wink at Maggie on their way out.

"Thank you," Momma mouthed back to Vernice. Then she turned her eyes to her girls. "Now. Finally. Alone with my best friends."

The girls stood frozen, clumped together on one side of Momma's bed.

"Can I have a hug?" Momma said.

Lindy bent to hug her mother first, careful not to break her. She kissed her cheek and was reminded of how soft Momma's skin always was. Baby soft like the cuddly tot on the bottle of Downy fabric softener. Therapeutically soft like comfort food for the touch. And right now sticky soft from the dew of perspiration that rose from her skin. Kissing Momma's cheek was like kissing a damp piece of chicken fried steak that had been tenderized in Downy. And it was wonderful.

Momma looked at Lindy. "Vernice said you helped her make salmon croquettes for your birthday dinner."

"She burned 'em," tattled Jo.

"That's OK, honey," Momma said to Lindy.

"I didn't burn 'em. Vernice did," Lindy said. "I just helped her mix 'em up."

"I'm sorry you had a lousy birthday," said Momma. "How was your cake?"

"Good," Lindy answered.

"Liar," Momma teased.

"Hey, I'm working on a big surprise to give you when you come home," Lindy said. She was so proud of her Green Stamps scheme that it took every ounce of her willpower not to blow the secret at this very minute.

"Well, it's a good thing I'm coming home tomorrow," Momma said.

"I have a surprise for you too," Jo piped up, not wanting to be outdone. "I've been sticking Green Stamps in books to buy you a present."

Lindy gasped. "You little spy." So much for no one questioning her time in the bathroom.

"Girls, don't fight." Momma sounded more tired than angry.

"But she's taking credit for my idea." Thank God Lindy hadn't yet traded for the tennis bracelet or Jo might have taken credit for that too.

Momma ignored her daughters' protests. "I want you both to listen to me. I want you to start taking care of each other. You're family. You're sisters. And even though you may not like that right now, the most important thing you have in life is each other. Nobody else knows you like the other one does."

She drew a long breath and looked at Lindy. "Nobody else has scribbled in your Dr. Seuss books and made you so mad you wanted to spit."

Her eyes moved the few inches to Jo. "Nobody else has come to your rescue when Vicki Mulberry hit you over the head with a toy shovel. Nobody else is your true 'buddy pal.' Remember when you used to call each other that?" She swept both girls up in her gaze. "You only have each other. Cherish that. Love each other. I know you don't believe me now, but someday you'll treasure those scribblings in your Dr. Seuss books." Then she smiled her smile. The smile that made the good better and the bad disappear. "Now, hug each other."

The girls stiffly did as commanded.

"One more thing. Life's too short. I want you to do what makes you happy." She opened her hand for Jo to take. "Model." She reached across for Lindy. "Sing."

"But you don't think I'm any good," Lindy said.

"Oh, honey." The word "honey" bounced around in Momma's throat. "It only matters what you think."

"You're talking like you're gonna die," Lindy said accusingly. It never only mattered what Lindy thought.

"I may die, but I'm never gonna leave you girls. I want you to know that. I'll always be with you." Maggie so wanted her girls to thrive. It would prove that her life had not been for nothing.

"Be with us how?" Jo asked.

"Well," Momma paused. "You know how Jesus is always with you?"

"Even though He's invisible," Jo answered.

"Right. I'll be with you like that too. Alongside Jesus."

"It won't be the same," Lindy said.

"Sure, it will. I'm ruder than Jesus. I'll butt in anytime. After all, I'll still be your mother." Momma was trying desperately to lighten the mood.

Lindy was in no mood for humor. Momma's casual tone made her defensive. "Are you really coming home tomorrow?"

"Yes," Momma replied. "So you can stop hating me tonight for being sick."

"I don't hate you," Lindy said.

"I know. But sometimes it's easier than loving me."

"I do love you, Momma," Lindy said. "I love you more than anything."

"Oh, sweetie. Come here." Lindy's tears mixed with Momma's as their soft cheeks meshed in a hug. Before they broke, Lindy heard a faint whisper in her ear, "I did the best I could. Please know that."

Of course Lindy knew that. What she didn't know was why Momma needed to say it. She was a terrific mother; anybody could see that. And tomorrow she would see that Lindy was a terrific daughter. She would have her gift—her gift, not Jo's—waiting when Momma came home. Momma was gonna love her tennis bracelet. And she was gonna love Lindy for giving it. Tomorrow, finally, Lindy was gonna win Momma's love.

~

"Will she be as comfortable at home?" asked Vernice, playing with the straw in her Coke.

"The doctor's gonna give her some pain killers. And the nurse recommended a hospice worker." Joe paused to take a sip of his coffee, burnt from sitting too long in the pot. He didn't notice.

"I can sit with her some, Joe."

"It's almost over. She knows it. I know it. The doctor's the only one who's out and out said it. They can't do anything. Hell, they couldn't do anything five months ago." He wanted to blame someone for this change in his life. This devastating, frightening, frustrating change in his life.

"Smiley and I'll do whatever we can."

"I appreciate your help. And for letting the girls stay over."

"It's been nice to have the company."

Joe didn't hear Vernice's words. His worries were too deafening. "I don't know how to tell them. Their momma's coming home to die."

CHAPTER THIRTY-FOUR

On the drive home that evening, nobody said much of anything, Vernice for fear of saying the wrong thing to the girls, and Lindy for fear of saying the right thing to Jo. She refused to let her baby sister off the hook for stealing her thunder; she just couldn't deck the prissy nincompoop until she got her alone.

Vernice stopped at the girls' house first so Lindy could check on Lulu. Lindy headed straight to the backyard, and Jo stupidly followed.

"You better get away from me if you know what's good for you," Lindy barked at her sister.

"I would've helped you with those Green Stamps if you'd just asked me. If you'd just let me in the bathroom," Jo said.

"I didn't want your help. I never want your help. You're a liar and a thief."

"I didn't steal from you."

"You stole my idea. You took credit for all my work."

"I just want Momma to love me too," Jo screamed.

"Isn't it enough that she loves you for everything else you do? Can't you leave some love for the rest of us?" Lindy shrieked.

"She doesn't love me! She thinks I'm stupid. I always hear her saying that to you." Jo's words echoed in the night.

Lindy looked at Jo, baffled. Jo did have a point. She was stupid, and Momma did always say that to Lindy. Did that mean Momma didn't love Jo either? Jo certainly thought so.

So if Momma didn't love Jo, and Momma didn't love Lindy, where did all of Momma's love go? Father didn't suck up that much of her love; she was too busy being constantly irked at him. Lindy was very confused. How could she win Momma's love if there was nobody to win it from? Was it possible Momma had an untapped vat of love ready to gush forth once she opened her dream tennis bracelet? That had to be it. That had to be the way to get Momma to love her. Momma couldn't just *not* love her. A mother couldn't just not love her daughters. One of them anyway.

Lindy's thought-bubble burst when she arrived at Lulu's doghouse. Lulu was just outside the door with one new puppy—one tiny blob of glop—fresh out of the womb. Lulu was in the middle of dogbirth.

"Yuck, gross," Jo said, stepping away from the mess.

"Oh, sweet girl," Lindy said not to Jo, but to Lulu. "Go get Vernice." This she said to Jo.

"Is Lulu gonna be OK?" Jo asked.

"She will if you'll hurry up. Go." Lindy prayed Vernice would know what to do.

She watched as Lulu eked out another head.

"So you're finally having those puppies, eh, girl," Vernice said, walking up. "About time. She's gonna be fine, girls. She probably doesn't need our help, but we'll give her a hand anyways."

Vernice sent Jo in the house for some old towels and Lindy for a bowl of hot water.

By the time the girls returned, the second puppy was out and the third on its way. Vernice and Lindy each wiped up a puppy with the water that had cooled to warm, then wrapped them together loosely in a dry towel. The two baby girls quickly snuggled with each other and were soon joined by their brother.

Lulu kept pushing as if there were another puppy to deliver, but no head appeared.

"Is that all?" Lindy asked.

"No, we don't have the runt yet," Vernice answered.

"She's stuck," Jo said.

"Yeah, I think it is stuck," Vernice agreed.

"What do we do?" Lindy was panicking.

"It's probably breech. We've gotta reach in and turn it around," Vernice said.

"What's breech?" Jo asked.

"It's backwards. Hind end first," Vernice said. "It needs to come out head first." Vernice took a ring off her right hand. "Will you hold this?" she asked Jo.

"You're gonna put your hand in there?" Jo asked, repulsed.

"I'm gonna try."

Lindy snapped at Jo: "Why don't you leave if you're just gonna whine."

"I wanna watch," Jo said.

"Then be quiet," Lindy said.

After a couple of tries, Vernice said, "I can't get my hand in there." Her large hooked hand with the two webbed fingers wasn't even close to entering the small basset.

"I'll do it," Jo said.

"No, I'll do it," Lindy said, blowing off her sister.

"The smaller the hand the better," Vernice said. "Lulu's in a lot of pain. If we can't get this puppy out, she might die before we get her to a vet. Jo, you sure you're up to doing this?"

Jo nodded and handed Vernice back her ring.

"OK, stick your hand in," Vernice instructed. "Lindy and I'll hold Lulu. You should feel the puppy right away."

Jo took a breath and held it and slid her hand in. "It's slimy." A chill ran down her spine and she looked for a moment like she might toss her cookies, but then a strange calm fell across the nine year old.

"You feel its head?" Vernice asked.

"Yep. It's pointing thataways." Jo nodded in the direction of Lulu's head.

"OK. Get a firm grip on its body and slowly turn it 'til the head's facing Lulu's hiney."

Jo grimaced and Lulu jerked and Lindy held and the puppy spurted out along with Jo's hand. It was the runt. The baby sister.

Vernice gently cleaned the baby and added it to the litter.

Lindy shook the cobwebs from her brain and tried to decipher what just happened. Lulu, four puppies, and...Jo? Who was that kid? Poised, calm, confident, competent. One minute she's a sniveling little brat and the next she's Marcus Welby.

And—shock of all shocks—Jo had done something *nice.* Something nice for Lindy. Satan must be bobsledding in Hades.

~

"I was thinking of naming the runt after you," Lindy told Jo later that night as they got into bed.

"Jojo? Like Lulu?" Jo asked.

"Sure." Lindy paused. "By the way, I forgive you for what you said at the hospital."

"About me filling up the Green Stamps books?"

"Yeah."

"And I forgive you for yelling at me."

Lindy gritted her teeth. Jo didn't made forgiveness easy.

"But I shouldn't have lied to Momma," Jo continued. "I just wanted to be a part of your present."

Jo's confession suddenly made Lindy feel very magnanimous. "Well, maybe we can both give it to her."

Lindy told Jo of her plan for getting the tennis bracelet tomorrow, all of which thrilled Jo to no end.

As she lay in the darkness, Lindy stared up at the ceiling to avoid eye contact with any of the antique anti-Christs. "Thanks for helping Lulu," she said, then added, "and Jojo."

"Jojo," Jo repeated, liking the sound. "Can she be my puppy?"

"Sure," Lindy said, for the first time wondering who would own the puppies.

In the glow of the moon, Jo asked, "Is Momma gonna die and be invisible like Jesus?"

Lindy pondered for a second. "I don't know."

"I talked to God about it. Told Him I'd do anything if He'd let Momma live. I'd give up my most favorite thing in the world. He told me to give up Dr. Peppers. For three days I haven't been a Pepper. Not at ten, two, or four. So Momma's gonna live." Jo looked up to heaven. "Right, God?" She waited. "Sometimes I wonder if He hears me."

"Me too," Lindy said.

CHAPTER THIRTY-FIVE

The next morning Lindy claimed to have a sore throat, which she didn't, but it was a convenient lie since strep throat was going around school. She easily convinced Vernice that she needed a penicillin shot, which she didn't, but it was the only way she could get a ride into Jessip. She had to trade for the tennis bracelet today. She had to give Momma her welcome home gift.

Lindy was prepared to suffer through an unnecessary shot, expecting Vernice to drive her into town, but as it turned out Smiley was going in for some parts anyway, so he dropped her off at the doctor's office. She waited just inside the door, hidden from the receptionist, and when Smiley drove away, she hightailed it out of there and ran the five blocks to the Green Stamps store. She made her trade—175 books of Green Stamps plus a crisp, new twenty dollar bill—and raced back to the doctor's office with a sparkling new rhinestone tennis bracelet in her jacket pocket.

She waited for Smiley on the sidewalk just outside the pharmacy. On the way home, she marveled at the perfect execution of her plan. One tennis bracelet and zero shots. What a great day.

Lindy was in such a good mood that she even told Smiley she felt OK and wouldn't mind going to school today. She chuckled; she must feel good about herself if she wanted to face the Fab Four. Make that the Fab Three. But she had a secret. She had the best gift in the world for the best mom in the world, and she was officially about to become the best daughter in the world. She was unstoppable. Besides, she had a test in English and knew that acing one of Mrs. Westmorland's exams while witnessing that illiterate Holly Breedlove fail it miserably would simply be icing on the cake of this fine day.

So Smiley dropped her at school—a move that he heard about when he returned home. Vernice couldn't believe he didn't know any better than to let a sick child run around and get sicker, not to mention spread the contagion to her classmates. Vernice felt very lucky to be able to use the word "contagion" in a sentence; it had been the word of the day on her daily calendar.

Smiley defended his actions on the grounds that the girl had gotten a penicillin shot, which he felt nullified the prosecution's...er, his wife's, arguments. Smiley loved *The Rockford Files* and was proudly picking up some of the lingo.

Lindy scored a perfect hundred on her English test and came home on the bus with the rest of the kids and her nonexistent contagions.

All day she had kept her hand diligently on the box in her pocket that housed the tennis bracelet, and now, as the bus turned down the caliche road that led to her house, she gripped it fiercely. Her moment of glory was only a mile away. Gosh darned, if she wasn't on the verge of a Magically Perfect day.

The bus rounded the circle drive in front of their house and she could see Momma's old yellow Ford parked on the side. Momma was home.

Lindy stepped to the front of the bus before it came to a stop, something you weren't supposed to do, but she didn't care. Momma was home.

She sprang off the bus, sprinted up the sidewalk, and flung open the screen door, not even caring that Jo was on her heels. Momma was home.

She hurried through the living room, barely giving a second look to her father who was sitting on the couch, cradling his face. "Momma in the bedroom?" she asked.

Father made an effort to lift his head. "Momma's not here."

This was not going according to plan. Lindy expected to rush in, present Momma with the tennis bracelet, see the excitement and joy and tears in her eyes, and at last truly know that she was loved. "She at Vernice's?" she asked as she headed for the front door.

"No, she's not," Father said.

Lindy turned back and truly saw her father for the first time today. His eyes were puffy. His jowls sagged. He had aged twenty years since yesterday.

"Momma died this morning," he said.

The girls stopped, and something in them died that instant too. Jo started to cry, and Lindy stood in stunned silence. Finally, Father spoke. He told them how he had stayed all night in the chair in Momma's hospital room, like always. Momma didn't wake up in the night like she usually did, and they both slept late this morning. Until 6:30. That's when the nurse came in to check on Momma and give her breakfast. Father was opening up the tiny box of Corn Flakes for Momma when the nurse told him that his wife had passed away in her sleep. Then the nurse went and got the doctor to confirm the death while Daddy watched over Momma. He had held her hand all night long. It eased some of the pain to know he had been holding her as she left.

Father's eyes started leaking, but his one-time show of emotion didn't register with his offspring. Jo had already lapsed into her fantasy world where dependable, fictitious Wendy was comforting her, consoling her, loving her. Lindy was consumed with the white hot coals that burned inside her belly as tears rolled down her cheeks.

For thirteen years, Momma had been Lindy's lifeline. She had made birthdays, holidays, all days special. She had healed the pain, the hurt, the boo-boos. She had made life worth living.

Now Lindy's lifeline had been extinguished. Momma couldn't heal the pain Lindy felt today or tomorrow or ever again, and pain was all she would feel for the rest of her life.

Life would never again be worth living.

CHAPTER THIRTY-SIX

Night demons lurked at the edge of the bed. Jo was sure they did. She refused to go to sleep. Momma died in her sleep. Sleep killed Momma. It might kill her too.

Lindy was haunted by her own night demons. If she dared doze off, gremlins would sneak in carrying nightmares, horrible illusions starring Lindy and Loneliness, in which a visible cloud of Loneliness would engulf Lindy until she suffocated. On the flip side of the double feature, Lindy headlined an ensemble cast consisting of horror-house hospitals, evil cartoon caskets, and rapidly disappearing quicksand graves. She played the hero trying to wrest her dying mother from the clutches of these antagonists, but she was always too late or too slow or too weak. The worst part was that when she awoke, she couldn't console herself by saying, *Don't cry, it was just a dream; Momma's alive and well.* The worst part was that her waking hours haunted her as much as her slumbering ones and there were no hours left to offer a reprieve.

So at night both girls watched the ceiling and stared at the walls from underneath their covers, afraid that closing their eyelids welcomed an ambush from the fears that lurked in their minds. And every now and then, when eyelids shut and sleep drifted in, one sister would wake the other from the grips of a night demon.

Prime among Lindy's demons—day and night—was her anger. It ate away at her nice-girl shell. She had been slapped in the face with the cold reality that life wasn't fair, and she had come to this conclusion: life stinks. Honest, hard-working, moral people didn't deserve to die at age thirty-four or to lose a mother at thirteen. The only entity she could think to blame for this injustice was God. God Almighty. If He was so Almighty then why didn't He save Momma? Was He a hypocrite who spouted rules on how to help others and then turned His back when others asked for His help? Or did He just have it out for Lindy? Did He hate her for some random reason? God of Love. Lindy rolled her internal eyes. *Yeah, right.*

~

As the sun broke on the morning of Momma's funeral, Lindy still wrestled with God's abandonment while Jo awoke, alive, and surprisingly demon-free.

"Did you sleep last night?" Jo asked her sister as Lindy lay hypnotized by imagined shapes in the clouds of the cottage cheese ceiling.

"Not much," Lindy answered. "How 'bout you?"

"I stopped being afraid to sleep."

"What'd you do, take one of Momma's sleeping pills?"

"I had a dream."

"Another nightmare?"

"A good dream," Jo said. "God tapped me on the shoulder and said Momma is with Him in heaven, and they are both watching over us."

"How do you know it was God?"

"That's what He said to call Him. Not Mr. God, just God. He's very informal. And He said Momma would be visiting us soon. In our dreams."

Lindy smirked. "So you're good friends with God now?"

"I think He liked me, yes."

"Did you ask him to say hi to the Fruit Loop people?"

"I'm not making this up," Jo insisted. "God's real. Not like the Fruit Loop people."

"So you admit the Fruit Loop people aren't real?"

Jo fidgeted. "God's realer."

"It was just a dream," Lindy reminded her sister.

"It wasn't just a dream."

"You made it up to make yourself feel better. Just like you made up Wendy."

Jo held firm. "God talked to me last night."

"And Julie Andrews sang me to sleep with 'My Favorite Things.'"

"I can tell you what God looks like."

"Big whoop. Everybody knows God is some white-haired old man with a long beard."

"Nuh-uh," Jo said. "God is a basset hound."

"What?"

"A basset hound. Just like Jojo."

Lindy snorted a laugh out loud, visualizing this latest of Jo's crackpot theories.

"Think about it," Jo went on. "It's creepy to believe in some grumpy old man God who watches our every move like a big old peeping Tom. But God as a cuddly basset hound is nice."

Jo had a point, and Lindy had to smile. "I can just see Lulu on a throne, God-like, wearing a crown and commanding her kingdom to get her more dog biscuits."

"And Jojo in a mini-throne sitting right beside her."

"The right paw of God Almighty."

Squeals of hilarity. The girls laughed until they cried. Tears of joy laced with tears of sadness.

Lindy wiped her eyes. "You really think that's what angels look like in heaven? Basset hounds with wings and halos flying around?"

"Sure," Jo said. "And they're making Momma feel right at home."

"Oh, yeah. Tracking mud in on her carpet and stinking 'cause they need a bath. I'm sure she loves that." Lindy chuckled again. "But I gotta admit it makes God a lot less intimidating."

"And it fits," Jo said. "Jojo loves me no matter what."

"Like Lulu loves me." Like God was supposed to love Lindy. Maybe Jo wasn't as dumb as Momma had always said.

"You know, I never knew I loved you before," Jo said through gasps of giggles.

Lindy's laughter eased. "What does that mean?"

"It means," said Jo, "I always knew I was supposed to love you 'cause I was told to, but now I love you without being told to."

"Oh." Lindy had heard monotone "I love yous" from her sister before—repeated upon threats from Momma—but she never believed them before today. Maybe Jo never meant them before, or maybe Lindy simply hadn't wanted to hear them. But with her family dwindling, Lindy hungered for those three little words that loomed too large for any adult Logan to utter. She found her reactions now slowing as they had that one time when Jo dared her to touch the electric fence that separated Smiley's property from the highway. The millisecond she gripped the live wire seemed like an eternity, and the tingle surged to her heart. Both then and now she experienced a cardiac jolt.

"I love you too," Lindy finally muttered with a degree of uncertainty. Did she say that because she felt obligated? Preprogrammed by Momma that thou shalt love thy sister? Or did she say it because she wanted to? She couldn't wade through the sludge of her sleep-deprived brain. She could only focus on her internal alarm that screamed *This Makes No Sense!* She didn't deserve to be loved. She hadn't earned it. She hadn't bought it. She wasn't famous. She wasn't even special. She was, in short, a nobody.

And yet she was loved. It made no sense.

The only thing she knew for sure was that God no longer seemed like the enemy. After all, He was really just a basset hound.

CHAPTER THIRTY-SEVEN

Momma's funeral was a blur. To Lindy at least. There were hymns and sermons and tears and Lindy sat stone-faced in her pew alone in a crowd, numb, and catatonic. She refused to acknowledge that her mother was dead. She refused to cry. She especially refused to dip her head inside the open casket when Birdy encouraged her to do so. Momma had always said Birdy was happiest at a funeral because there her martyrdom was appropriate. "Birdy's in a good mood. She's been to a funeral this week," Momma would say. And it was true. So when Birdy insisted Lindy view the corpse as a means to "closure," Lindy had replied, "Screw closure." She didn't want to see a withered Halloween corpse on a movie screen, much less a real corpse that was once her mother. Instead of pouring out her grief over her dead mother, Lindy turned her sadness into hate and aimed her darts of destruction in the direction of Aunt Birdy the corpse police. And in that, she found some solace.

Lindy allowed herself to be a little more present at home during the reception although her total rejection of the finger sandwich and pastries' table was indicative of just how deep into depression she had fallen. The thought of eating any of the many homemade casseroles or pies triggered acid reflux, and the only action that averted this desire to retch was her determination to eavesdrop on the conversation Father was now having with Birdy and Lolly.

They were huddled suspiciously on the front porch, the aunts pretending to nibble from their plates as Father leaned against the wrought-iron railing. Something was going on. Cole Porter may have gotten no kick from champagne, but Father got no kick from talking to Momma's sisters.

Lindy snuck around the side of the house to get a better vantage point from which to snoop, and, when some well-wisher distracted her father with a greeting, she hid behind the sturdy, old cedar elm that towered over the three-foot slab.

The well-wisher departed, and Birdy spoke first. "I'll take Jo, not Lindy. You know she cursed at me at the funeral. I don't need another Fay."

"Well, they never get along anyway," Father said, "so it's probably a good idea to separate them." *Never get along? What was he, high on tobacco?* Jo loved Lindy. Lindy loved Jo. He couldn't separate them. They were like Siamese twins, connected at the heart.

"Since Kate's graduating from high school, we'll take Lindy," Lolly said, adding, "We can only manage two kids at a time."

"Thank you," he said, nodding to both. "Now I can pick up extra work and start paying off hospital bills. I talked to a fella at the gin about working nights during stripping season, and 'til then I'm gonna do some truckin'. I'll send money the first of every month to help with the girls' food and clothes and stuff."

"OK," Birdy said. Lolly subtly elbowed her sister in the ribs.

"Joe, don't worry 'bout that," said the wealthier Lolly.

"Yeah," echoed Birdy. "We know you're in a bind not having any insurance. Not to mention your debts from before. It must feel like you're drowning in that mound of bills."

Lolly interrupted, "What my eloquent sister is trying to say is that she'll gladly feed and clothe and put a roof over Jo's head. And I will happily do the same for Lindy."

Father swallowed mightily and nearly choked on his pride. "Thank you. I'll help out whenever I can."

"That'd be nice." Birdy refused to make this easy.

"I think the sooner all this change can be over with, the easier it'll be on the girls," he said.

Hearing her father's final declaration, Lindy's mind went on auto pilot. This situation—Operation Separation—was drastic. It had to be stopped. Lindy had a mission. And she would accept it. She had to keep her family together.

At least what was left of it.

Lindy found Jo sitting in the backyard holding JoJo and quickly reported what she had heard.

"I don't wanna be separated," Lindy said, not even taking time to be surprised by the strength of her own conviction. She was on a mission. Operation No Separation.

"I don't wanna be separated either," Jo said with equal conviction, although the quiver in her frightened voice lessened the punch.

"Then we gotta show Father how well we're getting along, and rustle up enough money to help him pay off his bills so he can afford to keep us," Lindy said.

"I still have fifteen dollars left over from my hoeing money," offered Jo.

"And I could sell the tennis bracelet," Lindy said. "But we still gotta find a way to make a lot more money."

~

"Joe, perhaps you'd better step out back," Birdy said with some urgency when she found him standing in the hallway staring at the photo of Momma sniffing a yellow rose of Texas from the Tyler Municipal Rose Garden.

Joe was shocked to see that the majority of the mourners hadn't gone home like he assumed, but had instead migrated to the backyard. And when he looked over to see his daughters hugging as if on cue, he didn't know what alternate universe he had stepped into.

"Hello, Father," Lindy said, borrowing a measure of cutesyness from Jo's book.

"We're selling Lulu's blueblood puppies," Jo said. "Even Jojo. She's the pick of the litter."

"That's right," Lindy announced to the crowd, climbing atop Lulu's doghouse and barking her pitch. "Their mother's pure basset hound. Their father's one hundred percent Scottish deerhound. Talk about your all-purpose hunting dog." Then she went in for the kill, echoing a popular local ad where two little girls hawked automobiles for their car-selling poppa, "Buy a puppy from our father, he needs the business."

The crowd chuckled. Father did not.

"Girls, come with me into the house," he said as he yanked each inside by an arm.

"We already sold Rory," Lindy said, hoping to avoid trouble. Rory was the male. "For forty-five dollars. It won't pay off all our debts, but it's a start, right?"

Father didn't say a word or let go of anyone's arms until all limbs were inside the master bedroom. Then he spun both girls to face him and ripped his sentences with the rapidity of a machine gun. "You think you're so smart. Well, let me tell you, this is not funny, this is not cute. You think it's funny to embarrass me because I can't pay my own bills? To point it up to everyone here? To throw it in my face? You think you're so smart?"

Lindy thought none of the above, but the fact that she had never before seen her hot-headed father quite this livid scared her into muteness.

"Answer me." He shook Lindy by the shoulders. Hard. "Answer me."

Finally, Lindy found her voice. "I heard you talking to Birdy and Lolly. I don't want us to all live apart, and neither does Jo."

"That's right," Jo added, even though she had backed away and was cowering by the edge of the bed.

Lindy continued, "So we're raising money to help pay off the bills. I'm gonna start looking for a job tomorrow. School's almost out, and I can work full-time this summer. Or, even better, I can clean Momma's houses so we won't lose that money. I'll start right away, cleaning after school and on the weekends. That way you won't have to take a second job or a third one, and nobody'll have to leave anybody. Plus, we won't have to buy anything but groceries. I can get a deal on everything else we need from the Green Stamps store. I've got connections there."

Father released his death grip. He turned his back to the girls, and Lindy could visibly see his shoulders droop. His voice quaked. "I appreciate your trying to help. But you're too young to take a job."

"No, I'm not," Lindy said. "These are our bills too. If we're not too young to help get us into debt, we're not too young to help get us out."

"Lindy," Father faced his offspring, "you can't make the kind of money yet that's gonna make a dent in this debt. I plan on taking two jobs besides the farm, and I still don't know if I'll ever pay it all off."

"Then I'll think of something else," Lindy said. "There's gotta be a way. You can't give us up."

"I don't want to," he pleaded, his voice loud then soft as tears burst through an invisible dam. "But I can't. I can't. I can't take care of you by myself. I can't take care of you without your mother."

"I can take over Momma's responsibilities," Lindy volunteered.

"It's not right. It's not a proper home. You girls need to live in a home with..." He almost said a mother, but neither Birdy nor Lolly would ever be that to his girls. They could never replace Maggie. Nobody could. "Two adults."

"We need to live in a home with each other and you," Lindy said.

Father lifted his head and revealed his eyes and what lay behind them—defeat and doubt and fear. And one last time he said, "I can't."

It was then that Lindy realized her father was scared of her. Of her and her sister, the two foreign beings that were his daughters. And no arguing, or jobs, or money was gonna change that. So she dropped the subject. She would go live with Lolly. And Jo with Birdy.

Poor Jo. Poor Father. Poor her. She thought of Momma's favorite movie, one she watched every time it was televised and took the advice of Scarlett O'Hara. Lindy would not think about all of this today. She would think about it tomorrow. After all tomorrow was another day.

CHAPTER THIRTY-EIGHT

On the last day of school, Lindy said good-bye to her classmates—at least the few that said good-bye to her—and that didn't include the Fab Three. She hadn't bothered telling anyone she wouldn't be returning to school next year. There was no reason to. They didn't care about her, and she didn't care about them.

When the final school bell rang for the year, Lindy and Jo came home to pack for their second move in ten months. Tomorrow they were to be driven to their death sentences.

Cheery Lindy could be conjured no more.

Early tomorrow morning Father would drive Jo to Birdy's in Crosbyton and Lindy to the airport in Lubbock. Lolly had insisted on paying for her niece to fly to Dallas so she wouldn't have to endure the ten-hour bus ride. It would be Lindy's first airplane flight, and, OK, yes, she had to admit that this took some of the chill off the cold shoulder she planned to deliver to her new household.

All in all, Lindy figured, she had nothing to complain about compared to Jo. She got the favored aunt and the big city while poor Jo was stuck in the sticks with a cough drop-wielding Mennonite.

Crosbyton was night and day different from Dallas in the way that David was night and day different from Goliath. But at least Crosbyton was big enough to be considered a town—unlike Boudine—because it had that pantheon of West Texas municipalities. It had a Dairy Queen.

The Dairy Queen was the secular temple where the male elders would meet and greet, the shrine that displayed local milestones, and the monument that touted Crosbyton's famous sons and daughters. Like Deann Darby who actually won the National Spelling Bee. Or Ty Willis who changed his name to Ty Phoon when he became a weather broadcaster in Shreveport.

On Friday and Saturday nights, the Dairy Queen was taken over from the senior citizens by high school students. In between cruisings of the courthouse square, teenagers pit-stopped on restaurant row. The Dairy Queen was stop C on the tour and was preceded by stop B, the Sonic drive-in, which was always barren on the East side and jam-packed on the West side because only the cool kids parked on the West side and nobody wanted to be seen as uncool. But the marquee stop was stop A—the newly installed state-of-the-art Pizza Hut. In its day, the Dairy Queen ranked as stop A, but was now considered boring by these young upstarts. It was an acceptable place to go for ice cream, but never a main meal. Those country baskets were passe.

Such rules of restaurant etiquette were still a mystery to Jo, and, who knew, by the time she reached high school, the Pizza Hut might very well be a status no-no, replaced by the hip plasticity of a McDonald's or Taco Bell. Regardless, suffice it to say that Jo's formative years looked an awful lot like a string of fast-food chains.

Lindy didn't know a thing about life in Big D, but she knew there was a reason the town wasn't nicknamed Little D. Jo may be looking at a fast-food future, but Lindy could have that and access to life's finer establishments too. Like Bob's Big Boy. Bob's was located only in the really big cities like Dallas and Abilene. When the Logans stopped at them it was a sure sign of being on vacation. Now when she ate there it would be in her hometown. This was heady and terrifying at the same time.

Lindy had always loved the lights of the big city. She could remember looking out at Mobil Oil's red neon flying horse from their fifteen-story hotel room the time they stayed in Dallas and lost Soft Baby. She dreamed about living under the flying horse. But she dreamed of doing this as an adult, not as a kid. She was too small for such bigness. She didn't want to leave the only part of the country she'd ever known. It was bad enough having to leave Jessip—and don't get her wrong, she had no love lost for Grady County—but, holy cow, she was moving to Dallas! The biggest city in Texas! At least she thought it was the biggest city in Texas. Or was that Houston? No, it had to be Dallas; after all, they had the Cowboys, and nothing was bigger than the Cowboys.

Her heart beat to break free from her ribcage.

She already felt lost in the shuffle of the big city and she hadn't even gotten there yet. She guessed she felt lost in the shuffle period.

Don't think about that today. Think Scarlett O'Hara. Think about it tomorrow. Fiddle-dee-dee.

"Hey, look at this," Lindy said as she returned to rummaging through the shoeboxes of family pictures. "This would really freak Birdy out." She was looking for something, anything, to cheer her sister up; ever since they found out about the move, Jo had gone back to her Fruit Loop people and her invisible friend. Lindy didn't know if Jo had received any more personal messages from her basset-hound God, but if it made her happy, Lindy wished she would. Maybe she would pray about it tonight, that God send Jo more happy dreams, and, hopefully, her prayers wouldn't boomerang off the ceiling.

For her part, Lindy had turned to this photo project after virtually trying to polish the labels off her eight-track tapes and literally trying to knock some sense into her head by whacking it into the wall until she passed out. When she came to, Father consulted Vernice and she suggested that Lindy occupy her mind by filling up photo albums with the loose pictures in Momma's boxes. Then the girls could take some tangible memories with them. Lindy thought that was a good idea. Perhaps she *had* knocked some sense into herself.

"Huh? How 'bout it?" Lindy continued. "You can walk into Birdy's and show her this picture of Momma helping her to dye her gray roots? Or better yet put it on the refrigerator door when no one's looking and claim that Fay did it?"

Jo lifted her eyes from her suitcase. "I don't wanna leave you."

Lindy's heart cracked. "I know. I don't wanna leave you either." She watched her sister turn inward. "Are you gonna be OK?"

Jo nodded. "I've got Wendy. And the Fruit Loop people."

"Don't do that."

"What?"

"There's no such thing as Fruit Loop people and Wendy's not real."

"I know Wendy's only in my imagination. But she's the best friend I could imagine."

Not a bad way to go about this difficult business of making friends, Lindy thought. It made her lonely for as good a friend herself.

"Hang on." Lindy lifted her Raggedy Ann from its bookshelf pedestal. "I want you to have this. She'll keep you and Wendy company."

"But Momma made this for you."

"You can give it back to me when we're living together again."

"That's gonna be a long time."

"No. It's gonna be real soon."

Jo lifted Raggedy's dress to reveal the doll's hand-stitched heart, then smiled at Lindy. "I love you."

"I love you too."

Jo opened her arms and wrapped one around Lindy's neck and one around her torso. She gripped her big sister like a sucker fish suctioned onto aquarium glass. Perhaps she would freeze this way and they wouldn't be separated.

Lindy had never been hugged like this before. Like someone was desperate to love her. Like someone was desperate for her to love back.

"I wanna give you something too," Jo said, loosening her hug. She took Lindy by the hand and led her into the kitchen. She reached into the cabinet, the low shelf above the countertop where the cereal was kept. And from the very back, she pulled out an unopened box of Fruit Loops. "Here."

"I'm sure I can buy a box of Fruit Loops at Lolly's."

"You might need 'em before you get there. On the bus or something. I eat 'em when I feel sad, you know, like I'm gonna drown. I climb into an O and it keeps me afloat."

So all those drowning Fruit Loop people were really Jo. Jo wasn't saving invisible little people floundering in her bowl of milk; she was trying to save her floundering self.

"Thanks. You're right. I might need 'em."

They returned to their room and finished packing, promising to keep close by writing and calling. And Lindy vowed to keep Jo updated on all the good shows since Birdy refused to let her kids watch anything but religious programming.

"That just stinks," Jo said.

"Yeah. But at least Birdy's always got plenty of Dr. Peppers in the house."

Jo shrugged, remembering her pact with God.

"It's OK," Lindy said, "God won't mind."

"You think?"

"I know. And I know something else too. I swear one day I'll get you out of there."

As she lay in bed that night plotting ways to kidnap Jo from the beast that was Birdy, Lindy was surprised to find that her thoughts kept wandering to Amber. Of all people. Lindy couldn't care less about Amber. So why was she feeling sorry for her old nemesis? Lindy glanced at Jo and it hit her. Amber was isolated in a way that Lindy was about to experience for herself. Only Lindy had discovered that she had one source of love Amber lacked.

Lindy had a sister.

~

Father had studied for the last two weeks for his commercial driver's license so he could haul eighteen-wheeler loads during the lull that fell after cotton planting season. While he was waiting for the little stalks to grow—and praying for rain to help them do so—he could truck short distances for extra cash.

After he dropped Lindy off at the airport in Lubbock this morning, he had an appointment for his driver's test. He'd take the written test first and lease a cab for the driving test—that is if he passed the written test. He was sure he would. Well, not positive, but he could think of no other sure way to make quick money. He had to pass this test.

"Come on, Lindy. It's time to go," he hollered to his eldest. She was saying good-bye to Lulu.

"You be a good girl, you hear?" Lindy rubbed Lulu behind her ears. "I love you. You're gonna like your new family, and they're gonna love you. I'll never forget you, Lulu. You're the best dog ever." She kissed Lulu's head between her eyes and down her nose.

Smiley had volunteered to give Lulu to a family with kids about Jo and Lindy's age who desperately wanted a dog. Lindy was initially afraid Smiley would do away with the dog after what Lulu did to his ostrich, but Father promised that wouldn't happen.

"You mind if I say good-bye to Lulu too?" Jo stood behind Lindy.

"I think she'd like that." Lindy tried to hide her tears; as Momma would say, it's just a dog.

"You're a good dog, Lulu, and you birthed some good puppies." Father had eventually agreed to sell the rest of the puppies. Jojo went first, bringing the highest price. Her new owners looked nice, and Jo crossed her fingers that that was the case.

"OK, girls. Get in the car." Father had loaded all the luggage into Momma's yellow Ford.

Each sister gave Lulu one final hug and followed their father to the car. "It's crowded back there so one of you has to sit up front with me."

Lindy climbed into the front passenger's seat—Momma's seat. Three turns of the ignition and the old car sputtered to life. Lindy sat on her foot and craned her neck to see Jo's reflection in the rearview mirror.

"Stop the car," Lindy instructed her father.

"What? Why?" They were on the highway, but still only a mile from the house. "Did you forget something?"

"No. I just need you to pull over."

"Are you sick?"

"Father. Pull. Over. Please." Lindy could be pretty forceful when she put her mind to it.

Father pulled the car over as much as he could without falling into the deep bar ditch. Lindy got out of the car and opened Jo's back-seat door. "Get in the front with us."

"It'll be too crowded. Daddy won't like it."

"Father, Jo's gonna sit up front with us."

"It's too crowded," he said. "What are you doing? We were all arranged."

Without a word, Lindy slammed the front passenger door closed, reached over Jo and threw two small totes from the back seat to the front. She scrunched the rest over and crawled onto the half-empty bench seat. Lindy put her arm around Jo protectively. "We're ready to go now."

Father lurched the car into gear and headed up Farm to Market Road 651 to Crosbyton, scratching his head at those two little enigmas in the back seat.

Lindy smiled at her kid sister. "How's Wendy doin'? She need a Fruit Loop to float on?"

Jo smiled back and buried her head in Lindy's chest.

This moment will be over before I know it, Lindy thought. Crosbyton was only forty minutes away.

But, she reminded herself, she was loved now. No one could separate her from that.

The author and her sister hoeing cotton in West Texas circa 1976.